MIKE CANNON

LEE McKENZIE

MIKE CANNON

Lee McKenzie

Maple Leaf Publishing Inc. Alberta Canada

Mike Cannon

Copyright © 2020 by Lee McKenzie

ISBN Numbers:

Paperback: 978-1-77419-066-1

Ebook: 978-1-77419-067-8

MAPLE LEAF PUBLISHING INC.

3rd Floor 4915 54 St Red Deer,

Alberta T4N 2G7 Canada

General Inquiries & Customer Service

Phone: 1-(403)-356-0255

Toll Free: 1-(888)-498-9380

Email: info@mapleleafpublishinginc.com

Contents

Chapter 1

The after flames of the explosion had already engulfed the front of the building before Mike Cannon's Camaro came to a screeching halt.

He swore silently when he had to lean hard against the lock to get the door open. But taking into consideration the mounting list of serious mechanical defects that he had been ignoring, a sticking door lock was far from being priority, so he instantly dismissed the annoyance. Of all the important items on his agenda for that day, he was ill prepared for the carnage surrounding him. He and many others at headquarters were aware of the mounting tension between the drug-controlling factors in the city of Miami; they were also aware that sooner or later, a boiling point would be reached, resulting in a catastrophic eruption of violence, but the event of that day had surpassed the expectation of the most twisted imagination. The blast from several sticks of dynamite had blown away the entire front of an inner-city local ethnic food store—and with it nearly all of its early morning customers.

Mike paused and closed his eyes against the horror when the count reached twelve bodies in the street that had no reason to be still alive. The gruesome piles of body parts and the sickening smell of burning human flesh made him want to turn around get back in the Camaro and drive away from there. The little girl lying across the pavement was still breathing. All her clothes were burnt from her body, and the flesh on her face was melted like a wax doll. A chunk of glass was sticking out from her abdomen. She was trying to die. Her mother lying close by propped herself up on her one remaining arm and crawled toward what but a short while before was her five-year-old pride and joy. She ignored the pain from what remained of one of her legs that was pumping out blood as water from a punctured garden hose. She threw her remaining arm across the little girl, looked up pleadingly at Mike, and died.

Mike turned away, placed his hand over his mouth, and hurried to conceal his sickness behind a dumpster overflowing with days of rotting garbage. He had been a law veteran of many engagements and, as a lawman, witnessed more than he cared to remember, but nothing as gruesome as what he experienced that early Wednesday morning.

He jumped back to avoid the remains of his coffee, bacon, toast, and eggs from getting onto his recently polished shoes, and from the corner of an eye, he saw a young female rookie officer seeking the refuge of a nearby squad car. She had both hands cradling her abdomen while she wept and groaned as if she was in agony.

Mike hurried toward the open car door and placed a hand on her shoulder. He imagined she was hurt in the explosion. He asked, "Where is your injury, officer? Were you here when it happened?"

"They didn't tell me about this! They didn't!" she replied, tears streaming down her cheeks.

"Who are they? Who didn't tell you what?" Mike asked impatiently, waiting for an answer.

"At the Academy. They didn't tell me it would be like this. I am sorry, this is too much! I can't go back out there!"

Mike considered her statement and remembered he felt the very exact way his first time, but a job was there to be done, and unfortunately, that was her call—like it or not. So he took her by the hand and lifted her from the car. He held her by both shoulders, shook her not too gently a couple of times, and said, "Oh yes, you will. Now pull yourself together, officer. Go back out there, help to secure the crime scene, and do your duty as you had sworn to do."

The young officer suddenly straightened herself, squared her shoulders, wiped the tears from her face, and walked back to the disaster area.

Mike followed her back to the scene to where he had seen the mother dying, holding her little girl; he took off his jacket and covered both their faces. "They will pay for today, mother. By god they will. I promise you they will," he growled through clenched teeth, hoping she could witness his anger and hear his promise.

***

It was almost midday, and the coroner had gathered up the dead and their body parts from the street and pavement. The water from the fire hoses had washed away the blood, and where the store once stood, there remained only a pile of smoldering rubble.

Mike decided there was nothing more at the scene for him to do and walked toward his car. A neatly dressed young blonde in a blue business suit sporting a badge marked *Interpreter* hurriedly intercepted him, blocking his path. Beside her was a bearded middle-aged Hispanic male carrying a camera on one shoulder.

Mike looked at the badge pinned to her pocket and recognized her to be a reporter, and worse of all from the *Interpreter*. If anything could worsen the regrettable experience of that morning, it was about to happen. "Who the hell are you?" he asked, as if he did not already know.

"Kellie Drake," she replied, not in the least intimidated by Mike Cannon's demeanor.

"I could have guessed. Are you ready to apologize for all the garbage you and your paper have been printing about me? How I am more dangerous to society than the fictitious terrorist organizations I claim to be taking over the city? How there is no place in society for my style of law enforcement? Look around. Just how do you suggest I treat those responsible for your so-called fictitious occurrence of today?"

Mike was not about to allow her to interrupt his speech before he said what he so long wanted to say to her if ever he had the opportunity of meeting her face-to-face, and that time had just presented itself. She was then on his turf, and he was in charge.

It was evident she had made a mistake and chosen the wrong time and place for a confrontation with the enemy she had created, and she tried to regain her composure. But Mike would not allow her to, not just yet. He remembered how talented and effective she was with words, so he continued blocking every attempt she made to interrupt.

"Just as I thought, no answer. I have nothing more to say to you. Now get the hell out of my way. I have work to do." Mike walked around her and headed toward the Camaro.

Kellie Drake took offense at the manner in which she was being treated, worse of all in the presence of her photographer, an experience that was alien to her. After all, she was Kellie

Drake, and no public official who valued public opinion dared to earn her wrath.

Placing both hands on her hips, she finally regained her composure and retaliated. If Mike Cannon thought he could get the better of her for long, he was mistaken. She ran toward him and again blocked his path. She looked up at him and tried to control her anger. Her eyes narrowed into mere slits when she said with all the disdain she could afford, "What else can one expect from an uncultured egotistic police wannabe hero who allows brute force to replace judgment he never had? I suppose after today, the people of Miami can expect a spate of wanton Mike Cannon–style killings and police brutality as your answer for what is out there. The usual demonstration of your lack of self-control and civilize judgment. I see before me a semiliterate public servant who sets himself up as judge and jury because some fool official as himself pinned a badge on him and handed him a gun. I promise that will not be for long, Inspector Mike Cannon. The law-abiding people of the city of Miami will soon see to that. Of course my paper is against you and your kind. This is civilization, Inspector. Can't you tell? Wake up and smell the coffee. Or are you still asleep? You and your world are abstract relics of the past, fossils. Can you understand my words? You are not real. Wake up!"

She kept wagging her finger in his face, almost touching his nose, taunting him, hoping he would do something stupid.

But if Kellie Drake's intention was to have Mike assault her, she had chosen the wrong person even for that day. Of course he was angry at her and her sarcasm, but she represented only a tiny part of his anger. He was thinking of the fat rats who sat protected behind their desks in ivory towers, issuing orders that, for greedy selfish reasons, created disasters such as the city of Miami was experiencing. The time was ripe to send them a message, and what better messenger than Kellie Drake?

"Ms. Drake," Mike said, calmly suppressing the anger raging within. "In writing your next article describing your recent encounter with this prehistoric relic, please quote me in this message to the people your paper is so bent on protecting from this 'has been.' Tell them I know who they are, every single one of them. Tell them there is no protection from me now on this side of life. They have finally pissed me off, and as of this day, I will repay terror for terror and death for death. That is how it will be from now on."

Mike again walked around her and went into the Camaro without another word. In anger, he slammed the door until the glass rattled, turned on the ignition, and with a screeching of tires, pressed the accelerator to the floor, leaving Kellie Drake standing in the street.

Whatever she thought of Mike Cannon before, that day gave her reason to reevaluate her impression. Deep down she had to admit that Cannon was first and foremost a lawman and, in his own style, dedicated and focused toward a deadly purpose. She knew there was a high price that had to be paid for that day, and those who were guilty would pay and pay dearly. His methods were a bit out of time, but also was Mike Cannon. She feared the unfortunate occurrences of that day was all the motivation he needed to make his threats a reality, and she was right because when that finally happened, Miami was never the same.

Kellie Drake and her paper and many others of the media family had in the past willfully distorted the truth about him and, so doing, withheld the seriousness of the crime situation from the people of Miami. Their relentless crusade to smear him was at times unjustified. But who cared? That type of news increased ratings and sold newspapers. In Mike's opinion, they were no less guilty than those who gave the orders for what happened to Miami that day. But to kill a monster, one needs

11

to chop off its head. And that was his mission. He knew he had made a dangerous decision, and it would be bloody war. But there was no turning back.

He looked through the rearview mirror at Kellie Drake still standing in the street and wondered what worse thoughts she had of him after that confrontation. Really, he cared less. He had declared a state of war, and those not with him were the enemy. "To hell with you, woman!" he heard himself saying aloud. "I will do what has to be done regardless, and you and your paper and the gates of hell have nothing to stop me."

***

Several months had passed since that day that the people of Miami had named Bloody Wednesday, and the cleaning crew of the Everest Office Cleaning Company looked eagerly toward a few days' holiday when most commercial offices would be closed for Christmas. Some would be having an office party for the benefit of their staff, and that usually took place a few days before Christmas. The workload afterward would be heavier than usual for the cleaning crew, and the time taken could be twice as long. With regard to a particular establishment, that situation was advantageous to the members of the cleaning crew.

Who could suspect that these ordinary, everyday-looking people—with nothing more for lunch than a sandwich, a part-eaten hamburger, and a soda wrapped in a plastic bag and stuck into an overall pocket—were capable of successfully undermining the foundation of structured international organizations bent on destabilizing the greatest nation of the civilized world?

The offices of the South Atlantic Bank of Venezuela, an offshore banking institution in downtown Miami, were no exception, and at that particular Christmas, Detective Inspector Mike Cannon, head of a special undercover task force and president of the conveniently formed Everest Office Cleaning Company, had a special interest in the business affairs of the bank's chief executive officer, David Schulenberg, and his banking institution. The task force was created to infiltrate institutions responsible for high-profile criminal activities, including money laundering the proceeds of drug smuggling for terrorist support, kidnappings, jury tampering, witness intimidations, homicides, and bank robberies. Eddie Lang, an accounting specialist, and Danielle Mendez, a computer whiz, both members of the task force, were also part of the cleaning crew assigned to secretly investigate the bank's affairs during cleaning hours. Their inside contact was Elaine Bozzi, an undercover police officer who was recently appointed assistant to the executive secretary of David Schulenberg.

Mike was occupied with the report sheets that were coming off the fax machine on the small metal table by the side of his desk. The plastic tray was broken, and several sheets of papers were falling onto the floor.

Danielle Mendez got up from the chair across the office where she sat waiting for the better part of an hour. In her hand was a partly eaten hamburger that was supposed to be her midnight snack. She bent down and collected a handful of paper from the floor, then placed them before Mike. He looked at the residue of tomato sauce on most of the pages and began to get angry. He quickly controlled his anger as by then he had become accustomed to her insatiable appetite for fast food and her habit of satisfying her cravings in the most inappropriate places. But as a computer expert, she was a natural and the best the department could offer. The previous night she had worked two offices, and fatigue had taken its toll. It was evident she was hastily put together as her shoulder-length blond hair and makeup lacked the usual feminine attentiveness.

Mike glanced at the clock on the office wall and then on the watch on his wrist.

"Eddie said he may be a bit late, boss. He had to take his car to the garage, something to do with the engine overheating. I told him it could be the thermostat. I had the same trouble with mine," Danielle Mendez volunteered in defense of her workmate not being on time. She had a standing crush on Eddie Lang ever since she came on the task force. If Eddie Lang recognized it, he pretended not to. Although she had some claim to a certain degree of attractiveness, his family was his world, and after that his job. There was no space for flirtation in his well-organized life.

Mike selected a page from the bunch of papers before him. As he pushed back his chair, it made the usual disturbing noise that added to his annoyance. He walked toward a large detailed map of the city of Miami displayed on the wall, removed a green marker from the location of the South Atlantic Bank of Venezuela, and replaced it with a red.

Just then, Eddie Lang came through the door. He was breathing heavily from hastily climbing the stairs. He wore his gray overalls that had Everest Office Cleaning Company across the back.

Mike stared at him and said, "Take my advice and do something about your condition. Someday your life may depend on it."

Eddie Lang, in objection to the attack on his physical condition, said, "Not all of us can be Cassius Clays. I get along well with the person I am." He was obviously offended.

Mike ignored Eddie Lang's apparent annoyance and went back to his desk. "Pull up your chairs, and let's hear what the South Atlantic Bank of Venezuela is currently up to," Mike said.

Eddie Lang's defensive demeanor immediately disappeared, and he became excited. He leaned forward in his chair, both elbows resting on Mike's desk. He could not wait to report his findings. He was an exceptionally honest individual, and exposing the likes of David Schulenberg was his personal pleasure. "Mike, we have hit the jackpot. As you suspected, the bank is tied to a terrorist group, the World Liberation Brotherhood Organization in El Salvador. The bank over the past six months has been transferring on a regular basis small amounts to their account. But they are now up to something big. Pardon me, I should say bigger. Now they are planning the big one—a billion and a half in raw cash." Eddie Lang paused to study the impact the information had on Mike. He was not disappointed when he noticed the cloud of anger that settled over Mike's countenance.

"And how the hell do they intend to move that?" Mike asked, trying unsuccessfully to remain calm.

"Well, that was my question, until Danielle here went to work on it. Seven days ago, the bank made a transfer of funds to the Atlantic and Pacific Container Lines in Fort Everglades. So I asked myself what the bank would be transporting except money. That is how they intend to move it. The container company's head offices is in California. The other mystery was that the money transfer documents paying for the use of the container were made out in favor of a company in Argentina. Danielle traced the funds to a bank in Austria that further transferred it to an account in Ontario. Guess who is the account holder?"

Mike was about to explode with anger. That was no time to engage him in a guessing game. "Get on with it!" he shouted. "Whose is it?"

"It belongs to no other than our mutual friend, Fidel Castro."

To say Mike was not pleased with that information was an understatement. He pounded the desk with clenched fists until the veins in his forearm were enlarged almost to the point of exploding. Then he became calm, and a sadistic smile took over his countenance. It became clear as it would to anyone who was aware of his attitude when he was in the process of formulating a plan. He asked slowly, as if thinking between each word. "Who are the major clients of the Venezuelan bank?"

Eddie Lang reached in his overall pocket and produced a rolled-up piece of paper and handed it to Mike.

After examining the paper, Mike inquired, "And who is the CEO of the Biscayne Land Development?"

Eddie Lang hesitated, as if savoring his reply and the impact he knew his information would have on his boss. "His name is Donaldo Santiago, and one of his directors is no other than our city mayor, Frank Bukley."

Mike placed a hand to his cheek, as if waiting for the unsavory information to be digested. "You don't say. You don't say." He kept repeating this over and over, then he continued, "Oh, what a damned interesting web they weave."

Mike spent the remainder of that evening compiling a report he was certain his captain, Abe Duncan, would be pleased to read. Abe Duncan had to fight an uphill battle with his superiors when he insisted that the undercover task force be formed. But when he informed them that the leader would be the no-nonsense Mike Cannon, they had no doubt that it would make the difference the people of Miami were demanding.

***

It was the day before Christmas Eve, and everyone, including Mike Cannon, was looking forward to spending time away from the grind of their demanding jobs. Those with families were extra eager. The nature of their investigation required that for security reasons, minimum contact be maintained with their families. So for days the only contact was mainly with members of the group.

The telephone on the desk of the Everest Office Cleaning Company rang, and Mike Cannon answered. At the other end was Danielle Mendez. She was overwrought with distress and in tears.

"Control yourself, Mendez, so I may understand what you are trying to say," Mike shouted, knowing fully well that whatever was her dilemma, it would be of major importance.

"Mike, boss, Bozzi was just shot dead!" she exclaimed. "She is dead, Mike. I just saw it myself on the news. What are we going to do? She was on her way to her car parked on the bank's third floor parking lot when a hooded gunman attacked her and shot her in the back of the head execution style. She was not robbed."

Upon hearing the news, Mike's response was immediate. He said to her, "Contact everyone. Tell them to report here immediately. I don't know how, but I believe our cover may be blown."

***

When Captain of Police Abe Duncan entered the Eldorado Cocktail Lounge in downtown Miami at 4:00 p.m. that day, he found Mike seated alone at a table. He was on his third scotch. The captain paused before seating himself. He noticed the sullen countenance of the detective. Mike was in a foul mood.

"Hi, Cannon," the captain greeted.

Mike hesitated, then said, "Hi."

Captain Duncan overlooked the apparent insubordination and said, "You don't look like Christmas. More like your best friend had just died."

"You are dead right," Mike said without looking up. "Everest Office Cleaning Company just did. Our cover is blown. I don't know how. The woman shot execution style in the bank's parking lot today was one of ours. She was our contact in the bank. She was the assistant to the executive secretary of the CEO."

"Good god!" exclaimed Captain Duncan. "No wonder you are like that. You have got to pull out our people."

"I have already did," Mike responded. "The office was closed and the clients advised. By now most of them already know that the company was a sting. What are you going to do about the bank's movement of funds to El Salvador? Surely you guys have reported it to the feds."

"Mike, believe me, I think the feds already knew of the activities of the South Atlantic Bank of Venezuela."

"What the hell are you talking about? Are you trying to say our operation was only a sham? Damn it, man, a police officer has just been executed, leaving two young children. She was a single parent. I suppose the investigation into her murder will only be a formality? That is, if one will even be made. What sort of game you guys at headquarters are playing? And do you mean to say you were a part of this all along? I thought we shared most things about the job, and we were thicker than that."

"Mike, like you, I take orders," Captain Duncan said in his defense.

Mike by that time was furious but tried to control his anger. After all, Abe Duncan was his boss. "It may be politics to you and whoever is pulling your strings, but to us on the front line, it's life and death. Just as all the information I have been feeding you, there has been nothing done. No follow-ups. Not a single arrest. I should have known."

"Mike, it's all in a day's work. The politicians at the top meet and make decisions. Instructions are passed down to my superiors. They pass them to me, and I pass them to you. You know the drill."

"And what about the task force? What about us?" Mike asked, not concealing his frustration and disappointment.

"We do something different. Law and order have to be maintained with or without us. That is our job. That is how it had always been. And when we become too old, if we live long enough, others take our place," Captain Duncan replied. He had his personal ambitions, but that was not the time or place to disclose them. Mike was serving a purpose that supported his hope of climbing the departmental ladder.

Mike knew that speech by Captain Duncan was so many words and only for his benefit. "That's not good enough, Captain. For me, that is not good enough at all. I must believe in whatever I am doing. I must believe I am making a difference. For the sacrifice of being away from my family and putting my life on the line day in and day out, there has to be a better reason. Three months ago, I applied to the department through you for a change of duties because of personal family reasons. You told me that my request was under consideration. I now believe it was all a lie. I believe everything about the department is fraudulent. And you, whom I had believed in, turn out to be the biggest fraud of all. I intend to repeat my request come January, and if by the end of the month it is not granted, I will be turning in my badge."

Captain Duncan knew that Mike Cannon was a man of few words and usually meant whatever he said.

"Hold on there, Cannon, you can't be serious. You can't do that!" Captain Duncan exclaimed, fearful of having to face repercussions from incidents over which he personally had no control.

"Can't I? Don't you bet on it," Mike responded, expressing the firmness of his decision.

"But you are in the middle of things. If it were not for you, the streets of Miami would run red with blood. You have kept the Colombians and the Jamaican posse apart. You cannot turn them loose on the population of South Florida now," Captain Duncan pleaded.

Mike was a difficult man to handle in the department, but he was absolutely irreplaceable. The trouble was, everyone else was busy advertising their own indispensability, and no one bothered to acknowledge his contribution until it could possibly be too late.

"If it will help to change your mind, I will do something positive about your transfer. I promise. I give you my word. But in turn, you must promise me one thing. And that is never to let go control. Remain in charge until we do something permanent about those two groups. You alone can do it. I have no one else with the courage and experience. What do you say, is that a deal?" Captain Duncan stretched out his hand toward Mike.

Mike thought about what the captain had just said and was convinced of his sincerity, although he hesitated as he took his hand.

Captain Duncan breathed a sigh of relief. "This calls for a drink. Will you have another of whatever you have been drinking on me?"

Captain Duncan called the waiter and ordered two double scotches in separate glasses.

"What will you be doing for the holiday?" Captain Duncan asked Mike Cannon.

A smile replaced the seriousness on Mike's face. "Do you remember that Chinese place, Canton Palace, where we had lunch last year after we closed the Mexican kidnapping case? Well, I will be taking Kim and the kids there for Christmas dinner and try to make up for all the hard times I have been giving them," Mike replied.

"That's a nice quiet place. Good idea. Good idea," Captain Duncan said. He usually repeated himself whenever he was satisfied with achieving something important.

"And what will you be doing?" Mike asked the captain.

"Don't know yet," Captain Duncan replied. "I will think of something."

***

It was Christmas day, and the only thing observed missing in Miami was the snow. Church bells could be heard chiming from all directions. Bearded red and white Santa Clauses could be seen waving from behind almost every store window. The message of peace and goodwill permeated the yuletide atmosphere. It was Christmas and party time. The Canton Palace restaurant refused to be outdone. Entering through the door, it was plain to see that the Chinese management wished their many customers a sincere Christmas welcome. Banners were hung from the ceiling and on walls, wishing the best of the season, and the waiters and waitresses wore special red and white cone-shaped hats with shiny little bells on top.

When Mike thought of giving his family a special and well-deserved Christmas treat, he could think of no place more appropriate than the Canton Palace. Through habit, he chose a table where he could unobstructedly observe everyone, including those coming through the entrance door and the attendants coming and going to and from the kitchen.

Five-year-old Tommy, his son, knelt on the floor beside their table showing off his present, a new yellow and black sport Mustang. The noise from its tiny engine attracted an audience. Normally it would not be tolerated by the management or by the other customers, but it was Christmas, and as far as everyone was concerned, that gave him the right.

The attendants took longer than usual servicing the orders, but who cared? Everyone present was having a swell time, and no one that day was short on patience.

Being together was a rare occasion for the Cannon family, and each member was happy and mentally rejoicing. Those blissful moments touched deeply their emotions, and each of them reveled in their overwhelming joy as they looked at each other.

Mike reached across the table and held his wife Kim's hand. Their daughter, nine-year-old Diana, daddy's little girl, would not be left out, and she placed her hand on top of theirs. They anticipated an exceptionally perfect Christmas day.

But that expectation was not to last. Mike noticed a tall bearded and suspicious-looking character entering the restaurant, and he immediately sensed a numbing feeling in the pit of his stomach. He had once before experienced that nervous sensation in an unexpected shoot-out with two dangerous kidnappers. That time the warning saved his life. Not unusual for Florida, it was an exceptionally warm Christmas day, and there was no need for anyone to be wearing a heavy full-length winter coat.

Kim and Diana noticed the distressed look on his face and shared his concerns.

The suspicious character's menacing approach and nervous glances meant he was there for other reasons than a Christmas meal. Moments earlier, Diana saw her Chinese school friend Su Lee and her father being served at another table and called to her. Before her father could object, Su Lee hurried over to Diana for a chat before settling down to eat. They were on holidays and had not seen each other for many days. To close friends of that age, it could seem a lifetime.

At that very moment, the suspicious character opened his coat, produced an AK- 47 assault rifle, and began shooting randomly.

Panic stricken by the imminent danger to his family, the warning Mike tried to give froze on his lips. Finally he managed to cry out, "Get down on the floor! Now! For Christ's sake, do as I say! Do it now!" He kept screaming the warning over and over amid the roar of the assailant's gun.

Seconds afterward, his wife Kim screamed, "Oh my god! Oh my god! Mike, I am shot!" Then he heard the frightened cries of Diana and Tommy. "Daddy! Daddy! Please!" Those were the last words Mike heard from his wife and children. The memory of their cries would alter the course of his life. They expected help from him, and he was unable to give. The feeling of guilt would remain with him, eating away his very soul, transforming him into a victim of vengeance. For the lives of those taken from him, Mike pledged he would have no mercy on those who were found to be responsible.

For months after, Mike relived those terrible moments as he experienced them that never-to-be-forgotten Christmas day. He remembered seeing the events as if they were happening in slow motion. In his mind, he could still hear the reverberating report of automatic rifle fire in the confined area of the restaurant, causing panic among the unsuspecting men, women, and children. He could still see people being shot and heard them screaming. He could see the dead lying on the floor and across tables. Many threw chairs at the closed glass windows and were shot down as they tried unsuccessfully to escape the carnage. He remembered reaching under his jacket for the department-issue Glock 9mm weapon, standing up and firing several rounds into the assailant, mortally wounding him. He would forever see him in his dying moments firing his final rounds toward where he and his family were, transforming that area into a ghastly mass of shattered furniture and mangled flesh and blood. All those things that he wished he could forget, he kept remembering. Then there came the finale. A bullet penetrated the right side of his neck, and he felt a numbing heat spread upward to engulf his entire face, into his eyes, partially blinding him. Another two struck him in his abdomen. He could still remember that pain, which felt as if he had swallowed fire, and inside his body was ablaze just before he lost consciousness. And as they told him afterward, he fell across Su Lee, which probably saved her life.

***

The day before the massacre was Christmas Eve, and Kim Cannon climbed onto a chair to place the final touches on the Christmas tree in the corner of the family room of their Miami Gardens apartment. Diana stretched to her full height and handed her mother a silver star to be placed on the very top. That would be the final touch. Kim gave a sigh of relief. She had finally accomplished what she had earlier thought she would not be able to afford.

Tommy approached the tree, burst out into laughter, and clapped his hands with glee when Kim inserted the plug into the wall socket, and the lights on the tree went on. That was the first time that day he had displayed any evidence of yuletide emotion. Kim had stretched whatever funds she had to the limit, and a Christmas tree was not on the shopping list.

Almost everything was going toward saving for the closing on their new house just four weeks away.

With regard to this disappointment, Tommy entertained no part of an explanation. He went on a hunger strike and became a one-man demolition crew, tossing almost everything in his reach. It was then that Kim decided to take her gold watch, a present from her husband on her last birthday, to the pawn shop and see what the generous Italian gentleman would allow her. After receiving the money, she carefully placed the pawn ticket in her wallet and drove around for nearly an hour before Diana noticed a sign in the front of a supermarket advertising last-minute sale of Christmas trees.

Kim drove into the crowded parking lot and maneuvered the station wagon into the only vacant parking space available. All three of them searched through nearly a dozen fading trees and finally decided on the one dressed and proudly standing in the corner of their family room.

That area of dissatisfaction rectified, Tommy then assumed duty by the front window, staring out onto the parking lot, hoping to see the arrival of his father whom he had not seen for days. It was midnight when Kim heard the turning of a key in the front door. She was awake and waiting to welcome Mike home for Christmas.

To compensate for whatever inconveniences his long and frequent absence had caused the family, Mike invited them out on a much-deserved Christmas treat—an ill-fated decision he would regret the rest of his life.

***

The tragic incident hung like a storm cloud over Miami that Christmas day, blotting out any intention of a carefree festive season. Those who had to bury their dead went on with it, and the living who were able found a church and gave thanks. The media had their treat and hung on to it, reluctant to let go, until the people of South Florida said, "Enough is enough." It was days since the doctors agreed that Mike Cannon had passed the worst and could be transported out of emergency and into a private room. Captain Duncan had pulled strings and got the hospital management to cooperate to total secrecy of his survival. Two of his most trusted plainclothesmen were placed outside the door of Mike's hospital room night and day for his protection.

The department had assumed that in spite of the wholesale massacre, Mike was the target. Only two known criminal elements operating in the country would have decided upon such brutality just to take out one person. That was the Jamaican Posse and the Colombians. And since investigation had since identified the shooter as a Latino imported out of New York, the Columbians were the most likely to be blamed. Apart from that, the Jamaican Posse, which was composed mainly of Dreadlocks, was known for doing their killings themselves.

Mike Cannon, opening his eyes, recognized the unmistakable surroundings of a hospital room. He was alive. Of that, he had no doubt.

Where is everyone? There should be people around. In a hospital there are usually doctors, nurses. Why am I here alone? he asked himself, not knowing he had been there for several days.

Then it started to come back, the numbing fear. Forgetfulness slowly gave way to painful memories. He realized they brought him there because he was shot. He wondered how badly. Kim and the kids were also shot. He could remember voices saying so before he lost consciousness. He would have liked to get up from the bed to find out their conditions. He tried, but there was no strength in any of the movable parts of his body. His left arm was not working. He tried to swallow his saliva, and his throat pained. He also recognized the heavy bandages around his abdomen. He felt sick and helpless, and he was hurting all over. He had to admit, he needed help. There usually was an emergency button somewhere near. He looked for it, found it, and squeezed. Even that brought him pain.

Two anxious nurses rushed into the room.

"You are back!" the nurse in charge exclaimed, bending over him and adjusting the nasal oxygen hose. She was pleased. Sometimes during his unconscious state, she had her doubts. Almost everyone had their doubts. Trying to keep him alive was their duty, but the remainder was up to him if he wanted to.

"You were out of it for almost three days. Some thought you wouldn't make it. But I kept pleading with you not to die on me. I told you I would not give you permission to do so."

Cannon's first question was of his family. "Kim and the kids, how are they?" he asked. He was partly fearful of their reply.

The silence and abstract stares of the two nurses answered his question. He knew they did not make it. At that moment, he wished he had died with them.

Many days had passed since Mike regained consciousness. Captain Duncan came out of the crowded elevator and walked down the passage toward his hospital room. Captain Duncan was as a big brother to Mike. Mike considered him the nearest thing to family. The two officers guarding the door saw him approaching, put away the magazines they were reading, and got up from their chairs. Captain Duncan reached the door just as Dr. Edward McDonald came out of the room.

He recognized the captain from an earlier meeting the day Mike was admitted. He asked the captain to accompany him to his office. In his office, Captain Duncan impatiently waited while the doctor seated across the desk silently studied Mike's file. The seriousness of the doctor's countenance caused him concerns. He knew from previous personal experiences with doctors that the news would not be the best.

"I wish I had better news for you, Captain Duncan," Dr. Edward McDonald bluntly said.

Captain Duncan's heart dropped. That was not what he had hoped to hear, although he knew it was possible. He wanted an able Mike Cannon back, doing what he did best. "Whatever it is, Doctor, let's have it." Captain Duncan was surprised he said that. Truthfully, he was not ready for bad news.

"The patient is healing. His body, that is, except for an unexplainable lack of sensation in his left hand. Physically he is doing well. My concern is the psychological damage the traumatic experience had done to his mind. That will not be healing anytime soon. I believe he blames himself for not dying with his family, and no known medicine has a cure for that. He has not spoken a dozen words since he found out they were dead. Not to me or the nurses. He nods and shakes his head when questioned, but nothing else. "

"Do you mean he may commit suicide?" The captain knew Mike would not do that. He wondered why he asked. It was not in him. He may die in a shoot-out or something like that, but not by his own hands.

"Not a chance while the people responsible are still out there," Dr. McDonald said. "I mean, he may not be much good as an officer of the law for some time. The only thing on his mind at present is revenge. That will keep him alive. He is not the Mike you knew before. This is a new Mike in a new world he has created in which to seek refuge from his agony. Beyond patching up his body the best we can, there is not much more we can do for him. Does he have any close relatives?"

"He has none that I know of. Two older brothers both killed in Nam. A younger sister, she died of the AIDS virus. I am the

28

nearest thing to family he has. Some sort of a big brother and friend, you may call it. As an undercover officer, he is, or was, the best. Now I do not know what to say to him. The force was his life, second to his wife and the kids. Take everything away from him, and I don't know."

"Do not mention his family when you speak with him today, except if he does first. Speak of police matters. See if you can go around the hurt he is suppressing. Offering too much sympathy will be giving energy to his pain. Try and get him to talk, that's the most important thing."

"What about the lack of sensation in the hand you mentioned, will it be permanent?"

"That I do not know for certain. Blood circulation to the area is normal, he can open and close the fist, but below the wrist, there appears to be no feeling. It may heal with time. The body is capable of miraculous healing power. On the other hand, it could be psychological. Men have died from less than what he had been through. You know we will not be able to keep him here much longer. He will discharge himself."

Both men sat staring at each other, not saying anything more. Both understood clearly the gravity of the situation.

"I will see him now," Captain Duncan said. He shook the doctor's hand and left his office. At the door to Mike's room, Captain Duncan spoke to the two officers. "If Cannon tries to leave, do not try to stop him, but let me know immediately. A Chinese gentleman will be coming to visit him. He is okay. His name is Wang Lee. He was at the shooting. He says Cannon saved his daughter's life. You may let him through."

Mike stared at Captain Duncan seated on a chair beside his bed through cold emotionless eyes, as if they were total strangers. They both remembered their last meeting and all they said to each other. Captain Duncan wished he could know what Mike was thinking, and he also wished he could have avoided being there. Seeing Mike Cannon like that was too painful for him. He had a vested interest in him getting well quickly and going back to doing what he did best. Also as his superior officer, it was his duty to be there.

He thought of Mike as a hard and private man. And the last thing he would want is for anyone attempting to share his grief. He believed whatever Mike was going through would make him even harder.

He had been placed in almost a similar situation in Nam. Shot up and badly burnt from the navel down. When he thought of his partial disfigurement, the only one he wanted to see was a North Vietcong in the sights of his M-16. He remembered the comfort he found in embracing the emotion of revenge. It had an abstract sweetness that helped him to absorb pain, heal his body, and motivated him into going back into battle.

He considered Mike to be at that same place, only worse. He had lost more—his entire family. So both men stared at each other, silently understanding. Not a word was spoken between them. When they were saturated with each other's presence, Captain Duncan got up without saying a word, bent down, and touched his arm, then walked through the door.

Chapter 2

At midnight, Mike Cannon walked out of the hospital room, passed the two officers at the door unchallenged, and took the elevator down to the lobby. He waited for a few minutes to see if he was being followed, and when he was certain he was not, he walked slowly toward the hospital parking lot. Every step was a new adventure in pain.

Wang Lee was leaning against the black Cadillac sedan as was prearranged. In spite of his painful condition, he could not resist noticing how young and attractive he really was. Mike, being extra cautious, hesitated, looked around, and climbed into the front passenger seat.

Wang Lee immediately opened the glove compartment and handed him a Glock 9mm and a full clip. He stroked the weapon fondly, inserted the clip, and shoved it in his waist. He savored the confidence and security the feel of the weapon brought back to him. That gesture completed his assessment of Wang Lee. He felt completely comfortable with him.

For the first time since he had regained consciousness, he felt he was regaining some control over his life. Days before, when Wang Lee entered his hospital room, he had sensed something between them. He thought about the strange connection, at first warily, but afterward, he compromised his suspicions for comradeship. Wang Lee was there when his family died; he saw it all. They both came face-to-face with death. Perhaps

Wang Lee shared his anxiety that it would not be long before the bad guys discovered he was alive and try again, and maybe the next time would be for keeps. So Wang Lee invited him to stay at his doctor brother's five-hundred-acre Central Florida estate where he could remain until he was fully recovered, and at the same time give his brother the chance to use his Oriental experiences and see what could be done about getting normal sensation back in his hand.

What was always lingering at the back of his mind was how Wang Lee knew he was still alive since that was privileged in-formation. He thought about it often, but after a while decided that the point was not worth pursuing under the prevailing circumstances. Wang Lee had proven both helpful and useful at a time when those features could not be overlooked.

Ten Lee, Wang Lee's older and more enterprising brother, was not the usual run-of-the- mill doctor. He had at a very early age attended one of those Oriental Shaolin Kung Fu training institutions in China where he became a master of the art. There he also became acquainted with the various healing techniques associated with the training. Upon graduation, he expanded his knowledge by attending a medical college tutoring ancient healing customs. After graduation, he set up offices in Hong Kong, treating the rich and famous. At the age of thirty-seven, he amassed enormous wealth through various enterprises and migrated to the United States, settling in central Florida with his younger carefree brother, whom he rescued from the wrath of a notorious gambling establishment situated in the gaming district of Hong Kong.

The new environment enabled Mike to heal rapidly. Phys-ically removed from the proximity of the tragedy gave him the opportunity to think over the entire situation objectively and to arrive at obvious conclusions. The reason his cover was penetrated had to be a departmental leak. He reasoned he could have been killed at any time before the attack, but targeting his entire family was an intimidating message being sent to other members of the task force to stand down. His effectiveness undercover was ended and, in his opinion, also that of the other members of his group. As head of the task force, he kept to himself vital information, a part of which he only shared with his immediate superior, Captain Duncan. The captain suspected he was holding back, but patiently waited for when he was ready to make a full report. He assumed Mike had his reasons. Conclusive proof linking various members of local government and several members of the police force, including high-ranking officers, would soon be completed.

The network of corruption was so cleverly organized that the code protecting names could not be easily broken. Many would no doubt be indicted if he succeeded. He contemplated seeking outside assistance toward that end. Real estate developments and several prominent commercial enterprises were the channels for laundering the proceeds of narcotic smuggling. Mike hesitated in submitting his findings as he considered his submission could possibly be misdirected and fall into the wrong hands. He recently discovered that officers of various police departments throughout the state of Florida were instrumental in the spate of witness executions. Some important person or persons with much to lose could not afford those findings to be submitted.

With time on his hands, the opportunity to analyze the situation presented itself. He could no longer rely on the teamwork of the department for protection. He viewed the fraternity of the institution with no less suspicion than the criminal elements he spent his time investigating. As a loner, he had the best chance of surviving, and for his own security, he would have to go deeper undercover and experience being a fugitive.

His effectiveness in the task force nonexistent, and as a marked man with his family murdered, Mike's decision to place himself outside the restraints of police procedures to attain his objective was a natural reaction. Circumstances had left him no other option, which was to kill the enemy or be killed by them, and for the first, he was well trained and considered among the best.

For his special undercover assignments, Mike was required to be included in a lengthy self-preservation training program specially designed for agents of the Special Services. He was so naturally adapted to the special skills required that he was at times required to demonstrate lethal techniques to other members of the group. He now found that training to be his primary weapon adaptable to meet his new agenda, which was to penetrate and create havoc in the deepest recesses of the criminal underworld in South Florida.

***

On the top floor of a newly constructed multistory high-rise office building complex was the penthouse office of Donaldo Francisco Santiago, owner of a real estate oceanfront development empire in the city of Miami. The real estate on which part of his development existed was formerly government property. Most or probably all of these holdings were acquired through association with privileged local government officials.

Donaldo Santiago looked down from his office window at the ongoing development and entertained doubts regarding its future. The man beside him was city mayor Frank Bukley, and beside the mayor stood David Schulenberg, chief executive officer of a very prosperous offshore South American bank.

The three men were troubled and unusually silent. Things carefully and methodically planned were getting out of hand.

Finally, Frank Bukley spoke. "I could not dream it would come to this. I want out."

Santiago turned and stared at him in utter disbelief. The more he stared, the angrier he became. "Out from what! Out to where? The only out will be to the cemetery. Have you any idea the people we are dealing with? These are the South Americans. We made commitments. When you give your word to these people, you keep it. We all knew what we were getting into, that there could be down sides. Now the going gets a bit uncertain, you want out?"

"I wish I could give it all back," Bukley whimpered. His trembling voice revealed the extent of his anxiety.

"Do you wish to give back your position as mayor also?" asked Santiago, desperately trying to contain his contempt for his colleague. "Have you forgotten already where the money came from that made you mayor? And what about the mansion on the waterway, the sixty-foot yacht, the custom-built Mercedes—will you give back those also? What would you have left? You would go back to being nothing. That is, if they allow you to live that long."

"Gentlemen, gentlemen!" David Schulenberg intervened. "This is not the way. We all have a lot to lose. Let us sit down and try to find a way out. We have no choice. Things have gone wrong, we cannot change that. But there has to be a solution. My motto is 'Where there is a will there is a way.'"

"What solution can there be?" Bukley continued to complain. "I told you murder was a bad idea. People are dead. A police inspector is dead. How do you believe that you could murder two police officers and get away with it? Do you have the slightest idea what that means? Those are not drug dealers at the street corner."

"That's where you are wrong," Donaldo Santiago interrupted. "I was informed this morning he is very much alive. That is the reason I called this meeting."

"What! Cannon not dead?" David Schulenberg asked. He was disappointed to hear the bad news that their greatest threat had not been eliminated. The information turned his complexion completely pale. "Are you certain of that? But the newspapers said—"

"Forget what the papers say," Santiago interrupted. "Take it from me, he is very much alive. His family is dead all right, but Cannon is very much alive. That is our problem. There is no stopping him now. We have to find a way to finish the job. Frank, this is more your area. What action can be expected from the department?"

"The department may call in the feds," Bukley replied. "I doubt if the feds will wait for an invitation. If Cannon links up with the feds and turns over to them the information he has, especially what he has on us, we are finished."

Donald Santiago thought of what Frank Bukley just said and promptly refused to accept the statement. In fact, his annoyance could hardly be controlled. "You are wrong, amigo. You may be finished, but I won't be. This is my life. I work hard for all this. No one takes this from me. Not Cannon, not his task force, not even the feds. You know what, Bukley, I am not certain about you anymore. And when I am uncertain about anyone or anything, I usually do something about it. You have no fight in you. No guts. You lack backbone. In fact, that was my first opinion of you. It was David's idea to give you a chance. I would hate to think of you as the weak link."

"Hold on there," intervened Schulenberg in an effort to defuse the dangerous message Santiago was sending. "I said it before, and I will say it again. There usually is a way out of any situation. We can find it if we stick together. Look what we have achieved. We are almost there. We are almost on top of the pile. We must keep it that way. Unity is strength. Bukley, those were your campaign words, remember?"

Santiago was silent while he decided whether to make an unpopular but necessary decision. He was the strength behind the group. He brought it together, and with a strong hand, he intended to do what it took to keep it successful. It had served his purpose so far, but if it became necessary to restructure, he would suffer no discomfort in doing just that. In Cuba as a teenager, he hated Fidel Castro, but at the same time admired his strength. That day he thought of Castro's courage in holding the revolution together against all odds, against the opinion of most of the world. But he had to do what he had to do and was still doing it. That was his honest opinion of the Cuban dictator, and that was the path he decided to take.

"Let me tell you both a story," Santiago said after a lengthy silence. He was reluctant to disclose the intimate details of his past, but the occasion made it necessary. "I was seventeen years old when I decided that I had enough of Fidel Castro. My mother had died giving birth to my brother. Ten years later, my father fell from the roof of our old house he was repairing, trying to keep the water out when it rained. He later died from the effects of that fall, and we were left on our own caring for ourselves. I will not attempt to describe what life was for us in Cuba as orphans, surviving on a day-to-day basis. Stealing was our only way of life when there was anything available to steal. Fed up and sick to my stomach of our condition, I got on to an older friend and sold him the idea of coming to America. It would be just the three of us. We had no money, so we decided to do it the hard way. One thing was never lacking in me, and that was courage. Show me a difficult situation, and you see the best side of me.

"It took us four weeks to steal six empty oil drums. We lashed them together with wire and rope to form a raft and made four oars from pieces of board I ripped from the siding of our old house. We would not need the house anymore, so it did not matter. We packed as much food as we could find to steal, washed out two empty ten-gallon kerosene tins, and filled them with water. Each of us tied tin cups to our waists to drink from, and to avoid the Coast Guard Patrol, one dark rainy Sunday night at ten o'clock, set out for Florida.

"We soon found out what rowing a raft made of six empty drums across the Straits of Florida was all about. After we lost sight of land, we also lost our sense of direction. But we kept rowing, hoping that by some miracle, we were going in the right direction and would one day reach the Florida Coast.

"After a few days, nothing we had planned was going right. We had lost track of time, the food ran out, and also most of the water. The sun was merciless. My brother took sick and had a high temperature and kept crying for more water. Between the three of us, although we had cut the meager ration by half, the water would not last two more days. I had to do something. Then I saw the large fin bearing down toward us. It was a tiger shark. You could tell by the stripes. He saw us, and he wanted one of us, if not all three. He kept circling the raft, and by then I got an idea. The water could not last all three of us, and the shark's intention was clear. So I made a decision and did what I had to do. I kicked my best friend off the raft right in front of the shark, and he ate him.

"The story does not end there. Two days after, my brother died, and the shark came back. It had tasted human flesh, and this time it brought a buddy with him. They were so ferocious, they all but climbed onto the raft. I kissed my brother on the forehead and pushed him over. While they were feasting on him, I saw a fishing boat with two Cuban Americans aboard coming toward me, and my story ends there. So you see, gentlemen, when the situation calls for it, to survive, I do what I have to do."

Santiago had made his point, and the others got it loud and clear.

"From now on, guys, I will make the decisions. Whatever it takes, I will do." There was no objection to Santiago's takeover. His story said it all. He would not tolerate objections, and if there was a necessity, he would do what he had to do.

Turning to the mayor, he said, "Bukley, have a meeting with that Captain Duncan. Find out what he knows and what action the department will be taking. Try and find out all you can about Cannon. If he pretends not to know he is alive, you will know that he already knows something and does not trust you. Let us meet here same time tomorrow. By then I will formulate a plan to deal with this situation."

***

It was 4:00 a.m., and Santiago held the Daimler convertible at a steady sixty. There was not much traffic on the Interstate-95 going north that time of the morning. There was a slight drizzle, and he lifted the top and turned on the wipers. He was going nowhere in particular. He spent the night thinking and could not sleep. Although it was raining, he rolled down the windows so the moist rushing air would aid in clearing his head.

He drove for almost an hour when the phone on the dash rang. He wondered who would be calling his private line that time in the morning. He had calls transferred from his private line to his car. He turned up the windows to keep out the road noise before he took up the receiver.

"Yes, who is this?"

"Mendez. Carlos Mendez. Jack Kolaski gave me your number and said to contact you immediately I got in."

"That's a name I prefer not to hear. The fool he sent down here boshed the job, got himself killed, and got me into a hell of a lot more trouble. He has a nerve telling you to call me. What do you want?"

"What fool, what's going on here?" Mendez inquired. "I am here to do the job. I got into town an hour ago. Jack sent no one down here. I am the man."

"What the hell are you talking about? You are supposed to be dead. Took four slugs from the hit that is very much alive and is..." Santiago was confused. He had to think. He needed time.

"Are you there?" Mendez asked when the conversation was abruptly cut short.

"Yes. I am here. We need to meet. I have to find out what's going on first."

"You do that. I am at the Airport Marriot. Call Kolaski and straighten this thing out. If I do not hear from you by tomorrow afternoon, I am heading back to New York."

Santiago took the next exit off the highway, drove beneath the underpass, and headed back to Miami Beach. So much was racing through his mind, he had difficulty keeping the convertible on the road. His information network that previously served him well now proved to be obsolete. Who ordered the hit? If some unknown person starts ordering hits on people, anyone could be next.

The thought of being vulnerable began to erode his self-confidence. He realized Mike Cannon was not his only major problem. It was evident he was not the top dog on the block.

Santiago was mandate for the South American producers of top-grade uncut cocaine smuggled into South Florida. He answered to the head of an offshore international organization capable of displaying awesome political and financial power. Preferential opportunities placed at his disposal enabled Santiago to amass enormous personal assets. But instead of strengthening relationships with associates who were instrumental in his success, he was unfortunate to earn their resentment and also their dedication to his downfall. To remain top dog in the junglelike arena of the criminal underworld, he must rely on his cunning and ruthlessness, the effectiveness of which would determine his survival.

***

Many miles away from Miami, Mike sat on the edge of the swimming pool at Ten Lee's house with his feet dangling in the cool water. The heat from the sun at midday was merciless. He thought that was the reason why Florida was the Sunshine State. In most other states at that particular time, folks were shoveling snow from their driveways. In spite of his personal problems, he instinctively sensed a world of activity in the immediate vicinity, although there was no evidence of a single soul in sight, the feeling one gets when being spied upon by someone in hiding.

From the night he arrived at Ten Lee's house, he had not seen his host or Wang Lee, who took him there. It was the third day, and his curiosity was having the better of him. He was waited on by the exceptionally friendly housekeeper, Tai, who catered to his every need. Whenever he enquired about the two brothers, Tai would pat him on the shoulder and walk away in silence. In spite of his curiosity, however, his policeman's instincts told him he was in no immediate danger from his host.

Ten Lee's house was an imposing white two-story mansion of concrete and steel, with several adjoining buildings that must have collectively occupied over five acres of ground. Whatever operation the two brothers were engaged in had to be very successful. All around was evidence of an enormous amount of money being lavishly spent. However, other more pressing thoughts did not allow that matter further consideration, so he dismissed the subject for the time being. He gave thought to the discomfort he began to experience from his partly healed wounds and just in time observed a small Oriental lady walking toward where he sat. In spite of the state of his mind, he could not help noticing how beautiful and well formed she was. She stopped about six feet away from him, held both hands in front of her, and bowed gracefully.

"I am Goldie Lee," she introduced herself. "Wang and Ten said I should take care of your wounds. If you wish, you may come with me." Her voice matched her gracefulness and reminded one of rose petals floating down to fall on velvet.

Having made her request, she unhesitatingly turned around and walked toward one of the many adjoining buildings, expecting him to follow. So he did. Inside the building was a well-planned and professionally equipped clinic, more than would be normally required for tending the physical well-being of any ordinary household. It was evident there was a large amount of personnel in the nearby vicinity who presently or at some past time used the facilities.

Goldie Lee was no novice to the medical profession. No hospital staff could have performed a more efficient service. After the wounds were cleansed and bandages replaced, she went behind an enclosure that served as a miniature pharmacy and returned with a vial of capsules and a glass of water. She handed him the water and one of the capsules, which he took immediately. She advised him to take one daily, preferably after meals. This gave him the opportunity to ask when would it be possible to speak with any of her brothers, and she told him that it would be possible very soon. Although he was tempted, he had not wandered into the wooded areas of the estate. He imagined it bad taste to abuse the hospitality of his host by trespassing because of his personal curiosity and waited to see if he would be invited to do so.

More than two weeks had passed, and he felt almost as good as new. He still had not seen any of the two brothers. During that period, Goldie Lee had cared for his wounds several times. Finally, she thought it safe to permanently remove his bandages and for the first time showed some emotion. Mike sat on a stool while she applied ointment to the almost completely healed wounds.

"Mr. Cannon," she said, looking him straight in the eye, "you are a good man. You have suffered much, and you have lost those dear to you. Do not be consumed by vengeance. Be patient, justice will have its reward."

Mike imagined she wanted to say more, but hesitated, because just a few feet behind him stood Ten Lee. He had unexpectedly crept up behind him.

Ten Lee was a small man in comparison to Mike. He was five feet eight at most, 150 pounds. He had icy-cold eyes and a body of steel. He stared at Goldie Lee, and without speaking another word, she disappeared. It was obvious there was not much love lost between them. That she was terrified of him was an opinion immediately formed.

Ten Lee turned toward Mike and mentally measured him from his feet upward—all six feet three inches, 235 pounds of him. It was obvious he was not impressed, and he wanted Mike to know.

He gave a contemptuous smile. In spite of his mixed emotions in regard to Ten Lee, he sensed strength and forthrightness in his personality that left him confused.

"I apologize for being away, Mr. Cannon. I was away on the West Coast."

Mike suspected Ten Lee had not left the precincts of his estate.

"But now that your wounds are healed, let's see if we can do something for the other parts of you. We will begin with the problem in your hand." Ten Lee started by probing the left hand from the elbow down. The strength in his fingers all but penetrated the skin. He looked up in Mike's face to see if he would wince from the pain he knew he was inflicting. But he saw no sign of discomfort. Ten Lee smiled sadistically as he proceeded to probe the hands and fingers.

"I feel nothing in my hand and fingers."

With his hand still holding Mike's, Ten Lee said, "Make a tight fist." Mike closed his hand into a fist, and Ten Lee grimaced from the excruciating pain that was unconsciously inflicted. "Was that deliberate?" Ten Lee asked, still affected by the encounter.

"No, I have no control over what my hand does. There is no sensation, no feeling at all."

"Wait here, I will be back." Ten Lee left the room and soon returned with a length of two-by-four hardwood lumber about four feet in length. He placed one end on the edge of the table while he held the other end tightly. "Strike this," he said to Mike.

With no apparent effort, Mike's fist shattered the length of timber. Ten Lee gazed on the splintered fragments on the floor and then up at Mike. "Have you ever practiced any form of martial art?" Ten Lee enquired.

"No, never have," Mike lied.

"Well, you have now. I have seen this before. The phenomena may remain with you, or it may disappear during the course of time, depending on your mental attitude. In your situation, it could be physiological, introduced by a feeling of guilt. You could be subconsciously blaming yourself for not doing more to prevent your assailant from killing your family. You could believe you had been let down by an element you usually depend on. The mind sometimes works like that. I suppose you were left handed. It remains for you to come to terms with yourself. There is nothing anyone else can do. It depends entirely on you. You must now train your right hand to serve you as your left hand once did."

Mike accepted the diagnosis with reservation. He strongly believed that the situation was very temporary and that one day soon it would disappear. But from the recent demonstration of its capability, for the time being, its usefulness as a formidable weapon could be an advantage in the emergencies he anticipated.

"I suppose you will be leaving us now that you are as well as can be expected?" Ten Lee asked, which was meant more to be a suggestion.

"Speaking of 'us,' what has become of your brother Wang? I have not seen him since I was here."

In reply, Ten Lee explained, "We are extremely busy people, Mr. Cannon. Our business takes us all over the world at very short notice. My brother was called overseas and could be away for some time."

Mike was tempted to ask what their line of business was, but he guessed he would only be lied to. Somehow, he believed he would have cause to find out for himself, and he was almost certain it was centered on that very estate.

As Ten Lee escorted him out of the clinic, he said to Mike, "Whenever you are ready, I will have one of the drivers take you back to Miami or wherever you wish to go. You may inform Tai. He will arrange it."

That very night, Tai came to his room and informed him that his transportation was arranged as he requested, and a driver was ready to transport him to wherever he wished to go. Out in the yard he saw a parked jeep. An Oriental driver he had never seen before invited him in. The driver was of the same size and hardness of body as Ten Lee. Mike wondered how many more of similar types were residing on the estate and what their purposes were.

Chapter 3

It was a quiet Sunday morning, and the steady stream of expensive exotic automobiles turning into the gated entrance of the Lauder Hill mansion must have attracted some concerns. Jack Wall had acquired and lavishly maintained those premises in spite of objections from his professional neighbors when he inspected the real estate prior to purchasing. But what could the agents do but sell when he entered their offices one morning and dumped cash on the table?

Jack Wall was a successful international commodity trader, even though he was a Jamaican who wore shoulder-length locks. His father was African Jamaican and his mother Chinese, which created the ethnic mixture that may have contributed to the aggressive personality that qualified him for being successful in the dangerous lifestyle he pursued. His cunning and organizational expertise placed him at the head of the Jamaican Posse, one of the most daring criminal organizations to challenge law enforcement in the United States of America.

It was a poolside cookout that special Sunday morning at the Lauder Hill house, and the caterers lavishly supplied the trimmings for the two dozen Jamaican dreadlocked men and their families. It was evident that money was no object. Reggae Jamaican music served as background entertainment, and Jamaican Red Stripe Beer was the favored drink of the adult males. The many children happily running around and the young ladies in bikinis lounging on poolside deck chairs having a great time did not give any impression that the occasion was the setting for a sinister gathering of dangerous international criminals.

During the course of the day, the two dozen men retreated to the main building and occupied the large and comfortably furnished conference room of Jack Wall International Trading Inc., a home-based trading company that specialized in smuggling controlled substances into the United States. To be discussed that day were Mike Cannon and recent developments favorably affecting narcotic importation.

Jack, who controlled distribution in Florida, sat at one end of the table, and C. Perkins, called CP, who controlled Bronx and Brooklyn in New York, sat at the other. Supporting those two were their street soldiers. Before the meeting commenced, Jack placed his weapon on the table before him, immediately followed by the others. That display of hardware was for security purposes and was the standing procedure.

Jack carefully scrutinized each of the faces to be certain during the course of the meeting he could place the correct name to each one attending. To maintain their loyalty, it was important for the men to understand that there was a personal bonding between himself and everyone in attendance. They waited for him to speak, and after a few minutes, he did.

"First, I must thank you guys who came all the way from New York at short notice, but it was important for you to be here. There is a little problem we must get out the way before we get down to important business. I suppose everyone has heard of this policeman Mike Cannon who is trying to make some problems down here?"

"Yes, we have!" they all replied in unison.

"Well, some fool placed a hit on him and did not get the job done. What they did was to kill the man's family and left him alive with a few bruises. Thinking about it, I can't believe the Colombians would be incapable of completing a simple thing as that. So that rules them out. And I can't believe the Latinos would have the balls to even try."

"Why not?" asked C. Perkins.

"Well, think of it, CP. If they don't even have the balls to get rid of Castro, do you believe they would have what it takes to hit a prominent American police officer? Think of it. Do you think if Fidel was in Jamaica and smashing up the country, he would be still alive?"

"He definitely would not be!" some of the men shouted.

"But you never know, Jack," C. Perkins said. "If this guy Mike Cannon has a lot on them, and they have a lot to lose, they may not have the guts to do it themselves, but they could get an outsider. What about this opium business down here? Do you believe that may have something to do with it?"

"Don't know," Jack replied after giving the question some thought. "I can't see the reason why it should. As much as I am made to understand, they don't have a lot going on, only a small corner of the market. Think of it, opium is not very popular in Miami. There is really nothing to write home about. Except they wish to stir up something, like getting the law to blame the hit on us or the Colombians. Then if we are taken out of the picture, it would give them an open playing field to introduce their junk. But the law knows we do not play that way. They know that if we want Cannon dead, he is dead. That also goes for the Colombians. All I know is that this Cannon guy has lost his family, and he will be like a mad dog running wild. He will be out for revenge and could cause everyone some trouble. And you can't blame him."

"No, boss, he can't make any trouble for us," one of the soldiers from across the table interrupted. "I can take care of that. No problem. Just say the word."

"I will in time, Sammy, if it becomes necessary. Let me look into it first. Maybe this Cannon situation could be a good thing for us. I will let you guys know what's to be done. Give me some time. Well, enough of that, let's put this aside for the time being and get down to real business."

As far as the group was concerned, taking care of Cannon was no major problem that could be dealt with whenever the necessity arises. So that small item on the agenda dismissed, the group waited in eager anticipation for Jack to proceed with the important information that was the main reason for the gathering.

"Listen up, guys," Jack continued. "At last we have the break we have been waiting for. We can now compete with the Colombians with their own shit."I suppose some of you guys know that I went back home last week. It was to meet a certain important gentleman, a Cuban. You may be asking yourselves if I went to Cuba. The answer is no. He came to see me. Then you will be asking yourselves next, how could that happen when Prime Minister Edward Seaga bans any Cuban from setting foot on Jamaican soil? The answer to that is that I met him partway, out at sea."

"You must be joking!" exclaimed C. Perkins.

"No, I met Señor Ulises Artega at sea on a Cuban gun boat one night, one mile off Ocho Rios."

"I know Señor Artega," C. Perkins interrupted. "Short, stocky, with a scar across his forehead."

"Same, but how, when?"

"A few years ago, about a thousand of us Jamaicans were sent to Cuba by Michael Manley to be trained in guerilla warfare. He was prime minister then and invited Fidel to take over Jamaica. He knew that there would be a war because Jamaicans would not tolerate communism. We were supposed to be trained for his personal protection. We were called Brigadistas. Artega was the senior weapons expert that trained us. He is good. Among a lot of other things, he taught us to dismantle and reassemble an AK-47 blindfolded. He was trained as a terrorist by the Russians. At that time, Castro wanted Russia to attack the United States, and Cuba would control the Islands. Michael wanted us to be ready because he knew his life would not be worth a red cent. And believe me, eventually I would shoot him myself. Look how poor Cuba is. I hate poverty. I would not even be able to afford my BMW."

That bit of interesting information immediately added to the prestige of C. Perkins, whose notoriety was already known throughout the areas of Bronx and Brooklyn in New York. It was obvious he was pleased with the effect the disclosure of his military training had on the other members of the group.

"So, CP, is that the secret why you are able to take care of things so effectively in New York?" one of the men from Miami enquired.

C. Perkins smiled but did not reply. Jack in particular, for the first time, discovered the reason why C. Perkins was able to expand the market so rapidly in the most competitive area of his organization. He had no previous knowledge of C. Perkins's military background. It was evident that his position as second in command was well justified.

"As I was saying, this is how it went down," Jack continued. "The deal is straight from Fidel himself. The Colombians will fly the cocaine into Cuba. All uncut high-grade stuff. Fidel will pay for it from a special Russian grant to Cuba for the purpose of 'waging overt destabilizing war on the USA.' That is exactly how the man said it. Then we will get it from Cuba at the same bulk rate they pay for it and delivered to my man in Ocho Rios by Cuban Coast Guard. Remember, Cuba is only ninety miles from Ocho Rios. And listen to the sweetest part of the deal: we get it on consignment. We pay after we sell it over here to our contacts. They are prepared to try us first with two deliveries of 250 kilos each. If we play fair, they will up the amount monthly, and then sky is the limit. It's forever."

"So why could they not sell it directly to the American dealers themselves?" one of the soldiers asked.

"Because no American pilot will fly into Cuba, and also, Castro don't want to deal with Americans. He hates Americans," said another soldier.

"That's correct," Jack said in support of that statement. "So instead of flying marijuana out of Boscobel Airport, we fly cocaine. How do you like that?"

"Irie! Irie!" The entire group shouted and banged on the desk, expressing delight on the new deal and what it would mean to each of them financially.

To accommodate the expected increase in business, there arose the need for restructuring the operation, so Jack delegated new responsibilities. Some of the soldiers were promoted to new positions with fancy titles according to length of service and proven aggressiveness. The ensuing atmosphere was charged with excitement as a result of this gesture. In conclusion, the members of the group were eager to individually pledge support for the new organizational structure. There being no opposition or further business to discuss, the meeting was adjourned, and the remainder of that day was spent in celebration.

Jack Wall had researched the Cuban American relationship at his local library before he accepted the invitation of Fidel

Castro to aid his anti-American campaign. Jack personally witnessed at first hand the attempted takeover of Jamaica by Fidel Castro. He knew of his takeover of the island of Grenada and the American military intervention. He was aware that to aid the Cuban government in any way or form in their destabilization campaign against the American government, he was to become a traitor and an enemy of this country. As a renegade citizen of the United States, he decided to join the ranks of the enemies within. He held in his hand a copy of a document written by Professor Edward Samuel Graham of a renowned American university and read the following information.

"During the period of the Cold War, Fidel Castro declared that his true destiny in life is to be instrumental in destroying the United States. The Soviet Union refused from supporting his suicidal idea of waging war against this country and declared him a bloodthirsty lunatic. So Castro was forced to settle for the pursuit of his alternative overt strategy. To this end, he indirectly organized mass migration of Cuba's citizens into the country. The plan behind this massive exodus was to infiltrate the American population with dangerous criminals and his trained anti-American agents by mixing them with honest immigrants seeking a better way of life. At his victory celebration speech in Nicaragua, he boasted: 'We have agents of absolute confidence all over the United States ready to undertake whatever actions are necessary at the time of my choosing. The Americans cannot begin to imagine the capabilities we have in their country. We can accomplish things that would make the riots in Florida look like a garden party.'

"This is the very same Fidel Castro that is now trying to fool Washington that he wants peaceful coexistence with the United States. It is evident that Fidel is only biding time, waiting for Washington to relax by thinking that he is no longer a threat, and then his long-term conspiracy will be put into action. Most of those implants are now sleeper agents just waiting for orders. The plan to contaminate the population of the United States with cocaine is part of Fidel's overt strategy. Toward this end, the Russians had already established laboratories in Cuba for the purpose of adding chemicals into cocaine capable of being transferred through the systems of users down to their offsprings even to the tenth generation. This demoralizing agent would affect the armed forces, the civil services, undermine the learning capability of future generations, and in the long term create a population of degenerates. The potent additives can be increased at will for the purpose of creating criminal behavior of unimaginable magnitude. For security reasons and to avoid mass hysteria, this information has been willfully withheld from the general public." Jack read the document several times before he made a decision. He gave thought to the privileges being enjoyed by his family, which he was willing to compromise in exchange for personal power and monetary gain. Fidel Castro had scouts in the United States, Central and South America, throughout the Caribbean, and the continent of Africa, searching for people such as Jack. So to implement his strategy, Fidel Castro was introduced to the Jamaican Jack Wall and his Jamaican Posse, which consisted of hard-core criminal-minded Jamaicans residing in the United States. They were both convenient and willing, Jamaica being only ninety miles from Cuba. But to be successful, they must overcome the resolve of Detective Inspector Mike Cannon, who in his personal war had pledged to go wherever it led him and do whatever it took to rid the people of the United States of the imminent threat. It was such criminal elements that took the lives of his family, and his war was against them.

***

It was almost closing time when Mike Cannon pressed the bell at the door of the gun shop owned by the Austrian. He had four weeks of unshaven beard and shoulder-length hair. A cap and oversized shirt over baggy jeans completed his disguise.

Bill Kirsky, who preferred to be called the Austrian, came to the peep window in the door, took one look at the person on the other side, and walked away. Mike pressed the bell two more times.

The Austrian returned to the door and opened it. That time he was very angry. "What the hell do you want?" the Austrian shouted.

Mike took out his badge and held it up so the Austrian could see he was a police officer. It was then that the Austrian took a closer look and recognized Mike. Cannon was satisfied his disguise was effective.

"My god, Mike, you are supposed to be dead!" the Austrian exclaimed.

"Not quite," Mike said. "They tried to kill me, but they couldn't. Kim and the kids were not so lucky though. They are dead. Billy, they killed my wife and kids, the murdering bastards."

The Austrian then understood the reason for the disguise and decided not to make mention of it. "Let's go around the back and talk about it over coffee. It will do you good to get it all out. We are like family, Mike," the Austrian said.

He held Mike by the hand and commenced pulling him toward the rear of the shop.

"I cannot stop today, Billy. Today it's business. I need something from you," Mike said, declining the invitation.

Mike Cannon and the Austrian went way back to high school days. They were fighting comrades against the Canal Boys who daily picked on the Austrian because of his poor English.

Mike stood up for him and many times got both their butts kicked. After high school, Mike joined the police force, and the Austrian joined his father in the gun shop. Since then, never a week would pass when they would not get together for a beer or coffee. So it was obvious that the Austrian would be happy to see Mike alive and seemingly well, especially that he seemed to have a burden on his mind and wanted something from him to cure it. If it was humanly possible, he would be happy to oblige.

The Austrian said, "You can have whatever it is, just name it. If I have it, you got it."

"I need a handgun that can drop a bear with one slug at fifty yards."

Thinking, the Austrian scratched his head and said, "Mike, I have just the gun for you. What a beauty. I was keeping it for myself. But it would be a waste. What would I be doing with such a weapon?"

"What make is it?" Cannon asked, excited. He knew that whatever the Austrian recommended would be his best.

The Austrian searched through a mountain of papers in a desk drawer and produced an elaborately printed document. Reading from one of its pages, he commenced to recite the description of a weapon he was about to introduce to his friend. "It's a Bren Ten type 80 machine / automatic pistol. With holster and shoulder stock that goes with it, which can be fitted at a moment's notice so you may aim and shoot as with a rifle. It can be semiautomatic or single action. Accurate kill range of one hundred meters or more, with twenty rounds to the magazine." To impress Mike, he added features of his own creation. "It's yours if you like it," he continued. "I also have on hand five hundred special rounds to go with it. When you are out, just call in. I will get some more."

"I will take it if I can afford it. How much is it?"

"How much!" exclaimed the Austrian. "Mike, it's yours for free. You are family. Anything so you can get even with those murdering sons of bitches." The Austrian took a long box from beneath the counter, in which was stored the gun wrapped in oilskin and then in a canvas bag. After slowly and ceremoniously removing all the wrappings, with both hands extended, he gave the weapon and the attachment to Mike.

Cannon examined the gun as if it was a fragile and priceless archeological find. He attached the stock and held it to his shoulder. His eyes moved slowly along the barrel to rest on the sights, and then worked the trigger vigorously, as if he was blasting an imaginary enemy. He then removed the stock and tested the balance. He had an extensive knowledge of firearms. He knew of the Bren Ten type 80, that it was a special weapon usually carried by senior military personnel when moving around in light armored vehicles while in hostile territory. The gun was the one he believed could do the job in mind.

"Do you like it, Mike? Is it okay for you?"

"Suits me fine, Billy, suits me just fine," he replied.

Mike took position of the weapon and ammunition and gave the Austrian a hug. He had things to do, and there was no time for the usual formalities.

"Thanks, Billy, see you later," he said as he went through the door.

"So long, Mike. Take care." The Austrian watched as he walked up the street and mingled with the crowd. In his mind, he said a prayer and hoped that wasn't the last time he would see Mike.

Chapter 4

It was 2:00 a.m., and Captain Duncan was not pleased when he was awakened by the ringing of his bedside telephone. He had a long day and had retired after midnight. He took up the receiver and inhospitably asked, "What?"

There was no answer.

He was about to hang up when the voice at the other end replied, saying, "Mike."

"Mike! Mike Cannon!" the excited Captain Duncan exclaimed. "Where have you been? What have you been doing with yourself?" Captain Duncan sat up and held the receiver tightly, as if by doing so, he would not lose the voice at the other end. He seemed pleased to be contacted by Mike.

"I am getting my act together," Mike replied.

"I want to meet you, but not at headquarters," Captain Duncan said.

"I would not be coming there. I have not lost my mind. Captain, do I still have my badge?"

"What kind of a stupid question is that? You are still a police officer. Every damned thing seems to be happening since you were shot. They have kidnapped Eddie Lang's thirteen-year-old daughter. What for, we can only guess. There has been no demand as yet. All the other boys in the task force have moved their families to safe houses. We miss you, Mike. Something has to be done. You have most of the answers."

"I read about the kidnapping in the papers. That is why I am calling."

Captain Duncan was pleased to hear that Mike was concerned. He felt certain Mike would do something about it. Eddie Lang was a dedicated honest man and second to Mike in the task force. Mike thought a lot of him.

"Your piece is in my desk drawer. I took it after you got shot. How will I get it to you?"

"Never mind the piece," Mike replied. "Tell Eddie I will get his daughter back. And, Captain, find some way that I may contact you in an emergency. Consider me still on active duty."

"Mike, I will arrange that. And, Mike, try and play it by the book as much as possible. I know you are hurting, and that will be a hard thing to do, but remember, you are still a police officer." Captain Duncan stared into the silent receiver for some time before he realized there was no one at the other end of the line. Yet he felt a sense of relief hearing from Mike and knowing that if Mike Cannon said he was going to do something, it was usually done.

***

From his one-bedroom motel window, Mike could see the traffic moving up and down the Miami River close by even at that early time in the morning. It was 3:00 a.m. and still dark. He left the apartment and walked toward where he had left the Camaro earlier at the service station parking lot on Twenty-Seventh Avenue. Had the motel manager seen him that early morning, he would be confused. As far as he was concerned, Mike Cannon was an out-of-town drifter down on his luck searching for a job and barely being able to pay his rent. That was a part of Mike's disguise. That morning he wore black leather gloves, a black SWAT combat outfit, and black combat boots. Inside one of the boots was a backup Glock 9mm. Strapped to the other leg was a twelve-inch hunting knife in its sheath. The Bren Ten was in its shoulder holster. With that much hardware added to the mood he was in, he felt invincible.

After the Christmas Day shooting, Mike's Miami Gardens apartment was burglarized, searched, and his briefcase with vital information stolen. But days before, he had removed the most damaging evidences he had collected to a deposit box and hidden the key in the inside lining of his belt. From knowledge gained through his undercover experience, he could target the right individual responsible for almost any given unlawful act, and he knew where to obtain any information, depending on the nature of the case. He was prepared to operate out of or within the law, depending on the urgency of the situation and what procedure would provide the quickest result. The urgency of the situation at hand was one of those that did not afford him choices.

There was light in the two-bedroom Opa Lacka apartment when Mike walked toward the front door. At that time of night, that area was no place for the timid or unarmed. And if you were armed, you must be prepared to defend yourself.

Jay Gordon, one of Mike's informants, was lying in bed with a woman. On a chair seated by the bed sat Claude Perez. Their other associate, Pecan the Indian, was seated at a table in the outer room having coffee, his back turned toward the front door. The Indian preferred to be alone. He had no time for chitchat. Details were not his thing. Give him an order, and he would carry it out regardless of its nature. In short, he was an inexpensive killer for hire.

The sound of music and loud laughter could be heard coming from the bedroom, so Pecan the Indian did not hear when Mike picked the lock of the front door and entered. There was not much of anything in that front room except a small round oak table at which the Indian sat, three chairs, a leather sofa, and a nineteen-inch television set on a small table with a plastic runner. There were no pictures on the wall. One door led to the kitchen and another to the bedroom. Gordon did not live well, but he drove an expensive European car.

Mike had been to see Jay in that apartment several times. He knew Jay to be a double-dealing informant working both sides. That suited Mike well as apart from gaining important information relating to the bad guys, he would pass on through him just what he wanted them to know. If anyone had the particular information he wanted, it would be Jay Gordon.

Claude and Pecan the Indian had just completed their shift guarding a valuable item stashed in a Hialeah warehouse. They had been relieved by two others, one of whom was an off-duty Miami police officer. Jay had arranged the job for Perez and the Indian, and Jay wanted to discuss information of salable value pertaining to the guarded item. That was Gordon's line of business, selling information.

Mike approached the Indian with the hunting knife in his hand. As he got closer, the Indian instinctively turned around, sprang to his feet, threw the coffee at Mike, and went for the .38 Smith & Wesson in his waist.

With a quick fluid hand motion, Mike threw the knife. The blade entered the front of the Indian's neck and went out through the back. He grabbed the handle in an effort to pull the knife out so he could warn the others. But for his effort, only a crimson stream gushed out of his mouth. He fell back against the table and died, kicking both legs as he slid to the floor.

Claude heard the commotion, raced through the door leading to the front room, and was confronted by the awesome presence of Mike behind the Bren Ten aimed at his face. Claude saw the body on the floor, lifted his hands high, and backed into the room followed by Mike.

"Good morning, people," Mike said as he pulled out the electric lead that connected the radio to the wall socket. "Having a conference, are we? Now listen to this. I have a question to ask, and I haven't much time. One or all of you know the answer. The one of you who answers first gets to live. Now, where is the girl?"

As a further demonstration to get their cooperation, Mike struck the top of the dresser with his gloved left hand with such force that it splintered into fragments, as if hit by a sixteen-pound sledgehammer. No one in the room had ever before witnessed such an awesome physical display. Mike himself was surprised at his destructive capability.

"Okay! Okay!" They all shouted at once. "She is in a warehouse in Hialeah."

"Now, who answered first?" Mike asked, pointing the weapon menacingly from one to the other.

"I did! I can take you there," all three volunteered.

"What a shame," Mike said. "I only need one of you. Three is a crowd." Mike pointed the Bren Ten at Claude as if to shoot.

Claude Perez, a hardened professional criminal who was wanted for questioning in two homicides, in desperation lounged at Mike. Mike sidestepped and struck him with his weapon with such force to the back of the neck that he was dead before he touched the floor.

The overall level of violence was too much for the woman. She became hysterical and began to scream.

"Shut her up, or she is next!" Mike shouted, aiming the Bren Ten at her.

Jay grabbed her and held his hand over her mouth.

"Gag her and tie her up. You are coming with me." Mike watched as Jay took the sheet from the bed, tore it, and did as he was ordered. On the way out, Mike stopped and retrieved his knife from the body on the floor. He sensed a feeling of satisfaction. Payback had indeed begun.

Both men walked toward Jay's Volvo. Mike followed Jay ten feet behind.

"Don't even think of it. This Bren Ten type 80 can surgically take your leg off at fifty yards, and you will be still alive long enough to show me where the girl is."

Jay wondered how Mike could have guessed he was about to make a dash for the wall in the darkness.

Jay opened the door of the Volvo and sat behind the wheel. Mike opened the rear door and sat behind him. They drove in silence for five minutes. Jay wondered how he should begin negotiating for his life. "Mike, I thought you were dead. You should know I would have told you everything."

"You, tell me everything? You have never told me everything. I was on to your double-dealing tactics from day one. That suited me until now. But I give you credit. You have gone up in the world, from a snitch to a kidnapper. You have done well for yourself, Jay Gordon. There is only one thing wrong with that. The sentence for kidnapping in my book is death. You are a dead man, Jay. You die tonight just as your buddies."

"For god's sake, Mike, take it easy with me. We can still work together. You don't have to do this. You can see I am cooperating. I am taking you to the girl."

"You have no choice. It's the girl or your life right now. At least this way you will live a little longer."

"Will you let me live after I take you to the girl?"

"I don't know. Your life is not worth the girl's. You have nothing to bargain with. You are of no further use to me."

"Yes, I am. If I tell you what you don't know, will you give me a chance?"

"Keep talking. But I am making no promises. Depends on what you have to say."

Jay breathed a sigh of relief. That last remark of Mike's gave him a chance to put something to bargain with on the table. That Mike behind him was a stranger he had never seen before. Two people were already dead that night, and he had no doubt that whoever else must die, Mike would not care less. He must negotiate to live and do it before he got to the warehouse. He knew time was not in his favor. It was running out.

"To begin with, more than a dozen of your people are involved in what's going on. One is at the warehouse at this moment watching the girl."

"Who, what's his name?"

"They call him Jose."

"Tall, slim, graying hair, walks with a limp?" asked Mike.

"Yes, that's him."

Manaedio. Jose Manaedio, Mike said to himself. "And who else?"

"There is a Puerto Rican from New York. I do not know his name. He is one of those the House Man brought in two days ago."

"Is it the House Man who ordered the girl taken?"

"Yes, he orders almost everything."

"Did he order the hit on me and my family?"

"That I do not know, Mike. As there is a God, if I knew something like that, I would have warned you. But I can find out if you let me."

"Now, who is the House Man.? Have you ever met him? For the answer to this, you live."

Jay's heart dropped. The answer to that question he did not have. "As God is my witness, Mike, that I do not know. I do not know anyone who has ever met him or knows his real name. Jose has never met him, but he receives orders. Through whom, I do not know either, he never says. I get my orders from Jose. Give me a chance, Mike. I can find out all you want to know for free."

Mike's experience with his kind told him he was speaking the truth. "I will think on it. Depends on what happens at the warehouse when I try to get the girl."

Jay saw his chance to live, and he had no intention not to cooperate. As he approached the warehouse, he cut the head-lights and parked. He wanted Mike to notice he was doing everything to assist.

Mike waited for him to speak. If Jay was being sincere, he knew what must be done from there on and would do it.

"Mike, the girl is in the office in the back of the building. Jose would have the key to the office. There is only the one door in and out of the building. The rear exit door is boarded up for security. The building is empty except for empty crates and small boxes. They are armed, Mike. I will go to the door and knock. There is a code. They will let me in."

As they walked toward the door, Mike took the car keys from Jay, placed them in his pocket, and said, "Keep out of my way, or I will kill you."

"I know that," Jay said.

Jay went to the door and knocked five times. There was a pause of about five seconds. He then knocked again three more times.

"Who is it?" a voice from inside asked.

"Jay, open the door," was the answer.

Mike, standing about six feet away, heard the action of a bolt, saw the door began to open, and hurled his full body weight against it. The Puerto Rican from New York was hurled ten feet to the concrete floor. Mike did not hesitate when he entered. He shot him twice, once in the abdomen and once in the head. Jose Manaedio, taken by surprise at the effectiveness of Mike's ferocity, threw himself from the cot on which he was resting and barely had time to take cover behind a large wooden crate. Overcome by fear, he was unable to maintain control of his faculties. He commenced blasting away randomly with his shotgun.

Mike went into a roll on the floor and let loose a barrage of automatic fire into the crate behind which Manaedio found cover. The bullets splintered the crate and ripped his chest open. He made a loud scream and got to his feet. Still holding his weapon, he made a jerky step forward, and then fell forward on his face as another barrage from the Bren Ten literally cut him in half.

The girl hid under the desk in the office when she heard the shooting. She feared the worst.

Mike took the office key from Jose Manaedio's body and opened the door. When Mike found her, she was trembling from fear. She began to whimper and covered her face with her hands.

"Come, little lady," Mike said as he reached for her. "My name is Mike Cannon. I am a police officer. I am taking you home. The bad men are dead."

She looked at Mike in disbelief, put her arms around his neck, kissed him on the cheek, and burst into tears.

Mike lifted her in his arms, walked out of the warehouse, and took her to the car. Jay was relieved of the outcome; he had just earned his chance to live.

***

At 6:00 a.m., Captain Duncan was on his second cup of coffee. The newspaper was opened before him. He stared at the headline. It was about the kidnapping.

The telephone rang. "This is Abe Duncan."

"Captain, this is Mike. Tell Eddie to collect his daughter at the Miami Beach Police Station. She is okay and very hungry."

That news made the captain's day, but he wondered at what price.

"Mike, how many are dead?" the captain asked in little more than a whisper. He feared the answer.

"There are four for the attention of the coroner. One of them is ours," Mike replied and hung up. There was no emotion in his voice when he made the statement.

Captain Duncan sat staring into the half-empty cup. He searched for the words that would fully describe his concerns. When they came to him, he said to himself, God Almighty, I have got a tiger by the tail!

***

It was eight o'clock Saturday night, and the rain and clouds had given way to a moonlit sky. Pete Suarez, a member of the secret task force, sat in his beat-up Dodge pickup truck parked inside the cemetery on the driveway and waited for Mike, who was not usually late. He thought he would have found Mike in his Camaro there waiting for him. As a police detective and accustomed to death, he should not be feeling uncomfortable. But he did, and for a while, he gave it some concerns.

Mike had set up the meeting there to kill two birds with one stone. He had not visited the grave of his family for some time, and he wanted to place flowers. The other reason was that Pete had volunteered to get certain vital documents from headquarters that would shed some light on investigations he was still pursuing. It was of his opinion that the cemetery was being watched by some of the criminal elements he was investigating, but it would be unlikely that it would be at that time of night.

Pete saw a figure walking through the tombs and coming toward him. It turned out to be Mike with a large bundle of flowers.

Pete said, "I almost mistook you for a ghost, you walking through the tombs like that."

"A ghost bearing flowers? That would be a change. Only you would think something as funny as that," Mike responded in jest.

"Why walking? Where is the Camaro?" Pete asked.

"I had a funny feeling that I was being followed, so I parked it on the side street and came over the wall."

"That makes sense," Pete said. "Well, you go along and pay your respects. I will wait here until you return. And, Mike, I have the package for you."

Mike walked away toward where there were a cluster of new graves. Pete went back to sit into the pickup and turned on the radio. He did not see the black Lincoln reversing without lights to stop about a hundred feet from his truck. Two armed men came out and walked toward him. By chance he glanced through the rearview mirror and saw them approaching both sides and almost by the doors of the vehicle.

Mike heard him shout, "Mike, we have company!" And then Mike heard two shots. Mike raced toward the truck. Pete Suarez was slumped over the steering wheel dead, two bullets to the head. By then the Lincoln was slowly driving away.

Mike dropped to the ground and hastily attached the stock to the Bren Ten. He placed the stock to his shoulder and compelled himself to relax. The Lincoln was almost out of sight, but he could make out the rear bumper in the moonlight. He aimed just below it where he knew the bottom of the gas tank should be and squeezed the trigger twice. He felt the slight nudge to his shoulder an instant before the gas tank exploded. The Lincoln veered off the road and onto the lawn and was enveloped in a massive fireball.

Mike ran toward it, but the flames were too intense. He knew no one could have survived. When he went back to the truck, the package Pete had was missing.

Chapter 5

Jack Wall and four of his soldiers waited impatiently in a van concealed under the low branches of a tree on the edge of an empty and freshly cleared potato field in Redlands, a mile west of the old Miami Key West railway lines. They were waiting for the past four hours. It was 6:00 a.m., and the marker flares were long removed. Daylight made them no longer necessary.

Landing in broad daylight would certainly attract the wrong attention, and they had hoped to avoid that at all cost. Majority of the men feared the worst but were reluctant to say so. It was the first shipment of 250 kilos of cocaine coming in from Jamaica under the Fidel Castro deal, and the plane was overdue. The group had run out of small talk, which had served while waiting to take the edge off their growing concerns.

"Something is wrong. When I called Boscobel, Dave had refueled and left some thirty minutes before. He should be here more than two hours ago."

"That is true, boss. I believe he has engine trouble, but you know Dave, if anyone can make it, he will," one of the men said, reminding Jack of the reliability of the pilot based on past performances.

Dave Shon had been doing marijuana runs from Jamaica for over three years. He was an ace fighter pilot in Viet Nam, and for skimming the waves to avoid radar, he was one of the best. That was the criteria to successfully fly narcotics out of Jamaica, especially since Prime Minister Edward Seaga took office and resolved to put an end to narcotic smuggling from Jamaica and into the United States.

Jack came out of the van and strolled around the edge of the field to pass the time. He heard the spluttering of the engines before he saw the plane. It was coming in very low. The pilot tried to circle the field when both engines died. Instead of coming in from the edge of the field, the pilot was forced to bring it down in the center with not enough run to come to a successful stop.

Jack watched helplessly as the plane headed toward the trees where the van was concealed. The pilot saw the van too late. He tried desperately to avoid an accident, but the tip of one of the wings struck the front of the van, disabling it. A watchman in a nursery nearly a quarter of a mile away telephoned the police and reported the crash.

Within minutes, Sergeant Bill Comings and his partner, Beverly Glades, on routine patrol duty were headed to the scene. So were three other backup vehicles, fire rescue, and ambulances.

Jack and his men heard the sirens and thought of removing and hiding the cargo, but the police cruiser was halfway across the field bearing down upon them. The idea of being caught on foot with a crashed plane loaded with cocaine was not an option.

"Listen, boys, just keep cool. We will come out of this. Wait for my move. Do not do anything hasty."

As usual, they could depend on his composure when in difficult situations. Then one of the men remembered the pilot, dazed from the crash and still inside the plane. "Boss, what about Dave? We can't just leave him here."

"We have no choice. Don't you hear the sirens? He knew the risks. We all do," Jack said.

He decided on a bold plan of action.

The two officers came out of their vehicle with guns drawn and advanced toward the plane. That was what Jack expected them to do. He gave the signal, and a barrage of automatic gunfire from AK-47 assault rifles erupted from behind the van, killing both officers. Jack and his men raced toward the police vehicle, jumped inside, and sped off at high speed. As they cleared the field, they passed the backup police vehicles coming in. By the time the police backup reached the crash site and discovered what had taken place, Jack and his men had escaped. Dave Shon, hurt and dazed, stumbled from the wreckage and into the hands of the police.

***

At ten that morning, Captain Abe Duncan received the report that the burnt-out shell of a police cruiser was found deep in the mangrove off Old Cutler Road. The recent spate of unfortunate incidents were mounting, and he admitted to himself he was losing control. His ambitions to be chief of police was conditional upon his success in establishing and maintaining law and order, and his chances were diminishing.

After joining the force as a decorated Viet Nam war hero, he made rapid advancement to divisional captain. That morning for the first time, it seriously dawned on him that he was again engaged in a war, fighting the odds against achieving his career goal. But on that particular day, Captain Duncan's problems had escalated

At noon, there was a police emergency, and all available personnel were summoned to an explosion at a gas service station on US-1. An old Cadillac sedan, while obtaining gas, had conveniently exploded. That explosion had triggered explosions in several other vehicles obtaining gas. The entire station was in flames that threatened the adjoining buildings. The street had to be cordoned off, causing road blockage for miles. People were hurt, and the fire engines and ambulances had difficulty getting through.

Thirty minutes after the explosion and five miles south, five vehicles drove into the parking lot of the Homestead Police Station, and ten hooded men armed with shotguns and AK-47 assault rifles stormed into the station. The officer on duty looked up from the report he was writing and into the bore of a shotgun. He held his hands in the air and watched the other Dreadlocks calmly file into the station. Jack gave the signal, and they jumped over the counter and disappeared to the rear.

"What do you want?" the officer inquired, surprised he found the courage to ask such a bold question in spite of the fear that had his entire body shaking.

"My 250 kilos of cocaine, that is what I want," Jack replied.

"I do not know what you are talking about," the officer said.

"I can see I will have to do this the hard way," Jack said and pulled the trigger. The impact hurled the officer across the floor and through the door leading to the rear offices, where he died. The other officers in the rear saw the body on the floor and decided it was not wise to fool around.

"I repeat, where is my cocaine?" Jack said.

"It is locked away!" one shouted and threw the keys onto the floor.

"Take it up and open up wherever you are keeping it!" Jack shouted.

The officer took up the key and led them to the meshed safekeeping store where the cocaine was kept.

"Okay, guys, let's take our stuff and get out of here," Jack said. Pointing to the two officers, he shouted, "Give them a hand!"

The officers obeyed, and the cocaine was loaded evenly into the trunks of the five cars. When they were about to leave and consistent with the profile of the Jamaican Posse, Jack said, "We can't afford any witnesses. Shoot them."

One of his men lowered his AK-47 and riddled the two officers with bullets. They died on the parking lot.

***

At 4:00 p.m. that day, Jack Wall and five of his street soldiers sat in his office discussing the successful activities of that day. At a price they believed was worth it, they had obtained their objective.

"What next, boss? What do we do next?" one of the men asked Jack.

"Just sit back now and make some money. I mean the good old American dollar."

"What do you believe the Colombians will do when they realize we are selling to their contacts and selling much cheaper?"

"What would you do if you were in their place?" Jack asked.

"Fight, boss. I think they are going to fight. There will be a war."

"Now, why would they wish to do that? Why would they want any part of us, when all they have to do is give up a small part of the market?" Jack responded. "This is how I see it. The Colombians are the real enemy of the feds. They are the ones the feds want to put out of business. They make the stuff in their country. If they start a war with us, they would have to fight the feds on one side and us on the other. They are not that stupid."

"Then, boss—"

"What again, Sammy?" Jack interrupted.

"This is important, boss. Just hear me out. Suppose the Colombians stop sending the coke to Castro when they find out that we are getting it from Cuba to compete against them?"

"Good question," Jack said. "There is a bigger picture behind all this. There is a Colombian rebel group called the M-19. They are supported by Castro, and they also protect the drug lords in the jungle against the Colombian government troops. These M-19 guys want to take out the Colombian government, but find it difficult because the government is supported by the USA. If they stop sending the stuff to Castro, then Castro will stop supporting them. So it is in their best interest to continue. The whole arrangement is a conspiracy that works for us."

The telephone rang, and Jack hastened to answer.

It was the first of several calls from his new drug contacts to confirm that their orders of cocaine would be met. Days before, Jack had contacted several of the Colombians customers and offered a 10 percent discount on whatever price they were paying the Colombians. Jack was told if he could match the quality and deliver on time, which he promised, he could have their business. That was the buyers' conditions. Jack had made certain those conditions would be met.

***

It was almost closing time when Mike parked in the far end of the supermarket parking lot. Not long afterward, a late-model black Mercedes Benz drove up and parked about fifty feet away. Mike waited until the headlights of the Benz flashed three times before he removed the Glock 9mm from the glove compartment and placed it in his trousers waist. He approached the Benz, walked around it, opened the passenger-side front door, and sat down.

"I thought you may not be here," Captain Duncan said.

"Why not? I am the one who asked for this meeting."

"I know, but I do not know who or what to believe in anymore."

"Me included?" Mike asked.

"You not included. But I do not know if some unexpected god-forsaken incident may not have kept you away. Before I forget, I must say thanks for handling that kidnapping."

"Have I ever failed to keep my word to you?"

"That's the only certain thing happening to me of late. By the way, here is my number where I can be reached night or day. " Captain Duncan handed Mike a card.

He glanced at it and placed it in his shirt pocket. "I heard of the Homestead cocaine affair. You know that's the Jamaican Posse."

"We are certain of it. We have the pilot. He refuses to co-operate. But he will soon change his mind when he realizes he may be facing the death penalty. But to start a war with them now when I can't even trust my own men is too risky. The feds may come in, but I do not think they understand the delicacy of the situation, and they may not adapt the right approach. I would prefer they do not start what they cannot successfully finish."

"You could be right, although I do not completely agree with you. What is the use of power if you are afraid to use it? The answer is to declare war against those punks and wipe them out once and for all. The feds would do this if you ask their help. That is their agenda. With a few good men, I could get the job done if you give me the authority."

It was evident Captain Duncan wished to avoid that line of discussion. For his own private reasons, he procrastinated in dealing effectively with the situation. "Mike, why did you call this meeting? It has to be serious," Captain Duncan asked.

"It is. Does the name House Man mean anything to you?"

"Can't say it does. Should it?"

"Well, it should. The dirty cops in the department take orders indirectly from someone who calls himself the House Man. It is possible he is the one who placed the hit on me. I promise you, I am getting to the root of this. And when I do, I am taking him out and everyone connected with him."

"Then suppose he is not the one who placed the hit?"

"It does not matter if he is or not. As long as he is dirty, it will all be in the process of elimination. They started this, I will finish it."

That conversation was not going Captain Duncan's way. If the killings continued, it may give the impression that the situation had escalated out of his control. The press would have a field day, and it would be goodbye to his promotion. His idea in creating the task force was to get incriminating information on the perpetrators of the law, whoever they might be, and turn it over to the proper authorities for prosecution through due process of law. The authorities for personal reasons would decide who should be punished. But not for any single individual to be judge, jury, and executioner; that right was not available.

"Mike, we will have to put a brake on the killings the way they are happening. You know that is not the way of the department. It all comes back on me. I will be the one responsible. I expect the mayor to be in my office any day now."

"Not the mayor!" Mike exclaimed. "Frank Bukley is not in a position to point a finger. Wait until I submit the file on him. Captain, you would be surprised to know what is happening around you. I have opened a can of worms. I believe that is why my family is dead. Politics will not be able to save them when I am through. If they force you to take my badge, then I will turn over everything to the press."

"No, Mike!" Captain Duncan exclaimed. "What about me? Do you have any idea what would become of my career? Mike, this is something for the department to handle. We take care of our dirty linen."

"Let's hope it does not come to that, Captain. Once the avalanche starts, nothing or no one will be able to stop it." Rage mounted in Mike as he spoke. He remembered seeing his family killed. He was hearing their cries. As far as he was concerned, there was no reason to prolong the conversation as the captain did not seem to understand his pain. The discussion was not going well for any of them.

Mike Cannon was a man of few words. When he concludes what he has to say, he moves on. He meant no disrespect, but he wanted Captain Duncan to know his intentions and where he stood.

"Captain, you have nothing to fear. You are one of the good guys. I will not do anything intentionally to harm your career, if it can be helped. But justice must be served. Remember, above all, you had pledged to uphold the law, whatever it takes."

After saying that, he ended the conversation and returned to his car.

Captain Duncan remained in his car, thinking of the best approach in defusing the explosive situation he had unintentionally created. He observed a situation that had become alive and grown into a career-threatening monster. Mike had to be turned around gently, but he had to be careful, or his wrath would be directed in the wrong direction, toward him, and that could have tragic results.

After the meeting with Captain Duncan, Mike drove around aimlessly. He feared going to his apartment and being alone. He drove onto a McDonald's parking lot, turned off the engine, and just sat there. Watching people going about their business and trying to imagine what they were thinking acted as mental therapy. Anything to keep Kim and the children out of his mind was welcome. At intervals, he would direct his thoughts to think of Captain Duncan and the problems the department was facing. He was glad the problems were of a complex nature, as it gave him a lot to occupy his mind.

The light drizzle had turned into a deluge before he was aware of it, and there were only a couple of cars remaining on the lot. He started the engine, turned on the wipers, and headed toward his apartment that he had refused to consider as home. Driving slowly and absentmindedly through the rain and listening to the rhythmic swish swash of the wipers brought him a strange sort of comfort. It dawned on him how empty and unimportant his life had become when he had to embrace such minute incidents as reward for daily existence.

He was on South West Twenty-Seventh Avenue and only a few minutes from his apartment when he saw bottles of alcoholic beverages displayed in the window of a liquor store. He thought a couple of drinks may reduce his melancholia. Although he had passed that area dozens of times, he had not noticed the shop before.

He came to a screeching stop and reversed to a point near to the entrance. He came out of the car, walked through the rain, and entered the store. The middle-aged gentleman behind the counter was just about to close and was stocking notes from the cash register into a brown paper bag.

Mike went toward a shelf, removed a bottle of scotch, and presented it with a fifty dollar bill to the owner.

He noticed Mike's wet clothes and remarked, "Nasty weather we have been having. This should be good for business, but for some unknown reason, it's not. Hope this is the last of it."

Mike grunted.

The owner took the hint, made the change, and handed it to him.

The little bell over the door jingled, and three big Latinos wearing black leather jackets entered the store. The one in front had his weapon drawn and approached Mike from behind. "I will take that," he said and took the change from Mike's hand. Stuffing the money in his pocket, he pushed Mike against the counter and said from behind, "We are just in time, old man. Let's have the rest of it from the register."

During his speech, Mike was watching his colleagues through a mirror behind the row of bottles stacked on the shelf behind the counter. He noticed how relaxed and confident they seemed since everything appeared to be going their way. It was obvious they had a lot of practice holding up small stores, and the last thing they expected was retaliation. They had no way of knowing that their timing could not be worse. Mike was in one of those godforsaken suicidal foul moods. The sight of the gunmen reminded him of his recent ordeal and aroused a resentment of their kind that was festering too long in him.

Disregarding the danger to himself, he angrily shouted, "To hell you won't!"

The gunman, surprised at the unexpected challenge, raised his arm to pistol-whip Mike from behind.

Mike saw it coming, caught the arm, and threw him over his shoulder to land on his back amid the crates of bottles behind the counter. The others taken by surprise were a little slow getting their weapons from their coat pockets. Usually they relied upon their intimidating tough-man appearance, and one gun was enough to scare their victims to deliver.

Their unfortunate hesitation gave Mike the split second he needed. He instinctively pivoted on one leg and fired as he turned. The bullet from the Bren Ten entered the chest of the one nearest to him; the impact threw him across the shop to land against the entrance door, where he slowly sank to the floor and died.

The other stared at his dying accomplice in disbelief. It was not supposed to happen that way. It was the one behind the counter who usually died.

As Mike swung his weapon toward him, he dropped his gun and attempted to raise his arms. "Sorry, I don't take prisoners tonight," Mike said as he fired. The special bullet from the Bren Ten caught the crook between his eyes and blew off the back of his head. Blood and chunks of brain matter stuck to the wall behind him.

The owner had witnessed enough. What he saw was too much to bear. He panicked and ran from behind the counter toward the rear of the shop.

Mike peered over the counter at the first gunman, who was trying to regain his feet. As he stood up, Mike struck him with tremendous force in the face with the bottle of scotch. The bottle splintered and tore the skin and eyebrows from his forehead. Partially blinded by the blood from the wound, he cried out in pain and groped around in confusion.

By that time, Mike was as a mad dog loose. He had lost control, and all the frustration and agony he had experienced took over his intent. He aimed the weapon and kept firing until the clothes the assailant wore was almost torn to ribbons. The floor behind the counter was a reservoir of blood.

When it was over, Mike looked up in the ceiling, made a loud inhuman cry as would a wild animal, stepped over the bodies, and walked out of the store with the gun in his hand.

Chapter 6

Donaldo Santiago met Carlos Mendez in the Marriot Hotel Lounge for the third time. As usual Carlos Mendez was sitting alone at a small table in the shadows. His glass was empty and Donaldo Santiago ordered a refill of his favorite, Johnny Walker Black. Carlos Mendez had requested the meeting. He had complaints.

"There has to be a revision of job description." Mendez said. "This guy is now a public hero after rescuing that kidnapped girl. Also he is now on the alert. And from what I understand he is one tough son of a bitch. I hear that the so called bad guys on the streets are afraid to show themselves as they do not know when or where he may appear. He is gone underground and there is no pattern to his behavior. You haven't got the slightest clue where he is or where he will be at any given time. Those are the information I am supposed to have got from you. This is your town. In a matter of fact, I am giving you an advice and you may take it or leave it. If this Cannon guy suspects that you put a hit on him, and there is a possibility he already has, after what he has been through you need a body guard, may be two or three. You do not need me. For all I know he may be stalking you at this moment. It could even be dangerous for me to be sitting here talking with you. This guy is a pro. He seems to have eyes and ears every where. Did you hear how quickly he got back that kidnapped girl? Within twenty four hours. Did you hear how many of the kidnappers got killed?

And I can bet you anything there was not a single scratch on him. Isn't that something? How did you get on the wrong side of a guy like that? "

"Were you hired to kill him or sing his praises?" Santiago asked displaying his frustration. "You are the hit man you are not suppose to be scared. No one said it would be easy. I am paying enough." Santiago's concern for his own safety was growing momentarily. He began to regret his decision. It was not that he did not wish to see Mike Cannon dead, but that it may not happen, and he could possibly become Mike Cannon's next target and that would not be a good thing.

"You don't seem to understand what I am saying." Mendez said in an effort to convey his personal concerns. "I do not work miracles. I cannot kill who I cannot find. The information you gave me is now obsolete. If you cannot do better I am packing it in. I am out of here."

"You can't do that you have a contract." "What good is a contract to me when I am dead? Do you believe this guy would hesitate to take me out if he finds out that I am here and why? Wise up man, he now has the advantage. If any one else knows you brought me down here, I would advise you get rid of that person and do it fast. In this business three is a crowd."

Donaldo Santiago immediately thought of Mayor Frank Bukley. That was the underlying fear that had been haunting him; one he was reluctant to face. Confronted by the wisdom of Carlos Mendez's statement he spent no time in arriving at a quick decision of what he had to do. Bukley was a weak link that posed an indirect danger.

"Listen Mendez, there is a lot of wisdom in what you just said. I have an urgent job for you. I will meet you here tomorrow same time with details."

"I will need an advance. There will be expenses. And get me current information this time."

"No problem. Just be here." Santiago assured the hit man. After that they shook hands and he left. Mike Cannon was still his major concern, but first things first. He would take care of Cannon at the opportune time.

As mike Cannon drove into the Burger King parking lot he saw Jay Gordon's Volvo. He parked beside it but it was empty. He waited for ten minutes, and then Jay Gordon approached his Camaro with a paper bag in his hand. He opened the passenger side door then asked, "Do you mind if I eat in your car I am starving." Mike cannon smiled. Jay Gordon took it for a no, he didn't mind. Jay Gordon had contacted Mike Cannon that he had important information. The smell of food reminded Mike Cannon that he had not eaten that day.

"It better be good." "Oh yes it is. I know where to find your hit man."

"Every one knows that. He is in the morgue." "The dead one is. But there is another one very much alive. And he is also from New York." Rage mounted in Mike Cannon. He struggled with his emotion to remain calm. The incident that cost him his family reappeared before him. Finally he was able to speak. "Are you certain of this? "I am very certain. A reliable contact of mine is bar tender at the Airport Marriot. He was a port worker in New York years ago. This guy Carlos Mendez was a free lance hit man for the mob that controlled the union. Do you remember Santiago the Cuban Developer? The one you asked me to check out last year? "Yes I remember." Well he went to meet him many times in the Lounge where my contact works at night. Last night he met him again, and the subject of their discussion was you. They had an argument about the job. From the bits and pieces he could hear Mendez threatened to go back to New York. What ever they were upset

86

about was settled, because Mendez asked for more money and he promised to take it to him tonight."

"Do you know what time they will be meeting?" "In the next two hours at ten tonight. My contact heard Santiago telling him same time tomorrow night."

"Get out I have things to do." Mike Cannon said as he started the Camaro. "Are you leaving me something for this?" "You have your life isn't that enough?" Mike Cannon replied angrily.

Mike Cannon sat at a table in the Lounge of the Airport Marriot Hotel. He chose one of two tables that were in shadows on a platform not far from the counter. Except for two ladies, the lounge was empty. He ordered a beer, and a waitress promptly appeared with it, wiped the table with a napkin and set it down with a glass. She wanted to start a friendly argument, but Mike Cannon discouraged it. That would be the wrong place for her to be, taking into consideration what was on his mind. He anticipated a show down with a man who was in town to take his life. He did not have long to wait before Carlos Mendez came in. He knew it was Mendez, because he dressed like a New Yorker and from the bulge on the left side of his blazer he knew he was packing. Mendez walked straight towards the other table in the shadows and sat down. The waitress immediately brought him a glass with what appeared to be whisky. He appeared to be a creature of habit. That was very bad for a man in his line of business. Mike Cannon thought.

Shortly after Santiago came in with a large brown envelop in his hand.

Santiago sat opposite Mendez at the same table. Santiago was dressed like a man of means. There was nothing cheap about him, from the thirty thousand dollar Rolex to the six hundred dollar shoes. Mike Cannon saw that the man lived well. He knew of Santiago but did not have the pleasure of meeting him in person. "Without any small talk Santiago placed the brown envelop on the table, and shoved it to Mendez. "This is all you will need. It is all there."

Mike Cannon saw enough, he got up and walked towards their table. With the Bren-10 in one hand, he took up the brown envelop and said, "I will take that." Surprised, Mendez and Santiago exchanged glances. Mike Cannon appeared as intimidating as was described. They were momentarily disoriented by his disarming presence. Mendez, confused and not quite certain how to handle the situation, made a hasty and unwise decision and went for the gun in his shoulder holster. Santiago looked in amazement at Mendez's desperate play, not quite understanding what he hoped to achieve with Cannon having the drop on them. Mike Cannon shot him point blank in the face. The blast flung him backwards out of his chair, splattering the wall behind him with blood and chunks of bone and flesh. Santiago taking advantage of the commotion, tried to get away and in his haste fell over and got entangled with his chair. He extricated himself quickly and took a right swing at Mike Cannon. Mike Cannon smashed him with his weapon on his shoulder twice shattering his collar bone; the right arm hung loose. Santiago was not an easy man to take out. He bent down to get the weapon he had strapped to his leg with the other hand. Mike Cannon straightened him up by a knee under the chin that lifted him off his feet; he fell backwards hitting his head on the tiled floor, and remained there unconscious.

Within minutes an eager crowd gathered. Mike Cannon walked up to the counter and showed his badge. He opened the brown envelop and emptied its contents under the lights. To his surprise there were several photographs of Mayor Frank Bukley, a sheet of paper with written information on his habits, and twenty five thousand dollars advance payment in hundred dollar bills.

"Pass me that phone." Mike Cannon said to the bar tender. He took a card from his pocket and from the numbers on it made a call.

"This is Abe Duncan." The voice at the other end said. "Captain this is Mike Cannon. I am at the lounge of the Airport Marriot Hotel. Send an ambulance and the coroner. The replacement hit man is dead, and the person who hired him will need the ambulance."

"Who is it that needs the ambulance?" "The Developer, Donaldo Santiago. You will be surprised who the hit was on?" "Who, was it you?" "Not this time. Mayor Frank Bukley". "Are you certain about that?" "I am very certain. I have the evidence before me. You will have my report in the morning." Mike Cannon hung up.

Six a.m. the next morning and Mike Cannon sat in the Camaro at the gate of the Mayor's residence. It was one of those electrical contraptions which, except you had the code it had to be opened from the inside, after inside knows who it is on the outside that wants to enter. Mike Cannon knew Mayor Frank Bukley would not want him to enter except his lawyer was present. So he waited. The Mayor's house was a mini mansion you only hope to own if you won the roll over lotto jackpot. Behind the house was the inter-coastal waterway, and, docked alongside the water way pier was his sixty foot yacht. Mike Cannon thought it was no wonder the Mayor's assets attracted all sorts of attention.

At six thirty a lady in a green Toyota drove up to the gate. She punched numbers in the key pad and the gate opened. Mike Cannon figured her to be the house keeper. He drove in after her. The lady came out of her car and walked up to the front door. Mike Cannon followed her. She stopped, turned and looked at Mike Cannon and asked, "This is private property. Why are you following me?" Mike Cannon showed her his badge. "I am Detective Inspector Mike Cannon, and I wish to speak to Mayor Bukley on a matter of grave importance."

The lady rang the door bell and waited. After a couple of minutes the door opened. She went in and closed the door after her. Mike Cannon stood on the steps and waited. He was about to ring the bell when the door opened, and an attractive middle aged lady in her dressing gown invited him in. Mrs. Bukley the Mayor's wife introduced herself and asked him to accompany her to the study. "Please have a seat Inspector Cannon, my husband will be with you shortly." She spoke with a relaxed educated voice. Mike Cannon sat and waited.

As a young man Frank Bukley was an outstanding Afro American athlete. The various displays of trophies of silver and gold were every where. His academic achievements were no less conspicuous. Neither was the evidence of affluence in the array of expensive original antique furniture in his study. Mike Cannon thought, where ever money was flowing from there seems to be no obstruction.

Mayor Frank Bukley was fully dressed when he walked through the door of his study. It was evident he expected to go some where instead of a chat in his house. He did not sit around his desk. He pulled up a chair and sat beside Mike Cannon. He said in a soft and subdued tone as if surrendering himself, "Here I am Inspector Cannon." Mike Cannon looked him straight in the eye and he looked away. Whatever guilt he was carrying was weighing him down. "Mr. Mayor, do you know one Donald Santiago?" Frank Bukley did not answer. He was breathing heavily as if suffering from an asthmatic attack. Mike Cannon repeated the question in a more demanding tone. "Yes Inspector Cannon. You know I do. That is why you are here, isn't that so? Is this the part where I must say, I need to call my Attorney?" "I think you are jumping to conclusions.

You are not being interrogated. I am simply asking some questions. Do you know of any reason why Santiago should put a hit on you?" "Nonsense! I have known Donald for many years."

"There is no nonsense about it. I shot and killed the hit man last night, and confiscated these when Santiago was in the act of engaging him. Here is the evidence." Mike Cannon handed the large envelop to Frank Bukley. As he took the envelop he remembered the last conversation he had with Santiago in his office, and his hands began to shake. He attempted to open it and its contents fell to the floor. He stared on the several photographs of himself, the hundred dollar bills, and the type written information of his usual activities. "Take them up! Take them up! Look at them for yourself!" Mike Cannon demanded. Frank Bukley got up from the chair and backed away, as if he feared the objects on the floor would come alive and do him harm. He began to weep, but Mike Cannon felt no sympathy. Mrs. Bukley appeared at the door, looked at the items on the floor, then at her weeping husband, then accusingly at Mike Cannon.

"What have you done to my husband? You beast! This is our home. I think you should go," she screamed at Mike Cannon. "Frank, what is all this about?" She enquired of her husband. In response to the question to her husband, Mike Cannon said, "Mr. Mayor, should I explain to your wife that you are a criminal, and your partner in crime hired a hit man to kill you; or will .you do it?" "Frank, is this true? Tell me it is not so." Mrs. Bukley pleaded with her husband and hugged him protectively. But he said nothing.

Mike Cannon collected the items on the floor and replaced them into the envelop they were in.

"Mr. Mayor, for your information Donald Santiago is in the Jackson Memorial Hospital's Emergency Ward under police guard. The contents of this envelop will be sent to Headquarters later today. I think you understand there will be a Federal investigation into your association with Santiago. You know exactly what I mean. Take my advice and place yourself on the right side, it may be easier for you. Go down and see Captain Abe Duncan before the Feds come to see you. At this stage I have no alternative but to turn in my entire findings on yours and Santiago's activities. Good day Mrs. Bukley. I will see myself out." Mike Cannon walked out of the study without a backward glance.

Chapter 7

The last of six boats arrived alongside the Ocean Rose riding at anchor in Biscayne Bay. It was a rainy February morning and the weather report forecasted the showers would continue throughout the day. Usually there would be at least a dozen Spanish beauties sunbathing on its deck, and Sabas Betata Gonzalez would be lounging in his personal deck chair striving to arrive at a decision which of his very willing guests would accompany him to his ivory tower. Some would term The Ocean Rose a luxury yacht, but there would be no justice done to what was in truth a mini custom crafted ocean liner with comforts defying all imagination.

In the state room of the Ocean Rose sat six men, carefully recruited to control cocaine importation into the United States. Sabas Gonzalez, above all other virtues, recognized order. His lifestyle, his pleasures, and business, each personified this key element, which reflected in the efficient manner in which he streamlined merchandise distribution in its most demanding market place, the United States. So when it was reported to him that Donaldo Santiago was confined in a Miami jail like some common criminal, it demanded his special attention.

is an assignment that may be executed singly, or collectively. I hesitate to suggest how it may be accomplished. That is your area of expertise Gentlemen." "There being no need for questions, this meeting is adjourned." There is no question regarding the repercussions resulting from noncompliance to any directive given by Sabas Gonzalez. Punishment was usually swift and final. Had there been allowances for a debate, Sabas Gonzalez would be informed, that getting rid of the Jamaican Posse, and the narcotic competition they posed, was easier said than done. The arena of South Florida was not large enough to contain the level of violence that would result from such a misunderstanding. Also their organization did not possess the special skills that would be required to make that venture a successful one. Their main concerns were, which one of their group would volunteer to partake in such a suicidal assignment, as there was no question in their minds, that an attempt had to be made, successful or not.

Complying with Sabas Gonzalez's orders, bail was immediately arranged for Donaldo Santiago at ten million dollars, cash or bond. Considering the notorious reputation of the organization behind Santiago, bail was not contested by the District Attorney's Office. For special considerations, Frank Buckly agreed to testify against Santiago, and was placed in protective custody along with his family. On the advice of his attorney, and as one of the special conditions, he agreed to tender his resignation to the City Council before he left Captain Abe Duncan's office. Any fool would give odds against Frank Buckly ever testifying in court against Donaldo Santiago. Mike Cannon regretted not killing him when he had the chance at the Marriot Hotel. He believed Santiago would never see prison time, and justice to the people would eventually be denied.

Donaldo Santiago was the genius who under Sabas Gonzalez's instructions, successfully unified the distribution of his product line, and in turn processed its proceeds by circulating it through every major bank in Florida, right under the nose of the United States Federal Agency. That was what Sabas Gonzalez meant by organizational order. After waiting on him for more than an hour, and taxing the patience of the six men, none of whom dared to openly complain, he casually arrived dressed in a smoke jacket, deck slippers, and a glass of wine in his hand.

In an air of superiority, he glared at each of his exceptionally well compensated agents, and said:

"Gentlemen, I did not assemble this emergency meting for a lecture, or a discussion, or a debate. There is no democracy here. This is my empire and I am its only emperor. Now listen to this. I will be saying it once. Firstly, I want Santiago out of jail and replaced in a situation where he can do what he alone does best." His guests did not agree with that statement, but it not being debatable, they wisely kept their opinion to themselves. Donaldo Santiago had in moments of grandiose delusion, saw himself as top dog in the cocaine industry; and carried away by personal ambitions, ignored the principle of team playing. It would be only a matter of time before Sabas Gonzalez recognizes that his position as king pin, was being threatened. When that happens Donaldo Santiago would become history.

"Secondly," continued Sabas Gonzales recognize, "I want this black competition called Jamaican Posse terminated. They have no class, and are bad for business; and affecting our credibility. Distributing this marijuana junk, and crack cocaine to children is no good. Get rid of them. And most importantly, the orderly execution of these simple requests is the criteria. The least publicity it attracts, the better. This

After experiencing the effectiveness of the element of fear, the influence of money and political connections, Mike Cannon came to a conclusion that in the current environment fair justice could only be administered his way. His 'take no prisoners' principle, would not be compromised in the future, regardless of the offence to his department, or the effect on public opinion. Also, he saw no other way in which he could support in the name of the law, the insatiable crave for revenge that was his agenda..

Mike Cannon walked from his river side apartment and stood by the Miami River Bridge. He inhaled deeply the fresh crisp early morning air from the river. The bridge was opening to allow passage to a Haitian trawler, and a line of vehicles stopped to await its closing. He walked down Twenty Seventh Avenue towards the corner street where he hoped to purchase a current edition of the daily news paper. A group of Spanish speaking men congregated in a small plaza engaged in conversation. From what he could understand, the topic of their conversation was based on The Jamaican Posse. Mike Cannon bought a paper and on the front page was the picture of the tragic climax of a gun battle which took place in a Fort Lauderdale shopping plaza between two members of The Jamaican Posse and four Colombian gunmen. The incident which was reported to be drug related, resulted in the death of the four Colombians and one of the Jamaicans. The other Jamaican badly wounded, left the scene in a white BMW. The car was found by the police two miles from the scene with the driver slumped over the steering wheel dead. What was unexplainable is that there was no evidence of blood in the car, as if his body was drained of blood before he left the scene of the gun battle. The coroner, when questioned by the press, had no explanation how the gun man could have driven from the scene to where he was found, without enough blood in his body to support his life.

Describing the incident to a reporter one spectator stated that even after the Jamaican Dreadlock was badly wounded, he walked out into the open with apparent disregard for his own life, and continued to exchange gunfire, absorbing more gunshot wounds, and did not cease until the two remaining Colombians lay dead. Then he stumbled towards his car leaving a trail of blood, fell two or three times, got up and drove away.

Below on the same page was a report of a seventeen year old high school 'A' student who after school, engaged four others in a knife duel, and single handedly badly wounded the four It was reported that he kept slashing even after he himself was stabbed a dozen times. His wounds resulted in his death after he was air lifted to the Jackson Memorial Hospital. Doctors were amazed that he lasted that long as one of the wounds had severed an artery which should have had immediate fatal effect

When Mike Cannon entered the supermarket parking lot that night, he had to search for the Black Mercedes. He had expected Captain Duncan to be parked at the place they had arranged the last time they met. Instead he was parked against the wall with the front of the car turned towards the parking lot exit. He parked the Camaro and walked towards the Mercedes. Almost there, Captain Duncan called to him from the shadows of a tree at the far end of the lot almost as if he was hiding.

"Over here Mike." Mike Cannon walked towards the voice, and saw the Captain. "You can't be too careful. They tailed one of our boys from the Task Force last night to the safe house where his family was, and took several shots at him. It was Terry Blanchard. He took off and had his car badly shot up. We had to move his family today. They are fighting back Mike. They have declared war." "That is how I like it Captain, then I don't have to go looking for them. Captain don't you see that being under cover is no longer effective? Our covers are blown. Better we face these guys head on. Don't you see that the drug war is about to commence. Before they start hurting innocent people we have to take them out. That's what law and order is all about. You told me that when I came into your division. Why I asked you to meet me is on account of two articles in today's news paper. The Fort Lauderdale gun battle and the high school kid's knife attack. I want you to think Captain. That was no coincidence. The situations are similar. There is a connection somewhere. I would like to follow it and see where it leads. I am of the opinion that it's a part of what we are chasing. And if I am right, and I crack this one, you will have your promotion. More importantly, I am of the opinion that before I am through I will come face to face with the son of a bitch who had me shot, and my family murdered." Captain Duncan noticed the serious effect both incidents had on Mike Cannon. He rightly agreed that they were more than a coincidence, and there was a common factor connecting them. He knew that nothing he said would minimize Mike Cannon's interest, so it would be better to give his blessings, and hope that as a result there would be no requests for the coroner. Addressing the issue he said:

"Since you strongly believe they are connected to your ongoing investigations, you do not need my authority to proceed. Not that you ever need my authority for any of the things you do. But still keep me informed and I will back your play. You can depend on me to do that." "That is what I thought. I will keep you posted." Mike Cannon said, and returned to the Camaro. He was concerned over the nonchalant attitude of Captain Duncan regarding the hell that was breaking loose around him. He knew the Captain was aware that the situation would not correct itself or go away. He wondered if the Captain had more desperate emergencies attending to that he was not aware of? And wondered what could be more demanding, than the situation that currently confronted the department?

Captain Duncan was pleased with that short meeting. His thoughts were that Mike Cannon was more relaxed, and displayed a more responsible attitude to other vital issues. Although it was impossible to disregard the motivating forces of revenge that was driving him, he had time to be concerned about the welfare of those he was expected to protect. It was possible he was coming to terms with his losses, or found a formula to coexist with it. Not withstanding, he remained alert, because he knew there was a volcano beneath that calmness that could erupt at any time, and when it did, people usually die.

Mike Cannon left Captain Duncan and went straight to his apartment. It was the first time since he had overcome his injuries he had the courage to spend time with himself. Usually he was so exhausted he would fall asleep as soon as he went to bed. The thought of being single and not savoring being in bed with Kim, brought tears to his eyes. He tried to relive the night before the tragedy, to recapture the image of her sensuous body snuggled so close to him he could feel the beating of her heart. He longed to experience the fragrance of her hair, and feel the warmth of her breath against his bare chest. Then the memory of her face twisted in pain, and seeing the pleading in her eyes just before he lost consciousness, swept away the sweetness of his longing. To compound his torture, the voice of the kids as they cried out to him for help penetrated the defense his mind had created against the agony. "Oh God isn't death better than this" he moaned over and over. And his pain would find release in a load cry, as would a fatally wounded animal.

To expect Mike Cannon to behave as normal, would be hoping for the impossible. His daily duties were the distractions from his bereavement. So he would engage himself in the most dangerous assignments, hoping that one would terminate into a tragic conclusion. That was the ticking bomb that he had become.

11.30 am the following day Mike Cannon accompanied by two uniformed officers walked up the driveway towards the front door of number 1375.Hagley Avenue. He banged on the door most fiercely. He was in a foul mood. This was the house where the seventeen year old high school student that was stabbed to death lived. It was also the home of a police officer his father. Mike Cannon hoped to find evidence of the substance that had caused the unusual action of a normal honor student, ending in his untimely death. He had his suspicions. A woman in her early forties answered the door. Her eyes were swollen as if from weeping. "You Mrs. Blake?" He asked. She answered in the affirmative. "I am Detective Inspector Mike Cannon. I have a warrant to search the premises." Mike handed her the warrant. She glanced at it and handed it back to him. Mike Cannon and the two officers followed her into the house.

A man came out of the bath room. It was Police Corporal Steve Blake. Mike Cannon shoved the warrant in his face. Mike Cannon said to him. "Have a seat and see that you do not obstruct us. You know the drill." And to one of the officers, "See that he remains there." To Mrs. Blake, Mike Cannon asked, "Which of the rooms belong to your son?"

"Top of the stairs and left," she replied. Mike Cannon accompanied by the other officer, climbed the stairs, and entered the boy's room. Mike went directly to the bed and lifted the mattress. He retrieved a small brown paper bag half full of a white substance. He tasted it and identified it as cocaine. He came out and stood on the landing of the stairs and waited until his anger subsided. "Bring Blake up here". He called to the officer. Corporal Blake ascended the stairs followed by the officer. Mike Cannon stuck his finger in the contents of the paper bag, and showed Blake the white substance. "This is pure uncut cocaine, found under the mattress of your son's bed. Where is the remainder? Go get it."

Corporal Blake remained silent and uncooperative. "Do you want us to rip this house apart or not?"

Corporal Blake glanced at his wife then stared at the floor, and said. "It's in the garage." Mike Cannon and the two officers followed him into the garage, where he lifted an upturned metal box and handed one of the officers a partly opened package containing almost a kilo of cocaine. Mike Cannon said to him, "You murdering son of a bitch, you are the one responsible for your son's death. You deserve what is coming to you. You are under arrest for having in your possession a controlled substance with intent to distribute. Officer read him his rights." Mike Cannon started to leave when he stopped abruptly. Something about that double car garage was not just correct. Then it dawned on him. The space was about eight to ten feet short. Looking carefully he noticed an eight by four foot metal sheet concealing a padlocked door. He looked at both Steve Blake and his wife and they avoided eye contact. "What is behind that door Mike Cannon asked?" "Nothing," they both replied. "That's interesting, a locked door with nothing behind it. Open it up let's see." Mike Cannon ordered. "I had misplaced the key for several months but since nothing of value is in there I neglected to replace the lock," Steve Blake said, trying desperately to conceal his panic stricken countenance. "Stand back!" Mike Cannon ordered as he drew his weapon and blasted the lock.

Mike Cannon entered a well furnished room with photographic and special lighting equipment. In one corner was a small bed well made up, beside it was a television and video equipment resting on a small table. Two walls were fully covered with enlarged nude photographs of nude female children and teen age girls in various stages of sexual encounters.

One particular photograph of special interest was that of a fifteen year old high school girl who was reported missing over the past month. She was in the nude. Both hands were tied to the railing of the same bed in the room, with duct tape across her mouth. For an instant the strength drained from Mike Cannon's body and he commenced to tremble. Never before had he encountered such a nervous physical experience. He sat on the bed to await its passing while the tears uncontrollably rolled down his cheeks. He covered his face with his hands to hide his emotional trauma from the two police officers who also gazed in horror.

Steve Blake and his wife turned their backs towards Mike Cannon and faced the wall overcome with shame and fear.

Finally Mike Cannon regained his composure and got to his feet. The rage his body emanated charged the small room with an almost tangible vibration of aggressiveness.

Through clenched teeth he said to one of the officers, "Officer, remove the cuff, and both of you .wait in the squad car. You may leave us alone." The two officers looked at each other and refused to obey the command. "This is an order, leave us alone!" Mike Cannon shouted and drew his weapon. "I am sorry Inspector in your state of mind we cannot obey that order." Steve Blake and his wife fearing for their lives dropped to their knees and beseeched the officers not to leave them alone with Mike Cannon. They knew of the personal ordeal Mike Cannon had experienced and that he had lost his family. They also knew of his vendetta against crime on the streets of Miami that had career criminals running for cover.

Placing his weapon to Steve Blake's head Mike Cannon said, "This is your one chance to live. I will only say this once. Where is the girl tied to the bed? " Steve Blake's wife immediately replied. "Don't shoot Inspector. He sold her to the Haitian. The Haitian took her." For the better part of a minute no one spoke. There was a deathly silence as if time was suspended, and the occurrence taking place was a disturbing part from a harrow movie that would soon come to an end. Then Mike Cannon asked, fearful of the answers. "What did they buy her for? Do you think she is alive?" When he waited and there were no answers, he irrupted into a fit of anger and struck Steve Blake so forcefully with his fist across the temple that he rolled over unto the floor unconscious. He lifted his foot to stomp his head as one would crush a venomous snake, when Steve Blake's wife terror stricken shouted, "Stop Inspector! I will tell you every thing. Don't hurt him any more. The Haitian took her to their Voodoo Temple in Little Haiti. I do not know if she is still alive." "What about the others, were they taken there too?" "I don't know what happened to all of them, some went to an African with a boat. But that was a long time ago. I pleaded with Steve to stop. But he would not listen. I did not want our son to find out." "Where in Little Haiti the girl was taken? What is the address?" Mike Cannon asked. "Temple Of The Nile in Cannibal Street. The name of the voodoo Priest is Jean Biassou," Steve Blake's wife said. Mike Cannon turned to the police officers and ordered, "Declare this area a Crime Scene. Contact Captain Duncan and inform him of all that has happened here. Tell him I am going to find the girl if she is still alive. Tell him that I must do this alone, as a strong police presence may cause them to kill her if she is alive, or any one else they are holding. I will contact him later."

5.30 pm that day Mike Cannon drove into the premises of 777 Cannibal Street and parked the white utility van marked 'Bell South. The words 'Temple Of The Nile' were painted in huge Old English letters on the front of a white building; which was a restored cinema with red doors and situated on about three acres of ground. When Mike Cannon walked towards the rear of the premises and approached the middle aged Afro American security guard, he was immediately accepted as a telephone technician. "Hi there, I understand you are having trouble with your phone service." "I did not know of it. Any way the office is closed," the guard said. "When will I be able to check the equipment?" Mike Cannon glanced on the clip board in his hand and said, "It says here that it's urgent." "Not before 9 o' clock tonight. That is when they open. Some one was here earlier but she left. I understand tonight is special. People of the Order will be coming from all over." It was evident the guard was in a talkative mood and Mike Cannon decided to take advantage of it. "What do they do in there? The place gives me the creeps." "Mister you should be here at midnight. The chanting and shouting of that voodoo stuff when the killing and blood drinking takes place." "What the hell are you talking about? What sort of killing?" " Goats, sheep, .chickens, and it is rumored even people. But of course that would be hard to prove as only special members are allowed to partake at that level. That is heavy African stuff mister; these people are very dangerous. It's best to keep far from them. They deal only in fire and death. Tonight is one of their special nights."

Mike Cannon had learnt enough. Pretending he was scared by the account given by the security guard, he said to him, "I think they will have to open up the place in the daytime if they want their phone fixed. I will tell that to my office. Check you later." With that he walked back towards where the van was parked, climbed into it and drove off..

Mike Cannon parked the Camaro on the pavement about a hundred yards from the entrance of 777 Cannibal Street and watched the many vehicles turn into the premises. At 9.30 pm he came out of the car, willfully neglected to lock the doors and walked towards the temple. He was dressed in a white full length gown with a white turban on his head. His face and hands were darkened, and at a glance in the shadow he could be easily mistaken for one of the worshipers. In his hand concealed in a plastic garbage bag was a ten gallon container of gasoline. He walked up the steps and passed through the red entrance door unchallenged. He immediately walked directly towards one of the many rest rooms, placed the container in a litter box and covered it with paper. Assisted by the poor lighting he entered the temple hall and joined the congregation.

On the well lit stage was a sacrificial altar large enough to accommodate a human. It was inclined about ten to fifteen degrees with a trough at the lower end. Beneath the trough was placed a stainless steel bucket for receiving the flow of blood from the altar. Near by was a table over which was draped a white cloth. On the table were a number of small cups from which the blood was served to the members.

Mike Cannon sat patiently throughout the preliminary procedures leading up to the climax at midnight, when a side door was opened and the sacrifice was wheeled out on a trolley and placed alongside the altar. Immediately four men draped in black robes and black turbans came out of an opposite door and lifted the victim from the trolley and placed it onto the altar, with head towards the lower portion. They then ceremoniously removed the white robe into which the sacrifice was wrapped to reveal a young white female arms folded across her chest and lying perfectly still as if drugged.

Mike Cannon immediately got up from his seat and hastened towards the rest room where he had concealed the container with gasoline. He commenced to empty its contents on the floor of the rest room. It flowed along the passage and down into the temple hall where the congregation was by then on their feet chanting loudly in anticipation of the final moment, and swaying to and fro in a frenzy. A black robed figure emerged through the door from which the sacrifice was taken, bearing a large shiny dagger on a black cushion and stood beside the altar. Suddenly as if by some secret signal, the audience became silent, and out of the opposite door slowly emerged the High Priest Jean Biassou robed in black with the bleached skull of an infant attached to a chain draped around his neck, and approached the figure bearing the dagger. Mike Cannon quickly struck a match and lit the trail of gasoline that by then had made its way unnoticed throughout the unsuspecting congregation. He shouted, "Fire, the place is on fire!" The flames by then had set ablaze the robes of some of the congregation and were racing towards the stage; followed by Mike Cannon who had thrown aside his disguise revealing his black combat outfit and weapon in hand. He snatched the unconscious girl from the altar, hoisted her upon his shoulder and raced towards the emergency exit door. The High Priest Jean Biassou who had remained calm throughout the confusion, realized what was happening. He seized the dagger from where the attendant in his flight had discarded it on the floor, and pursued Mike Cannon. At the door Mike Cannon turned and fired, but the burly priest kept coming. Mike Cannon aimed for his head and the bullets from the Bren-10 disintegrated his skull.

When Mike Cannon got to the Camaro he gently placed the girl onto the back seat. Looking back he saw that the flames had already engulfed the interior of the Temple. He drove towards the nearest hospital where he placed the girl in the care of the nurse in charge. In the car he had partly covered her nude body with his combat jacket. "Who is this, and what is the matter with her?" The nurse enquired, looking suspiciously at Mike Cannon.

Mike Cannon showed her his badge. "I am Inspector Mike Cannon, and I have just rescued her from being sacrificed. I believe she is drugged within an inch of her life." He took a bit of paper from the front desk, wrote on it, then handed it to the nurse. "Call Captain Abe Duncan at that number and tell him we have found the missing girl Casey Andrews." As Mike Cannon turned away he said, "Good bye nurse, this has been a long night. I am going to bed." He yawned, walked through the hospital door and out into the night. . .

Chapter 8

The telephone rang on Captain Duncan's desk. He had just opened a box containing special fried rice his secretary Liz brought from the Hong Kong Star one block down the street. She knew the captain's passion for special fried rice and shrimp chow mein. Liz had previously complained that recently Captain Duncan was neglecting himself, especially his meals.

The captain said under his breath, "It better be good." He lifted the receiver and answered, "Captain Abe Duncan."

"This is Mike Cannon, Captain. Is this a wrong time?"

"Of course it is not," Captain Duncan lied.

Somehow Mike knew he did. "I won't keep you. About that white substance, did you get the result of the test?"

"I just got it an hour ago. You were right. It contained an added substance. Something the Russian scientists discovered during World War Two. They gave it to their special units when the Germans were at the gates of Leningrad. It turned the soldiers into superhuman beings, each having the strength of four or five men. Not mentioning their ferocity. It caused them to ignore personal danger. Unfortunately, almost all those particular soldiers died from heart attack within twenty-four months."

"Captain, does that ring a bell?" Mike asked.

"Yes, it does. Do what has to be done. We can't have that on the streets. The press is becoming suspicious. We can't afford the public to panic. "

***

When Mike entered the lobby of the Holiday Inn on US-1 in Coral Gables, Jay was on his second pint of beer. Mike sat beside him on a stool at the bar. Mike ordered a Miller Light and pretended he did not know Jay.

On the next order, Mike turned to Jay and said, "Would you care to have another on me, partner? Hate to drink alone."

"I can't say no," Jay replied.

"Bartender, another Light for me and another of what my friend here is having."

Halfway through the last order, and after an exchange of fictitious names and much small talk, Mike asked, "Did you hear of the shoot-out of the druggies in Fort Lauderdale?"

"Everyone has. That was between the Jamaican Posse and the Colombians," Jay replied.

Mike whispered, "Get me everything you can on the Jamaican Posse for tomorrow night. I will be in the parking lot outside. There will be something in it for you."

After finishing their drinks, both men shook hands, and Mike left.

The next night, Mike drove into the parking lot of the Holiday Inn Hotel at eight, as was arranged with Jay. The front section was filled with cars, most of which were probably belonging to guests and walk-ins, taking advantage of the famous creations of the hotel's Greek master chef. It was rumored that he was once chef to the famous Greek shipping magnate Onassis.

108

Mike drove to the rear of the lot where he saw Jay's silver-gray Volvo. Jay was waiting inside his car. Jay saw him and waited until Mike parked and walked over. Jay opened the passenger-side door and sat down.

"What have you got for me?"

"Not much. None of my contacts are willing to give up anything on those guys without something first. These guys are bad news, Mike. They kill first and ask questions after. And when I say kill, I mean everyone on the premises, including the cat if there is one. I did manage to get the name of the top guy though. His name is Jack Wall. He lives in one of those exclusive residential areas in Lauder Hill, Fort Lauderdale."

"What about his men? I understand he has an army."

"Yes, about twenty-five, all Jamaicans. That is why it is so difficult to get information. I need more time."

"This is what you must get. Their names, names of their contacts, where they live, and where they keep the drugs. You know the drill. Anything, even if it does not seem important to you."

"Mike, did you hear what I said? These guys are dangerous, almost not human. They will come and get you in police headquarters if they have to."

"Don't worry about me," Mike said. "I have no family, I have no cat, I am not at headquarters, and I will get them in hell if I want to. Here is five grand. Meet me here two days from now, same time."

Mike handed Jay a sealed envelope. He got out of the car, and Mike drove off.

***

Glenis Johns sat on his front porch and stared across the untended ten-acre homestead he owned in the Redlands. The road that entered his property was yet to be paved. After building the house, the car repair business off Krome Avenue took a downward turn. With him being alone for the past six months and the shortage of reliable labor, there was not enough money to do what was planned. His dejection was not an act of will; it was the result of an unfortunate condition thrust upon him. An accident at the garage while working alone had left his back in a state of no recovery, except he could get a windfall of cash to afford a specialist and the special medical attention that would be necessary after the surgery.

Mike drove slowly on the dirt road to avoid stirring up dust and stopped at Glenis Johns's house. He came out of the Camaro and walked toward the gate.

Glenis recognized him and asked, "My god, Mike, what are you doing way out in the boondocks?"

"I stopped by the garage to see you or Johnny, only to find it closed," Mike answered.

"Johnny is dead for the past four years, Mike. Didn't you hear?"

"Of course I did not. I would have stopped by. Johnny was one of my best. You know that. What really happened?"

"They killed him and his son. Come on in and take a load off. I'll tell you about it."

Mike climbed the steps and shared a metal bench on the front porch with Glenis.

"You remembered my grandson Ken?"

"Of course I remember him."

"Well, one day he came from school in Cutler Ridge in a mess. Three bigger boys ganged up on him and gave him the beating of his life. .It happened that they wanted him to assist in selling drugs to the other children in school. That had been going on for weeks, and neither Johnny nor Beverly nor I knew. Ken did not tell us. He thought he could handle it by himself. So one day while waiting on the bus, they jumped him and messed him up badly. When he came home, Johnny took him in the van and went to look for them to warn them off. Well, he found them and did warn them off. He told them he was going to report them to the police. As he turned to leave, one of them put a thirty-eight slug in his back and another in Ken. By the time the ambulance rushed them to the hospital, they were dead. I tried to run the garage on my own and was doing fairly well in spite of my age, until the accident."

"What happened?" Mike inquired.

"I was working late one evening fixing a transmission when the hydraulic on the lift failed. I had it in mind to repair the safety lock mechanism but really never got around to it. I was trapped with the full weight of the car on my back for nearly two hours, until a customer came into the shop and found me. I was in the hospital for nearly a month. I cannot work, Mike. No insurance, you know the rest."

There was silence.

"Well, enough about me. How is Kim and the kids?"

"They are dead. Shot down right before my eyes. And I could do nothing about it. I was shot up pretty badly too."

"I heard about that on the radio. But there were no names mentioned, so I couldn't know you and your family were involved."

"That is why I came by to see Johnny. I remembered how clever he was in creating things. I wanted him to fix a ram to the front of my car. I had in mind something that can be removed and replaced easily. I am assigned to go after the drug guys who are behind all this, and the car ram is a part of my plan."

"I know what you have in mind, Mike, and I can do something for you better. You know how Johnny is always thinking of going into the Big Wheel racing sport. Well, he fixed this black Dodge truck with big wheels and a new super-charged engine he bought out of state. He put on special shocks and special stabilizer bars. It has four-wheel drive and special reinforcing steel bars that protect the driver if the truck rolls. He reinforced the door panels for added strength with quarter-inch steel plates inside the doors behind the outer panels. Mike, it is rebuilt like a tank with top speed of one hundred miles per hour. I have seen him testing it in an open field, and he pushed it to sixty in a series of turns. It listed on two wheels with the other wheels off the ground, and it righted itself. I can lend it to you and the garage in which to store it when not in use. It is the side bay in the garage. It has its own remote door opener, so you can come and go easily. When in use, you can park your car inside. It can take two comfortably. How is that?"

Mike could make no comment for a while. He could not dream of a situation more suitable. "How much will it cost? I will pay whatever it is."

"I tell you what. Come tomorrow. Bring me whatever you can afford, and I will give you the keys. How is that?"

"Perfect. That is just perfect for me. Glenis, I meant to ask you, how is Beverly? How did she take what happened to Johnny and Ken?"

"Oh, she took it hard, Mike. A month after we buried them, she went and joined the Army Reserves. You remember she was technically minded, always fooling around computers? Well, after she completed her basics, she did so well that the army sent her out of state, to Virginia, I believe, for special combat training involving anti-espionage and a lot of other things. She was invited to enlist as a commissioned officer and promoted to captain. She is an instructor in special skills and combat training. She says when her term is up, she will be leaving the army. She always asks for you and Kim. Those two were always thick. I will tell her you came by next time she calls."

"Is she in Florida now?"

"Oh yes. She lives about fifteen minutes from here."

"Tell her I will make it my duty to get in touch."

Chapter 9

Jack Wall went to the ice cooler and opened another bottle of Red Stripe beer. He was on his fourth and the last before he retired to bed at midnight. The telephone rang, and he lifted the receiver from an instrument on a nearby side table. "This is Jack," he said.

"Perkins calling," the voice said at the other end.

"What's up?" Jack asked.

"Run out of merchandise. I cannot keep up with the demand. People love the stuff."

"It is the same situation down here," Jack said. "I contacted my guy and asked him to get in touch with you know who and ask if he could make delivery every two weeks instead of monthly."

"Any reply?"

"Not yet," Jack replied.

"Keep in touch if anything happens. I will try and keep the customers quiet at my end," Perkins said.

New arrangement was made to receive the drop at sea from the plane bringing the cocaine from Jamaica. A speedboat would recover the merchandise at a prearranged time and place. Jack decided on that alternative as another police encounter on land was too risky. The Castro cocaine had gained popularity on the market, and more of the Colombians' contacts were deserting to Jack. Users all across the country as distant as California were singing the praises of the effect of the "new stuff."

Meanwhile the media were reporting the unusual increase of violence and mass murders across all levels of the population. A college in Nebraska reported that a student shot his female teacher and five other students, killing all six before killing himself.

An army reserve shot his officer in the field and two other soldiers. Every day there were multiple reports of the increase in violence and the senseless killing of innocent people. A front-page report of the suicide of Dave Shon in his cell, the only witness tying the Jamaican Posse to the Homestead police killings, shocked law enforcement officials.

Mike was not pleased. Something he could not presently identify was gnawing away inside. Whenever he tried to focus on it, his own personal situation blocked his vision and prevented him from giving the feeling priority. One thing kept coming up, and that one thing was something Captain Duncan had said to him. Apart from being a crime fighter, Cannon was a scientifically minded detective. Before long, he would unravel the puzzle.

***

Donaldo Santiago, while recovering from his injuries, was forced to spend more time at home, from where he temporarily directed his business. At ten one morning, he received a phone call from a concerned colleague. "Donaldo Santiago. Who is this?" he asked.

"This is Pepe Perez. I want to talk privately with you. I am coming over."

"Okay, call when you get to the gate. I will let you in," Santiago said to him.

Donaldo Santiago had problems of his own. His priority for the time being was no longer real estate development, money laundering, or cocaine distribution, but ex-mayor Frank Bukley. If the district attorney succeeded in getting Bukley into court, he was certain to see jail time, which was not an option. Without Bukley or Mike Cannon, there was not much of a case against him. Since it could be difficult to get at Bukley, he should still try to silence Mike, since he was not under police protection, but moving around freely, creating a certain amount of havoc. He would place a bounty of 250,000 dollars on Detective Inspector Mike Cannon and a similar bounty on ex-mayor Frank Bukley.

Satisfied that at least he had made a decision to do something practical toward the solution of his problems, he sat down to await the arrival of Perez.

Driving across the bridge that led to Williams Island on which Donaldo Santiago owned his twelve-million-dollar residence was an experience in itself. Having your address there was the only reference needed to elevate you to membership of a select social group. Pepe Perez would be required to have a complete renewal of mind to even consider spending as much as a single day among the affluence of that island, as already while driving, the upscale environment was contributing to a certain amount of uneasiness.

He arrived at the gate and called Santiago. The gate automatically opened. He drove onto a circular driveway and parked. He came out of the two-year-old Cadillac sedan and wondered what looked more out of place, him or the car.

Santiago met him at the door. Seeing Santiago caused Perez to feel more at ease. At last he saw a living person. The first since he crossed the bridge to the island.

"We will sit by the pool. There are helpers all over the place, and that is the best place since what we have to discuss may be confidential."

Perez said, "It certainly is."

Donaldo Santiago led Pepe Perez across a perfectly manicured lawn to the far side of the front of the house to an imposing metal gate. It was difficult to know how, but the gate swung open automatically as they approached it. They entered a tiled walkway that led onto the back of the premises, which was fully tiled with white marble. In the center was a very large heart-shaped swimming pool, around which were deck chairs and tables with green-and-white umbrellas. There were marble statues and crouching lions all around the decking. At the far edge of the pool was a tiki hut in which a young man was restocking the shelves of the bar.

The two men sat at one of the tables, and the young man in the bar immediately brought them two glasses of orange juice with drinking straws.

Perez was impressed. He remembered what Sabas Gonzalez said at the meeting on his boat regarding the efficiency and orderliness of Donaldo Santiago. Perez thought, Whatever this man is lacking, style is not one of them.

Santiago looked at Perez, expecting him to speak. It was he who asked for the meeting.

"Donaldo, I brought you into this lifestyle. I introduced you to Sabas. It's over."

"What do you mean by 'it's over'?"

"I mean secure what you have before you lose it all. Do not underestimate the law. The law is the United States of America. That is as big as they come. You are an American citizen. That is as lucky as you can ever get. You value close to a billion dollars. What more can you want? Get out."

"Explain how I do that. Sabas will not allow it."

"Don't be foolish. He is only a man. He called himself an emperor at the last meeting on his yacht. That would make us his subjects. Hell, Donaldo, no way! You came here on a few oil drums tied together with wire. You watched your brother die in your arms running away from a madman. Are you going to let another madman own you? He is safe on his boat. Anything happens too big for him to handle, he sails away to somewhere else and finds others. You know who is left holding the dirty end of the stick? All of us will. Do you know you can be deported or imprisoned? Take your pick."

After that statement, both men were silent for a long time.

That thought was always at the back of Santiago's mind. But he was reluctant to make a move, not sure of support from his colleagues. In fact, he was uncertain how to propose it. If he made such a suggestion, he would first have to be very certain it would be entertained. But if Pepe Perez suggested it and believed it would succeed, it was good enough for him. Perez was the only man he knew who stood up to Fidel Castro face-to-face, called him a mad fool, and lived to talk of it. He trusted and respected Pepe. He was extremely wealthy, but modest enough to keep a low profile.

"What would you suggest?"

"First, are you with me on this? I will need you to swear on your children's life."

Donaldo Santiago had no further reservation regarding the subject. He raised his right hand and said, "I swear on my children's life I am with you on this. But before we can do anything, I must get rid of Mike Cannon and Bukley. They can take everything away from me. I have decided to put a bounty of two hundred and fifty thousand on each of them. That ought to get it done. It would be suicide for any one of them to show himself anywhere in Florida."

"Who did you get this time?"

"There is no one yet. It will be an open contract. Anyone who delivers gets paid."

"Hold on there. If the word gets out that you are the one who placed the bounty, your bail will be revoked. Also, Mike Cannon will be coming after you. And believe me, this time he will kill you. Leave it to me. I know how to get it done without you being involved. Just keep out of it. Make the transfer to my account, and consider it done."

Donald Santiago felt satisfied that if Pepe Perez, his good friend, made that commitment to him and took his money to get it executed, he had nothing more to worry about. Pepe had always come through for him.

Perez drove back slowly toward his home in Hialeah. He had accomplished what he had planned for many days. Years ago, he had placed Donaldo Santiago on top, but it all got to his head. He abused the privileges of power. He had to be stopped before he pulled down everyone with him. He had no intention of placing a bounty on anyone. He would take Santiago's money since he had no better use for it.

Chapter 10

M ike Cannon placed the list he received from Jay Gordon that night on the table in his riverside apartment. Beside the list was a copy of a map of Dade and Broward counties. There were eight names and current addresses, including that of Jack Wall on that list. When he got the list, he reminded Jay that the person or persons he received those information from will be informing members of the Jamaican Posse for a price, that there were inquiries being made of their whereabouts. He paid an extra two thousand to Jay and advised him to become scarce for a while, or he could be the next casualty. Jay advised Mike that he was aware of his danger and had already taken precautions.

The names on the list were the only men of Jack Wall's group trusted to make deliveries and collections. He was also informed that a shipment of cocaine was expected from Jamaica in three days from that date. Satisfied of his progress, it being after midnight, Mike went to bed.

Early the next day, Mike drove to the garage off Krome Avenue where the Big Wheels was parked. He was about to lift the door by remote control when he noticed a note pasted on it. He got out of his car and read the note. It was from Beverly Johns, and she wanted to see him. Also on the note was a telephone number. He made the call from a phone booth and drove to meet her.

Mike wasted no time, and within an hour, they were both having a meal at a nearby Denny's on US-1.

"Mike, I heard all that has happened to you and Kim and the kids. What a damned shame. Nothing could be worse. I have been there. I will not say you will get over it because that would not be true. Things like what we have been through never leave us. In time you may adapt to the situation, but that's all we can hope for."

While she was speaking, Mike noticed the dramatic changes she underwent. Gone was the shy, frail-looking young woman who used to frolic with his wife Kim. Before him was an athletic dynamic female, oozing self-confidence through every pore, and something much more he could not identify.

"Beverly, you look great, simply marvelous. Tell me, what you have been doing?"

"Long story, Mike. You must have heard from Johnny's father that after Johnny and Ken's death, I joined the Army Reserves. As you may remember, I was good with computers. After the basic training, what they gave me to do was working with computers. The basic military training was terrific. For one, it was very intense. It helped me to forget my pain. At nights I just fell asleep. I was not awake long enough to grieve. My sergeant could not understand my motivation. The more they threw at me, the more I asked for. They did not know I had just lost my son and husband. I excelled in every phase of the training.

"It so happened that the War Department sensed some crisis in homeland security and required that personnel from every branch submit the best of the people they have for special training. Those they required must be also technically mind-ed in the field of communication. They sent me and another soldier to a special training camp in Virginia. Mike, that was no training camp, it was a human restructuring factory. The training group was made up of military personnel, male and female, who were sent to every corner of the world to master every art of warfare and self-defense each particular country had to offer. When they returned, they combined all the arts into one program and molded it into us. Or better, us into it.

"Mike, they made our bodies do things that were considered physically and psychologically impossible. We were transformed, each of us into a weapon. We were known as units with numbers. Our human identities were stripped from us, and we became just another piece of artillery. We were trained to kill with no emotion capable of mercy. In combat, we would not know how to take prisoners. We were trained to become almost amphibious, mastering an ancient Greek technique that enabled us to hold our breath for several minutes underwater that would render an ordinary individual unconscious. We were trained to eat portions of flesh from animals that were not yet dead. Raw fish while it was still alive, tear frogs and lizards apart and eat them raw without puking. We were taught to jump from incredible heights without breaking our bones or damaging our limbs. From a Chinese art, they trained us to run up perpendicular walls. There is hardly any condition under which we could not survive.

"I did not only survive, I excelled. I was invited, or better to say forced to join the ranks as a commissioned officer, passing on my special skills to officers wanted for covert operations.

"Unfortunately, Mike, I am barely human. That loss, I do regret. Sometimes I yearn to feel like a woman again."

Mike listened attentively to what Beverly had to say. He tried to sympathize but could not find any reason to. She was a superwoman and perhaps one of a dozen in existence. Was that such a bad thing? He was yet to decide. Had Beverly Johns decided? he asked himself.

"Why did you want to see me?" Mike asked.

"To see you again, for one, and to be a part of what you have in mind. My time in the army is almost up, only a few months to go. I want to use my training for something worthwhile. I want to help and clear the human garbage from our streets and try to get back our country from the criminals, the drug dealers, and the gunmen. I want to do this for Johnny and Ken."

"Beverly, are you serious about this?" Mike inquired. Scarcely believing that providence could be so benevolent as to supply the finishing ingredient to what he had secretly created. He had hoped that a partner motivated by a similar purpose would become his crime-fighting partner. But hoping for a Beverly Johns would be stretching his faith.

To be certain he did not misunderstand her offer, he found himself asking her, "Are you ready to do whatever it takes?"

"As ready as anyone can ever be. Together we could be a formidable force."

They stretched across the table and held hands.

"To Cannon Force!" she said.

"Yes, to Cannon Force!" Mike responded. He liked the sound. He felt the energy it represented.

***

It was 4:00 a.m., and Captain Duncan had been driving for almost four hours. He had been making that secret journey every month for too long. Circumstances had placed him in a position that he mentally termed a straitjacket. As a younger man with suicidal courage as Mike, the situation could not

123

have existed. But Abe Duncan was conscious that the youthful sparks of courage that were once his driving force had been extinguished. He was holding the only card fate had dealt him in his latter years, and he was reluctant to make a desperate play. He hoped that an unexpected chance would present itself that would automatically serve his purpose without any exposure that may affect his career or possibly his freedom.

He was caught in a web of his own weaving and irrevocably compromised the only friendship that he could have relied upon for help.

Mike had noticed the changes and surmised that whatever the burden, it was overwhelming enough to cause him to place his responsibility to law and order on the back burner.

It was early morning when he finally drove up to the large impressive double iron gates. He edged near to the metal stand on which the keypad was placed and punched in the special numbers. Both gates swung open. He could see his final destination a thousand yards or more in the distance; the red roof of the colossal residence sat among large oak trees.

He slowly drove along the driveway and parked at the end of it. The individual who held power over his life expected his arrival. He came out of the house and stretched a hand to greet him.

If only I could shoot you dead this instant, Abe Duncan said to himself as he took his hand.

"Go to your usual room and rest, Abe, you must be exhausted. I will send up refreshment." Ten Lee made no attempt to conceal the contempt that showed on his face. Contempt cultivated over the years for a man whose mental weakness allowed another to methodically manipulate him without any resistance.

Captain Duncan, after he properly rested himself, met with Ten, Wang, and Goldie Lee to give a detail report of the month's activities that could possibly affect the expansion of their business. He listened to criticisms and repulsive opinions pertaining to decisions he was compelled to make without the Lees' agreement. He made apologies and gave promises of better performance in their interest during the ensuing month. He was compelled to compromise the authority of his office to satisfy the ambitions of the Lees. He asked himself why the feds were so reluctant to get involved as they usually do. That would be his way out. And he would not be held responsible for bringing down the Ten Lees and others like him, who evidently enjoyed preferential privileges that allowed them to defy law and order.

Ten Lee, during the course of discussions that day, detected changes in the personality of Captain Duncan. During his experiences as a medical physician, he had at some time in the past called upon to diagnose and treat the psychological malady he detected. Away from the others, he invited Captain Duncan to accompany him in a walk in the wooded area of the compound. During that walk, he disclosed to him the reason for his presence in the United States and a situation the magnitude of which deserved his pledge to secrecy. The burden of that disclosure bore heavily upon him, and if Ten Lee believed it would act as a remedy to his desperation, he was mistaken. On the contrary, it made heavier his burden.

A subdued Abe Duncan, after spending the entire day, found himself on the long journey back to Miami. That meeting was more distressful than any that preceded seeing he had been forced into agreeing to conditions that he knew he would not be in a position to fulfill, although he sincerely hoped he could. He had noticed during discussions that frequently the opinion presented itself that Ten Lee was not completely in charge and was operating under duress. Not withstanding the mental pressure of his situation had become unbearable, and he was approaching the breaking point. For survival, he began to contemplate taking the only exit that presented itself. That is, to disclose the entire situation to Mike, ask his assistance, and face the consequences.

Captain Duncan sat in his Mercedes Benz, a picture of utter dejection, and watched the steady flow of people going in and out of the ABC Cinema off US-1. One show was over, and another was just about to commence. Nearby, a couple came out of their car and passed close by him. The man was in military uniform, and the lady was an Oriental.

His memory went back to a year before the campaign in Nam ended, and he was just married to the most charming Oriental girl he had ever seen. He was near the end of his leave of absence after his hospitalization. The day he got hit, he was in terribly bad shape when they shoved him into the chopper with three other guys. The pilot took one look at him, the blood spewing out of several bullet holes and the bottom half of his body badly burnt, and said to his buddy, "Pump some morphine into him and get him a padre immediately we touch down." But he was too angry with the bastards who did that to him to agree with the pilot. He was not ready to die. Right then and there, he vowed he would get at least one more shot at the enemy before the war ended.

After nine weeks of cutting and patching and rehabilitation, he was about ready to have another go. There was a comedy showing in a cinema in the center of town, and he wanted something funny to watch. He sat beside an attractive Oriental lady and asked her if she wanted to share his popcorn with him. The offer was so amusing that a conversation started. Six months after, he was married. She was not turned off because of his disfigurement caused by his burnt lower body, and he figured he was getting the better part of the deal.

Just as he started to enjoy the comforting effect of his trot down memory lane, Mike appeared, opened the passenger-side door, and sat down.

Mike was in another foul mood. He said, "My snitch told me he got it from a reliable source that it was the Lee brothers who put the hit on me. But it doesn't make sense. Wang Lee's little girl was almost killed. He was also there in harm's way. Why would he be there?"

"You are right," Captain Duncan agreed. "It really doesn't make sense why Wang Lee and his daughter had to be there, except he being at the hit was an accident. The hit was to get you any place, any time convenient. That means you were being tailed from your house to the restaurant. Wang Lee does not know you or expects any danger. But being Chinese, he was at a Chinese restaurant with his daughter having a meal. It could be purely coincidental. He could have also been hit. What I cannot understand, if he wanted you dead, why didn't he finish you off while you were way out there by yourself?"

Mike was very quiet. He began to think. A few things the captain said and also didn't say in that conversation did not add up. Why didn't he ask why the Lee brothers wanted him dead? One would believe that would be the first question he would ask. It was as if he already knew. Another thing, he made the statement "when you were way out there." Only the Lee brothers and I knew that I spent time getting well at their place.

He was also concerned over the feeble excuses Captain Duncan gave him when he asked why he was reluctant to mobilize effective police force to halt what could be considered the unchallenged takeover of the city by criminal elements.

Captain Duncan realized that somewhere in their conversation, he had given Mike cause to be unduly thoughtful. And to make it worse, Mike left his car without saying another word.

Captain Duncan remained in his car deep in thought for nearly an hour. He blamed himself for not taking the opportunity that presented itself and disclose everything to Mike and ask his assistance. Instead, he imagined he no longer had Mike's trust, and that was a disturbing conclusion.

That night, a thoughtful Mike went back to his apartment to make a decision on what would be his next line of action. He sensed a web of conspiracy he neither had the inclination, time, or resources to unravel. Being undercover and disregarding the acceptable methods of procedure, he had decided on a hit-and-miss process of elimination. By challenging suspects involved in serious criminal activities, the person or persons responsible for the death of his family could possibly be caught in the net. The result of that decision caused him to feel exposed and vulnerable, knowing that it was a negative one and would be counterproductive. For the first time, he became completely convinced he needed a trusted companion such as Beverly Johns who shared his passion and resolve.

Chapter 11

Jack Wall had secured his next drop shipment of cocaine from Jamaica and was making elaborate preparations to distribute to his wholesalers. He realized that a certain amount of exposure was created because of the overwhelming demand for his merchandise. To keep it undelivered and in one place would be unprofessional and dangerous, and that's what Jack was not. Grapevine would place on the streets the time of the arrival of the shipment, and his competitors or some enterprising adventurer could have ideas.

To offset any misadventure, he decided that all deliveries should be accompanied by an additional armed escort vehicle. That was ten men for each delivery. Undelivered merchandise posed an element of risk, so to minimize the risk factor, he decided on two deliveries per night, made simultaneously. So doing, he would exhaust the shipment in a couple of days, and also, if he lost one shipment, the other one would get through. It stood to reason that a hijacker could not be in both places at the same time.

Jack was never on a delivery, but he had the cars carrying the merchandise equipped with car-to-office radio contact so communication at all times was possible.

Through his information network, Jay Gordon was able to convey the information to Mike the night when the deliveries would be made, although the exact time was not available to him. He was also able to tell who would receive delivery any particular night, and also where it would be delivered. This was possible to enable the mules to plan individual deliveries ahead of time, which was a good and orderly marketing procedure. Some carriers were required to travel as far as places in Georgia and to areas on the Florida west coast.

Jack divided the shipment and placed a certain amount with trusted members of his group. That member was responsible for its security and prearranged delivery. The loss of any amount would result in assassination, painful and swift.

Jay, equipped with the names and addresses of members trusted with delivery, placed early surveillance on them on the particular night deliveries were scheduled to be made.

Mike Cannon and Beverly Johns had set up secret headquarters in the closed garage of Glenis, where the Big Wheels was kept. Mike would deal with one delivery group, while Beverly had no difficulty in convincing Mike that acting alone, she could effectively intercept and permanently wipe out the other.

Beverly would drive the Camaro, while Mike would drive the Big Wheels. Each vehicle was equipped with several Molotov cocktails, as it was arranged that the vehicle with the cocaine must be destroyed on the spot without sophisticated explosives that could possibly get innocent people hurt and attract negative public opinion.

Mike sat and waited, dressed combat ready for the occasion. Beverly went into the restroom of the garage to change. The surprise was what came out. She was dressed in a black Delta Force–type combat outfit with a ninja–type mask across her face. She was armed with everything capable of wiping out any enemy patrol. Mike had no doubt whatsoever that she was trained by the military to do so.

At midnight, the telephone rang; Mike took up the receiver and listened. He nodded to Beverley Johns, and they both drove out to individually intercept the enemy.

***

Mike saw the two late-model BMWs following one behind the other. They were observing the speed limit of thirty-five miles per hour like good law-abiding citizens. They did not want any confrontation with the police. Not with the drugs on board.

He allowed two vehicles between the Big Wheels and the escort car. Because of the height of his vehicle, Mike could look across the vehicles between them and into the escort vehicle through their rear window. Three Dreadlocks were seated in the back. That made five persons in the car. Most likely the merchandise would be in the trunk of the lead BMW. Mike hoped that the delivery point was a secluded area where innocent people could not get hurt.

At an intersection, the two vehicles between turned off, but the BMWs continued straight ahead. Mike held back to allow impatient motorists behind to pass him and fill the vacant space. A black SUV and a red pickup truck did just that. Mike continued in that formation for about four miles.

At another intersection, the two BMWs turned right, and Mike knew that they were headed under the bridge to a large open field where a large number of houses were demolished. That road was a cul-de-sac, and there was nowhere else to go. For the last one thousand yards, there were no houses on both sides of the road and also no streetlights.

Mike cut his headlights and slowly followed. When they entered the field, he stopped and observed through his night-vision goggles. There were two vehicles parked side by side facing the entrance to the field with their park lights on. The BMWs approached them abreast with full lights on and stopped about sixty feet away. For about two minutes, nothing happened. Then one man emerged from the escort vehicle, and another came out of one of the opposite cars. They commenced to walk slowly toward each other with arms stretched sideways, palms down, to show that they had no weapons in their hands. They talked and returned to their respective vehicles. The occupant from the BMW went to the lead car and spoke to the driver, and then the five men came out.

The occupants from one of the other two cars did the same, except that one of the men had a briefcase in his hand. The driver of the lead BMW popped the trunk and went to the rear of the vehicle, as if to remove something. That was as far as they were allowed to proceed.

The lawman turned on the headlight high beam and pushed the accelerator to the floor. The engine roared, and the front wheels raised high off the ground as the Big Wheels charged across the field like a rampaging elephant. Those who were out of the vehicles scattered and fled in all directions, scaling the walls and fences, leaving whatever possessions they had. The Big Wheels mounted both BMWs from the rear and squashed them, trapping whoever were left inside. It then raced toward the other vehicles. One of those drivers kept his nerves and raced away from the charging monstrosity and escaped, but the other was flattened.

Mike turned around and faced the damaged vehicles. He raised a bullhorn to his lips and shouted, "This is the police! I will be giving you only one warning. However you may, come out of the vehicles with your hands up. Leave your weapons inside. If I see a weapon, you are all dead. I will be torching the vehicles."

The four Jamaican Dreadlocks temporarily trapped in the BMW that contained the cocaine in the squashed trunk compartment managed to squeeze out of the wreck and assembled on the opposite side away from Mike. One of them said, "It's only one man in there, Rasta, who the f— — he think he is? He is not burning our drugs tonight. Come on, what the f— — you waiting for?"

Mike had expected that reaction from men of the Jamaican Posse. He knew they would not surrender. He had the Bren Ten on automatic and ready.

The Jamaican Dreadlocks came charging toward him from the front and rear of the wreck, their automatic handguns blazing. The men from the opposite vehicles saw the move of the Jamaicans and were motivated by their daring. They squeezed out of their wrecked vehicle and joined the charge.

Mike knew he only had twenty in the clip and could not afford wasting bullets. He would remain calm and deal with the Jamaicans first, as they were nearer. He squeezed on the trigger and felt the Bren Ten jerk as it delivered instant death. As if it happened at once, he saw the charging Jamaicans hurled backward and stretched out on the ground.

The men from the other car was midway toward Mike and observed the dying Jamaicans. They tried to turn back, but it was too late. The flashes from the Bren Ten were already delivering their deadly message. They also died.

Mike waited for about a minute, then lit two of the Molotov cocktails and walked around the bodies toward the BMWs. He threw the torch. It ignited both vehicles as it splintered, spreading the flames. The ruptured gas tanks exploded and hurled both vehicles into the air. He calmly walked over toward the other wreck and did the same. Then he picked up the briefcase abandoned during their dash to safety over the wall. Mission completed, he climbed into the Big Wheels and drove away.

***

While Mike was trailing the two white BMWs to their delivery point, Beverly was also trailing a black BMW that was acting as escort for another black BMW two car lengths ahead. She held back the Camaro two or three vehicle lengths so that the occupants would not become suspicious.

The occupants were so confident of their firepower that they were not very cautious. There were five young Dreadlocks in the lead car. In the trunk compartment was a collection of assault rifles, M-16s and AK-47s, and a leather bag with twenty kilos of cocaine. The men in the escort vehicle were also heavily armed. Aside from their handguns, they had two double-barrel sawed-off shotguns inside the car with them.

After about fifteen minutes, the vehicles being followed turned onto a lonely stretch of road and slowed down to twenty miles per hour. Beverly realized they had discovered they were being tailed and intended to put an end to it. She had no option but to slow down as well. Then they came to a full stop. She did the same and stopped about forty feet behind the escort car.

The four doors of the escort car opened at once, and the five men came out. She immediately reclined her backrest and jumped over to the back seat and prepared to meet the oncoming confrontation. There were two men with shotguns and the others with handguns. The two with the shotguns advanced while the other three stopped. She immediately flattened herself on the floor. They did what she anticipated.

They emptied all barrels through the windshield, shattering the interior of the car with flying glass.

Confident that they had accomplished their objective, they came to both sides of the door to confirm. Her two German Mauser C-96 pistols, one in each hand, blasted their faces off, hurling their bodies to different sides of the road. The other three started blasting away. Their bullets ripped the padding from the front seat backrests, behind which she took cover. She did not return their fire. They thought she was dead. They did just what she hoped. They cautiously advanced to investigate. At that time the occupants of the lead car, supposing that the danger was over, all came out with guns drawn and joined their buddies. The group of eight came closer.

She took the M-16 from where she had placed it on the rear seat for such an emergency and opened fire. The three nearest were cut to pieces, while the others dashed for cover behind the escort car and started firing. Bullets ripped through the interior of the Camaro. One of the men broke cover and tried to make it to the lead car and was immediately cut down. In another desperate attempt to save the cargo, another tried and suffered the same fate.

Beverly aimed for where she knew the gas tank of the escort car should be and blasted away. The BMW exploded, and the explosion lifted it into the air. The sudden blast set ablaze two men who sought cover behind it. They screamed and ran out into the open. She aimed and fired, putting them out of their suffering. The confusion gave her chance to open the door of the Camaro and rolled out into the street. She continued to roll until she was in a position to shoot off one of the rear tires of the lead car.

The shooting stopped, and there was silence. Beverley Johns waited where she was lying, the M-16 ready in her hand. By her count, one was still unaccounted for. "Come out and show yourself. Now!" she shouted.

"God damn, it's a woman!" a surprised voice exclaimed. Then his macho ego took over. He broke cover with guns blazing and advanced to the direction from which he heard the voice.

Beverly rolled as bullets thudded into the ground where she was. She opened fire and blew his legs from under him. The gun flew out of his hand and landed across the street. She got up, walked over, and stood looking down on him. She removed the mask from her face.

"Woman, who the hell are you?" he asked.

"Cannon Force," she replied and shot him in the chest. She went back to the Camaro and drove by the lead car. She lit the Molotov cocktail and threw it in. Flames immediately engulfed the interior. She drove to the top of the street and waited for the explosion. When she finally heard it, she slowly drove away.

***

Jack Wall sat by the telephone and waited. In spite of his precautions, he was still anxious. It should have been confirmed that both deliveries were successfully made more than two hours ago. He opened another Red Stripe beer, his sixth. He felt something had gone wrong. He pictured in his mind all possible misfortunes that could possibly cause the lack of news.

At 4:30 a.m., the telephone rang. He caused it to ring twice before he answered, afraid of what he may learn.

"Boss, is that you?" The voice was broken and faint.

"Of course it's me. What the hell happened? Was the delivery made?"

"What delivery? We were attacked, and almost all the boys are dead. I barely escaped by jumping over a wall. I have been walking ever since. I just got home."

"Then what about the package?"

"That I do not know. While I was running for my life, I heard a loud explosion, and when I looked back, I saw a fire that lit up the sky."

"What about the buyer with the money?"

"That, I do not know either. Some of them got killed. Some jumped over the wall with me. I believe they may have left the money behind. I am not certain. They knew our movement, boss. They knew everything. What about Delroy, boss, have you heard from him?"

"Not a single word. This is the first phone call. I can imagine what also happened." Jack held the receiver in his hand for a long while before he hung up. He sank back in the chair and sat staring at the ceiling. "What the hell is this? What could have gone wrong?" Jack repeated to himself over and over as various possibilities went through his mind. His best-laid plans were breached. That had to be the work of an organization. But someone had to tip them off. But who could that be? It had to be the feds who did this. Only the feds had that much firepower to do that much damage in two different places at the same time. They were the notorious Jamaican Posse. No one attacked the Posse. That was the nature of his thoughts. He found it difficult to accept the unacceptable reality.

At 7:30 a.m., the telephone rang. Jack was sitting in the same chair. He grabbed the receiver.

"Mr. Wall?" That was not the voice he expected.

"Yes, this is Jack Wall."

"This is Ben. Ben Hyman. Where is my package?"

"Don't know. You should have had it from last night."

"Have you listened to the seven o'clock news?"

"No, I have not."

"Well, you should. All your boys are dead. I am canceling my order while I am ahead. I heard through the grapevine that another customer was not so lucky. He lost his money and also good men."

The police reported that at one location, six bodies were found and three vehicles crushed and burned in an open field. In another location, nine bodies were found and two burnt-out vehicles. Most of the dead were identified as Dreadlocks connected to the Jamaican Posse. One Jamaican, who was critically wounded, died on the way to the hospital. The police reported that before he died, although incoherent, he mentioned that it was a ninja woman that did it, burnt their cars and the cocaine they were carrying. Both incidents were reported to be drug related. They also reported that both incidents took place at approximately the same time. The police had no further comment.

***

Captain Abe Duncan listened to the news with mixed emotions. The statement that there were two separate incidents occurring simultaneously scared him. He hesitated to imagine the existence of another Mike Cannon. Yet he could not ignore the evidence that there existed an efficient operating organization of awesome destructive force, taking the law into their hands. Mike had gone too far; he had to be stopped. But how could even Mike be in both places at the same time? Then what was that report of a ninja woman? To accuse Mike without proof would be a costly error. Yet the description of both events bore his trademark. That was enough proof for him. He decided it was time to do something.

At 8:00 a.m., his decision to do something was executed. He opened the secret compartment in the dresser in his bedroom and took from it a small black book. He sat down and made a call.

The answering voice at the other end said, "Exman."

Captain Duncan said, "D day" and hung up. From the same book, he made another call, that time long distance. When he got an answer, he said, "This is Donald. The lid is off." He hung up.

To ask Mike to turn in his badge would be a decision too dangerous to make. He would take his undercover findings to the press, and the feds would be forced to be involved. It was possible that Mike had career-threatening information that could affect his career and possibly freedom. There was no way of knowing what he knew. He sensed from the result of their last meeting that Mike was suspicious, and an exposure was eminent. Cannon, by that day's news, had created an army of enemies. If anything had to be done, it had to be then. The time was right. It was Mike Cannon or Abe Duncan.

***

Mike walked around the Camaro and shook his head. Over a hundred bullets had punched holes into the body. The front windshield and the upholstering on the front seats were blown away, and the radiator was damaged beyond repair. The engine had overheated, and it barely made it back to their headquarters.

"This is finished. You had been through hell," Mike said to Beverly.

"I had been there before and back. You should see what I did to the other guys' cars. We will need to find something else."

"Never mind, we can surely take care of that. Just look what we have." Mike went into the office followed by Beverly. On the desk was a black briefcase. "This belonged to the bad guys. They were in a hurry and forgot to take it."

Mike opened the briefcase, and it was full of packages of hundred dollar bills amounting to hundreds of thousands of dollars. "There is more than enough here to meet our expenses. Crime fighting is expensive."

Chapter 12

David Schulenberg sat across the desk from Donaldo Santiago in Santiago's penthouse office. The ivory palace of cards was tumbling down. Frank Bukley was in a safe house somewhere under police protection. He was key witness against Santiago for conspiracy to murder a police officer and may give evidence in another unsolved homicide involving Santiago. A federal investigation of the business affairs of Santiago, which would certainly involve David Schulenberg's Venezuelian offshore bank in money laundering, was eminent. The meeting that evening was to inform David Schulenberg that it was in their best interest to wind up the money-laundering section of his affairs and become totally legitimate.

"Donaldo, my friend, that is more easily said than done," David Schulenberg said, looking away from him.

"And why is that so? I was under the impression all these years that you were in full control of things. You were the man."

"To an extent, I am. But the politics of international banking goes much further than you and me. When I agreed to back your scheme, I told you I would handle the politics, and you the other phases of the business. I know international banking. That is my business. I do not try to get involved in yours, unless it threatens to interfere with the operation of my bank. Since it comes to this, I will now fill you in with details you previously had no reason to know.

"To begin with, Sabas Betata Gonzales is the wealthiest and the most powerful man in all South America. He is responsible for placing in power, and removing from power, more presidents and dictators than any other man in the western hemisphere. One of his close relatives is head of a growing radical socialist group that aims to one day take over the Venezuelan government and nationalize all the country's natural resources. Don't for one minute believe Washington does not know of his affairs. But to interfere with the operation of Sabas Gonzalez would be to disturb the delicate balance of United States–South American relationship. Therefore, his primary function is to make certain that American relationship on the South American continent remains unstable. So it is important that he maintains cordial relationship with Fidel Castro, who is the creator of overt destabilizing activities in the central and South Americas.

"Sabas Gonzalez controls mining and is indirectly behind all narcotic operations in South America. He supports cocaine smuggling and considers its production one of the continent's most lucrative agro industries. He is the owner of my bank and several other offshore banks operating in this country. In short, he allowed you to be one of the beneficiaries of the proceeds of his international operation. Now, how do you think you can extricate your interests from his because you were advised by some uninformed fool or fools to do so? Where would you go? Venezuela, Argentina, Colombia, Chile, Peru? Tell me where. Certainly you could not remain here. Except as an inmate in some prison and experience the federal government confiscating your assets as the proceeds of money laundering. Whoever advised you to even think of making this suicidal decision is certainly not your friend. And I can bet you everything I own, by this time Sabas Gonzalez has already learnt of it and has made arrangement to dispose of you."

After that lecture, Donaldo Santiago realized he had spun his web and got caught in it. He became conscious of being the victim of treachery. Since Pepe Perez was in the first instance influential enough to place him in the confidence of Sabas Gonzalez, everything he had just learnt, Perez already knew. He made current errors in judgment that had affected more people than he imagined. When he was placed in jail, those individuals thought that was the end of that, and he would be got rid of. But Sabas Gonzalez through his influential connections arranged his release. And unknown to him would have also arranged that he be cleared of all charges. But he had taken it upon himself to contemplate another hit on Mike Cannon and also on another witness under police protection, Frank Bukley. That would further upset the existing order of things. To remove Donaldo Santiago, the relationship and confidence he enjoyed with Sabas Gonzalez had to be undermined. It was cleverly executed and already done.

"David, I need your advice here. What do we do next?"

"I do not know what you will do. But I do nothing. I continue managing my bank. As long as I remain loyal to Sabas Gonzalez, nothing will happen to me. The worse is that I will be recalled to Argentina and sent to somewhere else to manage another one of his banks. The feds certainly will not mourn my departure, and life will continue."

A wave of loneliness then swept over Santiago. At the last meeting, he took over control unopposed and unwittingly did to his business and personal affairs just what he had condemned in Castro. He tried his hand at being a dictator.

"How much money can I take from my account without raising a red flag?"

"That would be about half a million. But you have done that already. The transfer to Pepe Perez's account was completed today. I am certain Sabas will instruct head office to terminate your line of credit facilities. And you must remember that a bond was pledged for your release from jail. You, my dear friend, are no longer liquid. You are cash poor."

Donaldo Santiago's back was against the wall. He was no stranger to that situation. He waited impatiently for the inspiration that so often supported him to come to his aid and instruct him what to do.

It was after midnight when he retired to the back of his residence to seek refuge in the darkness of the compound. He turned off the lights around the swimming pool so that none of his family or resident house staff could observe his melancholy and desperation. He threw himself in a deck chair and called upon his survival instincts to send him instructions what next to do. In the darkness, he observed the affluence of his environment, an expression of his personality, the interpretation of his American dream. Mentally he wished he could hold back the night, as at daybreak his dream may vanish. And vanish it did, because in spite of his personal contribution and dedication to the prosperity of Sabas Gonzalez's questionable enterprises, two days after, the loan to his organization was called in, and overnight, he became financially destitute.

Grapevine had circulated the downward spiraling of Donaldo Santiago's fortune. In situations such as that, men as Santiago become desperate and seek ways to get even by taking others down with them.

***

Mike that evening sat alone at a table in a Cuban restaurant in Coconut Grove. He had chosen a table where his back could

144

be against the wall, and he had an unobstructed view of the entrance door. He knew that various factions were gunning for him, and enormous bounties were most probably placed on his head. But when he received the invitation from Santiago, an established enemy, to meet him there on a matter of grave importance to him, he just could not resist.

Across the room at another table sat Beverly Johns. In a very large handbag, the Mauser C-96 was in easy reach. No one suspected she was connected to Mike. She had ordered a salad, and it took some time in getting to her, which suited her fine. She was in no hurry. Mike ordered coffee and was on his second cup. The Bren Ten was in his waist concealed by his sport jacket. Santiago, according to arrangement, should be there any moment, but Mike, being the strategist, was there thirty minutes before he said he would.

Earlier, a plainclothes detective driving an unmarked car spotted Mike as he stopped by the intersection of Douglas Road and US-1. He immediately made a call and was advised to follow, but under no circumstances should he engage.

About that same time, Donaldo Santiago drove across the bridge on his way from his home in William Island to keep the appointment with Mike. He did not wish to be late. He rehearsed how he would present the information he had to Mike in a manner that he would be taken seriously and believed. Mike knew in the past he wanted him dead. It would be difficult to gain his trust. Mike would be expecting a trap. So occupied in thoughts, he did not notice the black SUV with tinted windows tailing him.

Mike saw Santiago as he entered the restaurant. He was on time. He paused, cautiously looked around, walked directly to Mike's table, and sat down. Where he sat, he had a plain view of the entrance door. The tension was noticeable as they stared at each other in silence, both men remembering their last encounter.

Beverly, at alert at her table, slowly ate her salad with her eyes on the door and on both men.

"Cannon, we will not pretend not to dislike each other, so I will say what I am here to say, whether you believe me or not."

"Get on with it, while I am still undecided whether to kill you here and now or not."

Santiago stared in Mike's eyes to decide how serious his last remark was. He knew how unpredictable and dangerous Mike had become. In spite of his immediate concerns, he decided not to be sidetracked from his purpose.

He continued.   "Two weeks before the attack on you and your family, for which I was not responsible, a Chinese gentleman came to me with a proposition. He wanted to expand his distribution of opium on the South Florida market. I guess you already know that I am connected indirectly with the Colombian cocaine exporters. I asked why is he speaking to me, what he does is no business of mine. He said it was in a way because unless we could get rid of the Jamaican Posse, we may have conflicts over territorial divisions escalating into a drug war because there was not enough room in South Florida for three competitors. I advised him that it was a risky proposal as the Jamaicans would not take that decision lightly and without doubt retaliate by turning South Florida into a war zone. He advised that he had the backing of a prominent senior police official, and he also had a secret powerful organization at his disposal capable of taking care of any opposing situation that may present itself. Nevertheless, he would prefer our allied interests rather than hostile competition."

Santiago paused to see how his information was affecting Mike.

"I need the name of this Chinese person," Mike demanded.

"His name is Wang Lee. There are two brothers."

"I now need the name of the police official."

"His name was not told to me. He said for the time being he will refer to him as the In-House Man. I afterward discovered that he is the one ordered to put a hit on you because you were getting too close to his identity and other secret connections. I believe the connections had something to do with the Vietnamese War. And for your information and for what it's worth, I no longer have any interest in your death. The person who will be placing a hit on you is Pepe Perez. And the one who ordered it is the South American Tycoon Sabas Betata Gonzalez. He comes in once per month on his yacht and meets with the biggest cocaine wholesalers in Florida. He spends two days and—"

The information was interrupted by a signal from Beverly. When Mike looked at her, she pointed to five armed men crossing from the other side of the street toward the restaurant.

"Mike said, "Santiago, if you set me up, you get it first."

"No, Cannon! I believe they may be after me," Santiago said.

"Well, there is no time to find out. If you have a weapon, get ready to use it." Mike immediately overturned the table and took cover behind it.

Santiago raced across the room to secure a table for himself, behind which he hoped to take cover. But he exposed himself racing across the room and in plain view of the first gunman who entered through the door. He fired, and the bullet struck Santiago in his chest. Another bullet caught him in the abdomen just as Mike cut the gunman down.

The other four men jumped over their colleague's body and immediately sought cover behind upturned tables. The one nearest to Mike grabbed a table and advanced behind it, holding it before him as a shield.

Mike pumped two bullets from the Bren Ten into the table. The assailant's table splintered from the impact, and the bullets followed through and entered his chest. He was dead when he hit the floor.

When the shooting started, Beverly ran through the door that led to the restaurant kitchen, out through the back door, onto the pavement, and came in through the restaurant entrance door behind the gunmen. Their backs were turned to her, and they did not notice. She had her weapon pointed at the one nearest to the door, who knelt behind an overturned table and was shooting at Mike. The exchanges were so fierce from the high-caliber handguns that it was almost impossible to see through the smoke. The gunman nearest to the door turned instinctively to look behind him and saw Beverly's weapon leveled at him. He tried to roll out of her line of fire and caught a bullet in his head. The other two realized they were caught in a cross fire and decided the encounter was not going in their favor. Both abandoned their covers, jumped to their feet, and were about to discard their weapons and surrender.

But they were a bit slow. Before the guns left their hands, they were cut down, one by Mike Cannon and the other by Beverly Johns.

Mike walked across the floor and examined Santiago. He was lying in a pool of his own blood, dead.

The plainclothes police officer, who was told only to observe, saw five men enter the restaurant, and only Mike and Beverly came out. He ran to his car parked around the corner away from the restaurant and took off at high speed. He stopped at a phone box and made a call. "Bad news, there was a lot of shooting, and they did not come out. I think they are dead," he reported.

"Did you see Cannon?" the voice at the other end asked.

"Yes, I saw Cannon, and a woman came out with him. I was too far to recognize her."

"Damn it, what the hell will it take to kill that man?" was the disappointing response.

Chapter 13

Mike Cannon stood by the front door of his new black Cadillac sedan and watched Jay Gordon driving around in the McDonald's parking lot. Jay was looking for the Camaro. Mike had forgot to tell him he had changed his car. Jay parked and decided to wait.

Mike walked through the rows of parked vehicles toward his Volvo and sat beside him on the front seat.

"What happened to the Camaro?" Jay asked.

"Like everything else, there comes a time when it outlived its usefulness," Mike replied.

Jay had vindicated himself, and Mike had appointed him as his private investigator, with salary and expenses. He handed Jay a sealed envelope. When Jay opened it, he counted twenty thousand dollars. He had a sudden intake of breath and looked appreciatively at Mike.

"Don't be carried away, you have plenty to do to earn it," Mike said. "Now what have you got to report?"

"The word on the street is that the Colombians have all but wiped out the Jamaican Posse. Jack Wall has sent his family out of the state and is recruiting a new set of soldiers for war. He has lost his contacts because some of his boys were ambushed, and a contact buyer lost a lot of money. You remember Santiago, the one who tried to put a hit on you?"

"Yes, I remember him. How couldn't I."

"Well, he double-crossed his group, and he was gunned down in broad daylight in a restaurant in Coconut Grove. The strange part of it is that two customers in the restaurant, a man and a woman, shot the five men that killed him. What can you make of that?"

Mike smiled and said, "You never know, what goes around comes around."

"Jack Wall is still in business despite of what has happened. He is sending all his shit to his people in New York. He has just received another shipment, but no one seems to know where his drop zone is," Jay continued.

Mike was satisfied with his report, and except for some minor details, they were correct. "Now that the seven o'clock news is finished, two things I want you to do," Mike said. "Do you know of Sabas Gonzalez?"

"Who does not know of Sabas Gonzalez? He is the big man behind the Colombian cocaine. He sails into Miami once every month to have high-level conference with his wholesalers."

"That's him," Mike said. "Find out when he will be here. Is that possible?"

"Everything is possible. All it takes is money," Jay replied.

"Well then, you should have no problem. The other thing is a bit more delicate and time consuming. I want you to put a tail on Captain Duncan of the Miami Police. Everywhere he goes I want to know, and if possible, who he meets. I suppose you know I will deny this if you mess this up."

"Have I ever messed things up?"

"No, but this is different. It could possibly be dangerous. Keep in touch. I have to go." Mike walked back to his car and drove out.

Jay sat for a while, thinking. His association with Mike got him thinking as a detective. He noticed Mike was not surprised at anything he had to say, as if he already knew it all. Would it be possible that he had some hand in the misfortunes of the unfortunates? Thinking of it, nothing that happened was beyond the enterprising Mike Cannon.

***

Mike drove to his secret headquarters, where he met Beverly. To pass the time, she had dismantled the Mauser C-96, and the components were scattered over the top of a table.

Mike, who came later than was previously arranged, paused to stare at the collection of parts and asked, "Will you be able to put all that back together?"

"Blindfolded," was her reply. "It was due for a good cleaning. I am surprised at myself allowing such an important matter to slip my mind." While she meticulously cleaned and reassembled the weapon, she noticed that Mike had slipped away to sit in the far corner of the building. She observed a noticeable change when he came in that morning. His eyes were discolored and swollen, as if from weeping. Mike was a hard man, but human.

She remembered her period of grief and its periodic overpowering influence. At those times she wished to be alone, to be comforted by feeling sorry for herself. Mike was at that place in his healing experience and wished to be alone. So the morning choir completed, she quietly slipped away. She knew that after that period of depression, he may attempt doing something dangerous or possibly something he could regret.

***

That evening, Mike met Captain Abe Duncan at a seaside park in Miami Beach. He was aware of the millions of dollars of bounty placed on his life, but he was prepared to meet the threats head-on and refused to be in hiding. He was fully armed and of a resolve to take as many as he could with him if such an emergency was forced upon him.

Captain Duncan parked his Mercedes Benz, locked the doors, and walked across the sand to where Mike sat on a bench looking out to sea. Mike felt his approach but did not turn around. Captain Duncan sat beside him and said, "Hi, Mike."

Cannon did not answer, although he was the one who invited the open meeting. He believed that would be the last secret meeting he intended to have with the captain, and if he was going to be attacked by known or unknown, it would be better dealt with in the open.

From the moment he asked Mike Cannon where he wanted to be met, and Mike said it should be in the park in broad daylight, he realized that he was added to the list of suspects. He also went fully armed, with a backup weapon strapped to his leg.

Mike took his badge from his shirt pocket and placed it on the bench between them. Captain Duncan looked at the badge, then looked away. Mike said, "When I have finished saying my piece, you may want my badge, so I am making it easy for you."

"Cannon, what is all this about? If I wanted your badge, I would ask for it and take it. You know the procedure."

"You possibly want more than my badge. May be you want my life."

Captain Duncan turned and looked Mike in the face and said in a cool authoritative manner, "I am your superior officer anywhere, in or out of my office, and there is no reason for me to sit here and be insulted by a renegade, lunatic police detective. In the future, if you have something to say, make an appointment and come into my office." Captain Duncan stood up to leave.

Mike, still staring out to sea, said slowly and calculatingly, "One step before I am through saying what I came here to say, and I promise you, it will be your last."

Captain Duncan felt his legs became weak, and he slowly lowered himself back onto the bench. The tiger he caught by the tail was staring him in the face. Mike never said what he did not mean. Captain Abe Duncan of all persons knew that.

"I know you had my wife and children killed and almost murdered me too. You are the only one who knew that I was taking my family to that restaurant. I absentmindedly told you the evening before. You personally know the place, we had been there before. I subconsciously refused to piece those facts together because I believed you were my superior and also my friend, and I could not accept what was staring me in the face. Now the evidence is overwhelming. But there are a few pieces remaining that will make the package complete. When that happens, then I kill you. Abe Duncan, it will be slow and barbaric. It will continue as long as it takes the venom that poisons my soul to flow out of my system. It may be tomorrow, next week, or next month, but it will happen. From this moment on, we are at war. And the day you think of bringing the resources of your office to assist you will be the day I take the entire package of your conspiracy and filth to the press. I will expose your corrupt organization of dirty cops, the association with your Oriental opium-smuggling friends, the skeleton in the closet that is giving them a hold over you. For that, I will be considered a hero for taking you out. Do you see how efficiently I execute my assignments? You cannot run, and you cannot hide from me. You are finished. In the meanwhile, with or without your cooperation, I will continue to do the job I am being paid to do."

With that said, Mike got up, took the badge he had placed on the bench, and started to walk across the beach toward his car.

And then he heard what Captain Duncan said without turning to look at him. "Now that we are at war, this is what you must know. You are rocking my boat. But when I am ready, I will take care of that. You are no match for me, Cannon, but we do things differently. And this is one for you. I am being set up. I did not order that hit on you. If you do find out who did and circumstances permit, let me know. I am curious."

Abe Duncan lacked the courage when the opportunity presented itself to do what would be most ideal. That would be to fire Mike then and there. But pouring fuel on the already explosive situation was not his idea of surviving. He would survive in spite of the deck stocked against him. Abe Duncan did not have to guess what was in store for him. Mike was an upfront guy. He preferred the enemy to see him coming. Abe Duncan thought that was his weakness; it gave him the edge.

The highlights of his life over the past decade passed before him, and he came to terms with his new situation. There were so many things, if he had the opportunity, he would have done differently. Crossing Mike Cannon was one of them. But that happened all by itself. In spite of the threat to his life and career, he wanted Mike on his side. He respected him as a man. But the ghost that had been chasing him had finally caught up with him, and he would have to turn around and face it. He wondered if the confrontation was worth it, or if it was not too late to avoid it.

Almost an hour had elapsed in assessing his possibilities. His mind made up, he finally drove away from what he knew was his last secret meeting with Mike. He was once a military man, and armed with that experience, he would plan his strategy for a war he did not want.

***

That night, what Captain Duncan said to him that day added to Mike's list of regrets. The web of conspiracy was getting more tangled each day. He knew from experience with Abe Duncan he was telling the truth. He did not place a hit on him. He regretted handling the situation the way he did. But that was his style, whether it made him popular or not. He would always take the bull by the horns. He wondered if he was going over the edge and had become his worst enemy. For many reasons, he was relieved to know he was wrong about the captain organizing the hit on him. But if he did not, who did?

Chapter 14

As part of Captain Duncan's assignment set by the Lee brothers, he should report any threat to their operation he was unable to rectify within the scope of his official capacity. So it became expedient that Captain Duncan report that Mike was under the impression that they had organized the hit that killed his family and vowed to bring down their operation to get even. That was part of Captain Duncan's strategy, which he hoped would mobilize the powerful forces that Ten Lee disclosed was at his disposal against Mike.

Ten Lee got up from where he was seated, paced the floor, and said, "Had Duncan taken care of things in his own way as he had suggested in the beginning, we would not be in this particular dilemma." He stopped pacing the floor to stare at Goldie Lee, who pretended not to be concerned. "I said from the beginning that bringing in an outsider was not the answer and would create too much exposure if not successful. Whatever Duncan had in mind may have possibly solved the problem. At least it would be done discreetly, and his family would not have been hurt. Now, Mike Cannon is a threat that we may be unable to deal with."

"Wait a minute before you continue to criticize," Wang Lee protested. "Duncan has never done anything well in his life. You know that. Tai is a living witness to that. That man I hired came well recommended from the top. I was told he had successfully completed other assignments in Miami before. I even jeopardized the life of my daughter and myself by being there to make certain that the hit was made without any slip-up. It meant that much to me. I agree being there may have been a dumb thing, but I had no way of knowing he was an alcoholic and would go on the rampage. It was not supposed to go down like that. The fool was supposed to be there earlier as a customer. I would go in and discreetly finger Cannon and leave. If he was not stopped by Cannon, he would have killed everyone, including Su and myself. So I had to bring Cannon here to you. I had to gain his confidence to get him to come. Why didn't you finish him off?"

"Should I, in cold blood as a common murderer?" Ten Lee asked. "I was not trained to do things that way. That is something expected of you, Wang, being a person without honor or moral principles. For god's sake, the man had just saved your daughter's life."

At that last remark, Wang Lee turned angrily toward his brother. "Maybe you could explain what is meant by that statement about moral principles?"

"Goldie, you tell him what that means," Ten Lee said, staring accusingly at Goldie Lee.

But Goldie Lee refused to respond. Instead, she hastily got up and left the room.

"You tell me yourself, you made the statement. May be we can settle it here and now."

"That may be a good idea," Ten Lee said and menacingly rushed toward Wang Lee.

Wang Lee quickly got up from his chair and seized a ceremonial sword displayed below a mirror on the wall. He chopped twice at Ten Lee. Ten Lee dived under the next swing and speared him in the middle. He dropped the sword, held his abdomen, and grimaced in pain. Ten Lee, enraged, quickly took up the sword and, without hesitation, pierced Wang Lee through. He stood swaying briefly, cried out, then fell dead.

Goldie Lee heard the cry, rushed in, and knelt beside Wang Lee's body. "shy?" She asked, looking up accusingly at Ten Lee. "Why did you do this?"

"You know why? I did it because he deserved it," Ten Lee answered, and without any evidence of remorse, he walked out of the room.

***

Mike and Beverly met over dinner at the Steak House. It was one of those times when he truly felt dissatisfied with himself. He had confronted Captain Duncan and accused him of planning the murder of his family and drew the line in the sand. He was amazed at his self-control in overcoming the overwhelming impulse to kill the man, which would be an unforgivable mistake.

Beverly noticed he was in one of his pensive moods and waited patiently for him to explain.

Finally after dinner and two beers, Mike said, "Beverly, I was wrong about the captain. He did not order the hit on me and my family. I met him and declared war. What Santiago told me about him was not correct. The real reason for that may be revealed to me somewhere down the line. There is a conspiracy somewhere. As of now, I am confused about what is what. I still believe the captain is not leveling with me. I believe he is mixed up somewhere. But I would hate to kill a man for something he didn't do, especially a man who was once as close to me as the captain. The one thing I am certain of is that organized crime took my family and your husband and son from us. I know that what we are doing makes a difference. I feel comfortable with that. Do you feel comfortable with that?"

"Unlike you, Mike, I think and function as a soldier. I do not allow my emotions to get in the way. Point me in a given direction, and I go. Tell me to take that person out, and that I will do. Until the void in me is satisfied, that is what I prefer to be. In reality, I am a female animal that has lost her mate and her cub. I am vicious and hungry for revenge anywhere it can be found. Need I say more?" At that statement, her countenance changed, and an unexplainable hardness distorted her features. She placed the beer to her lips and drained the last drop from the bottle, then slammed it down angrily on the table.

Mike waited until she had composed herself and her countenance had returned to normal. Certain questions had crossed his mind, which he thought an opportune time to have answered. "I have been thinking of the metamorphosis you experienced during your Special Forces training," Mike said, trying to come across in a way that would not offend. "Do you, at any time afterward, ever experience feminine emotions?"

"Do you mean to ask if I ever feel the need for sex?"

"Yes, that is what I really mean."

"Then why don't you come out and say so? To answer that truthfully, I really do not know. Before all that I went through happened, the army included, I was conscious of an inexhaustible emotional fountain inside that I could drink from whenever I was ready. It provided inner beauty, a sort that cannot be described by words. I suppose that is what being in love with everything around you means. When Johnny left, I mean when he died, my soul went with him, and I wait for it to return. If it does, I hope enough of me will be still there to embrace it. Where my baby is concerned, I can still feel him in my arms. I believe if I live to be a hundred, that unfulfilled yearning will still be there. The part of me I fear most is the urge to kill during a hostile confrontation, as if should I shed enough blood it may fill the painful void that exists where my love used to be. I know that is wrong, but that's how it is." Beverly remained silent while Mike tried to feel some of what she had just said. And then she said very softly, "I hope you understand what I feel when I am feeling."

For several minutes, they sat staring at each other, experiencing the bond of comradeship that was being forged. Both gave a sigh of relief as if it was prearranged, and then they burst out in laughter.

"In the meanwhile, where do we go from here?" Beverly asked, getting back to business.

"Since you should ask," he replied, "I understand that the price on my head has gone up. My worth dead to any street thug is approximately one million dollars. At this point in time, I could not go to the supermarket without being killed. The highest price, I understand, was placed by Sabas Betata Gonzalez, the big bad South American drug tycoon who the American government is reluctant to take down because of international politics. He states that I am a destabilizing influence to his empire. That has been confirmed by my contacts on the street. I even have to be doubly cautious whenever I meet any of them. I never know who will become overly ambitious.

"Since Sabas wants me that badly, I think we should pay him a visit before he pays me one. What Mr. Gonzalez does not know is that I am not a politician, and I am not impressed by his political affiliations. I am an American and a policeman paid to do my duty. And my duty, according to my job description, is to uphold the law. And Mr. Gonzalez is breaking the law. It has been said that heads usually roll if his orders are not executed. Now that's a dangerous man. If you are up to it, I think it is time that he goes out of business."

"I hate to be inactive and put all that training to waste. When do we start?"

"We start right now. Señor Gonzalez will be arriving in his miniature luxury liner and will drop anchor in Biscayne Bay three days from today. True to habits, he stays for two days. The first day is business. He meets six of his generals in a top-level conference in his stateroom. He does things in style, money being no object. I fail to believe though that narcotics are all the business they discuss. I believe something more sinister to our security is afoot, and that floating palace of Señor Gonzalez is nothing short of a Trojan horse. I think we should find out."

"What do we need that we do not have?" Beverly asked.

"We need explosives."

"Name the type. I can have that in two days. I can make almost anything."

"We may have to place it under water if we do not get the chance to place it inside his yacht. The engine room would be the most effective place though."

"Consider explosives taken care of," Beverly said, bubbling over with excitement. The thought of a dangerous assignment gave her a rush. It was impossible to understand how such a beautifully feminine individual could be so dangerous.

"I understand that he has a crew of nineteen, aside from the captain," Mike continued. "Some are mercenaries and his private bodyguards. The business associates go aboard in their private speedboats, which are tied alongside during the meeting. After the first day, he usually throws a wild party inviting many willing Latino beauties. Whatever we do, must be on the first day."

"Since when are we interested in numbers? The more the merrier. Just get us a print of the interior of the yacht if you can. If you can't, we will have to make do," Beverly said.

Mike looked at her, shook his head in admiration, and smiled. In his mind he said, I believe both of us could take an enemy town if we had a mind to.

They came out of the Steak House and went into Mike's Cadillac parked near the parking lot's entrance. They sat in silence for a while, absentmindedly observing the parked vehicles and people going in and coming out of the establishment. Beverly placed her hands over her mouth and yawned. After her emotional release in the restaurant, she felt relaxed and sleepy. She said, "Mike, drop me home. I feel sleepy for the first time in months."

"Okay, I think I should do the same. Tomorrow could be an interesting day. Let's go."

He slowly drove out of the parking lot toward US-1 and skillfully maneuvered into the caravan of traffic going south. He stopped by the intersection at 152nd, and the big Lincoln Continental behind stopped about three car lengths away from his. He thought it unusual and became suspicious. He closed his eyes briefly and mentally went back to the parking lot he had just left and remembered he saw the same Lincoln with a similar broken roof antenna and tinted windows halfway down, parked with people inside. He immediately felt the familiar numbing sensation in his abdomen and imagined the remainder of the night would not be to his liking.

"What are you packing?" he asked Beverly.

She immediately turned to look through the rear windshield at the suspicious Lincoln behind and answered, "Just the Beretta. I came light tonight."

"Damn it, I am light myself. I only have the Glock."

When the lights changed, he accelerated to sixty, and before the other vehicles could move, he crossed over to the outside lane. The Lincoln dangerously did the same. They were then certain they were being followed.

They continued to observe the Lincoln following for the next three miles, and when it was safe to do so, at high speed, Mike unexpectedly turned right at the next intersection. Mike knew it to be a long dark and lonely road. The Lincoln did the same and closed in on them.

Looking again through the rear windshield, Beverly shouted, "Mike, we have more company. There are now two cars following us!"

Just then, the person in the passenger side of the Lincoln leaned out the window and began blasting with a high-powered automatic weapon. The rear windshield of the Cadillac was shattered, and a bullet passed dangerously close by Mike's head and penetrated the front windshield.

"Hold her steady, Mike!" Beverly shouted. "I am going to do some shooting of my own." She climbed onto the back seat, lay on her stomach, and rested the Beretta where the rear windshield used to be. She aimed to where the driver of the Lincoln should be sitting and fired. The first bullet struck him squarely in the face and went out the back of his head to hit one of the backseat passengers in the chest. The Lincoln went out of control, climbed the banking on the left, rolled over, and settled across the road.

The car behind following at high speed was unable to come to a stop and crashed into the disabled Lincoln and burst into flames. Suddenly there was a loud bang as the right rear wheel of the Cadillac exploded. The car swung off the road to the right, climbed a low grassy embankment, and plunged into a large canal that flowed parallel to the road. As the car began to sink, a survivor from the burning wreck approached the scene with an automatic weapon and emptied the magazines into the roof of the Cadillac as it began to submerge.

When the Cadillac went out of control, Beverly was in the rear compartment. She knew the vehicle was headed for the canal, and she also knew those canals were infested with alligators. She yanked open the rear door and rolled onto the embankment into a cluster of tall rushes at the water's edge. From there she watched the Cadillac disappear into the murky depths with Mike trapped inside. Just as she had imagined, the splash the car made when it entered the water attracted two enormous reptiles. Should Mike free himself and come to the surface, he would certainly be eaten.

The man with the empty automatic stood on the bank of the canal and watched the alligators circling around and gave a sadistic burst of laughter. It was time for Beverly to do something if she was to assist her companion. She quietly crawled up from among the rushes in which she was hiding and came up behind the amused gunman. One powerful kick sent the assailant sailing through the air to land ten feet or more into the water. The unfortunate man screamed as he was immediately set upon, and in an instant, both creatures disappeared beneath the surface with their prey after tearing him to pieces.

Seizing the opportunity, Beverly dived into the water, pulled open the driver's side door, and found Mike unconscious, slumped over the steering wheel. Releasing the seat belt, she brought him to the surface and swam with him toward the embankment. She commenced to pull his body out of the water when she saw another alligator less than six feet away from Mike's legs and closing fast. With a tremendous heave, she got him onto the embankment. But his body was too heavy to get him quickly out of reach of the man-eating predator that had climbed the embankment and, with open jaws, was closing the distance between them.

In a moment of desperation and with no other option, she grabbed the empty assault rifle thrown aside by the doomed gun man and rushed between Mike and the creature. With all her strength, she began to strike it in the head. "Get away from him!" she screamed over and over as she fought off the beast.

The alligator made a ferocious lunge toward her. As she jumped backward, she slipped and fell, and it rushed to seize her. Without thinking, she threw the weapon into its mouth. The alligator closed its jaws upon what it thought was a body part of its prey. It rolled over in its death roll and, with awesome speed, slid back into the water.

Beverly hastily got to her feet and hauled the unconscious Mike over the embankment and onto the center of the road where she immediately tried to resuscitate him. For several minutes she labored without success, and she began to believe she had lost him. Frustrated, she cried, "Damn it, Mike Cannon, don't you die on me!" And with full force, she struck him across the face.

Suddenly he retched and vomited, and moments later, he opened his eyes. It was then she noticed that one of the bullets had grazed his head when the vehicle was fired upon in the canal. A few seconds more under the water, and he may not have survived.

Cannon tried to get to his feet, but he was too weak. "What really happened?" he asked.

"You wouldn't like to know," Beverly answered and burst into uncontrolled laughter.

They both sat on the ground soaking wet and heard the approaching sirens.

"Let's get away from here, Mike, before someone else tries to collect that bounty." She helped Mike to his feet, and with his arm around her shoulder, they hastily left the scene. Barefoot, they walked off the road and made their way across a freshly planted tomato field. In spite of the recent experience, they were back to their usual good humor.

"Now that you have done your good deed for the day, I suppose I will not hear the last of it," Mike jested.

"Cut the speech, gator bait, and let's find a ride from someone somewhere so we can get out of these wet clothes and take a closer look at that wound. In the meanwhile, you would like to know that from now on, I have decided to be more selective of the company I keep. Recently I have been shot at, almost eaten by alligators, been vomited on, and in the middle of the night find myself walking barefooted dragging a wounded man across a tomato field—all of that in one day. Nothing could be worse."

"Listen to you moaning, and you know you would not have it any other way," Mike said.

After crossing a couple more fields, they came upon a main road and waited. It was not long before they saw the lights of a slow-moving vehicle approaching.

Beverly walked to the center of the road and waved. The vehicle kept approaching not intending to stop, but she stood her ground. The vehicle came to a screeching halt just feet away from her. "What the hell are you trying to do? Are you trying to get yourself killed?" the driver shouted at her, hanging his head out of the window.

Mike approached from the shadows and walked toward him. The driver panicked when he saw him and was about to drive off when Mike held his badge to his face. "Mister, I am a police officer, and our vehicle just went into a canal. See, we are dripping wet. We need a ride."

With that, the driver relaxed and said, "The lady can sit with me in front, but if you don't mind, you will have to climb into the back. There is room among the crates."

"That's good enough for me, mister. Thanks," Mike said as he walked toward the rear, hoisted himself up, and sat upon a crate of oranges.

Before they parted that night, Beverly thought of the near encounters with death they had just experienced and said, "You know what, Mike, a million-dollar bounty is hard to resist, especially by the criminal elements we are doing business with that evidently don't think much of us. If we plan to remain alive much longer, we have to remove the temptation. If there is no one to pay the bounty, there will not be any bounty hunters. We must do what we have to do, and do it now."

Mike agreed.

Chapter 15

The sea in Biscayne Bay was calm and silvery in the moonlight. The only sound was a low splash as the oars of the three occupants of the inflated raft touched the water. The Austrian was flattered by Mike's confidence in him when he was asked to be a part of what could possibly be a dangerous assignment. He could scarcely contain his excitement.

The three of them had rehearsed the part each would play so there would be no confusion when the action starts. The Ocean Rose was anchored one mile off shore, and the Austrian would remain on the raft and await the return of Mike and Beverly, who would swim the last thousand yards.

The duo reexamined each other's package strapped on their backs and silently rolled off the raft into the water. Mike had learnt from his contact that four armed guards would be patrolling the deck at all times. At about fifty yards away, the silvery hull of the vessel illuminated the water in the moonlight, so they approached with caution. They could plainly see a guard flick the remains of a lighted cigarette over the rails into the water and then moved on.

Beverly touched Mike, and they both went into a dive. They approached the bow under water and found the anchor chain. Mike started the climb, followed by Beverly. At the top of the chain, Mike crouched, and Beverly climbed onto his back. He then stood up, allowing her to reach the rails, and swiftly flipped over to stand on the deck. Looking around, there was no one in sight, so she bent over and helped Mike over.

Without speaking, they moved out in different directions to take out the four patrolling guards. They thought it unnecessary to remove their weapons from their packs as they were confident they could deal with that situation with their bare hands, and weapons were not necessary.

From where she crouched in the shadows, Beverly saw a guard approaching with an automatic assault weapon under his arm. He was eating what appeared to be a chicken portion. He threw the bones overboard and wiped his mouth with the sleeve of his shirt. He paused to look toward the city, as if admiring the lights. She crept up unobserved and, with tremendous force, brought up her foot between his legs from behind. He dropped the weapon to clutch his testicles; so agonizing was the pain. Like a mountain cat, she was upon him; she seized him behind the neck, and with all her weight, she sent his face crashing downward onto the metal deck. She pulled the unconscious body into the shadows and threw the weapon overboard. She was convinced he would be out for a very long time.

She silently crept about the deck looking for another and came upon Mike.

"What, no guards? Mike asked.

"Only one so far, and he is out."

Just then they heard low voices and saw the other three guards coming from belowdecks, each with a disposable dish of food in his hand. They had their weapons over their shoulders, and they ate with their fingers while walking, two abreast and one a few feet behind. They had to pass where Mike and Beverly were hiding.

Mike seized the last one as he passed and applied a choke hold from behind. He pulled him into the shadows and silently lay him down when he lost consciousness. For keeps' sake, he smashed him in the temple with a tremendous blow from that left hand.

Beverly trailed silently behind the other two, who were unaware of the fate of their companion. One instinctively turned around, saw her, and dropped the food to get his weapon from his shoulder. Using her thumb as a spike, she rammed it into the front of his neck, crushing his larynx. He opened his mouth to scream but could manage only a gasp. He fell writhing on the deck, unable to breathe. She knocked him out with a short right to the jaw and put him out of his misery.

Mike jumped over the prostrate body and engaged the other, who attempted to flee and was a few yards away. He tackled him from behind, taking him down. As the man fell, he rolled onto his back and tried to make a fight of it. A short left hook from Mike's sledgehammer fist landed just below the ear, splintering the jawbone. The man stopped struggling.

They heaved both men and their weapons over the rails and into the sea. Mike went back to the one on whom he had applied the choke hold, pulled him toward the rail, and also threw him overboard.

Satisfied that the deck was secured, they went below, and from the drawings Mike had studied, they found the engine room unchallenged. When they entered, they found only one attendant. He was on his knees carefully wiping a smear of oil from the floor. He turned and stared at them, at first not knowing what to make of the intruders. Then he made up his mind they were the enemy and rushed toward what seemed to be an emergency warning device.

Beverly sailed through the air and caught him with a drop kick dead center between the shoulder blades. The force of the kick sent the attendant sailing through the air to land face-first against the chrome-plated manifold of one of the engines. Blood spattered the engine from his broken nose. He sank to the floor unconscious, in a heap.

Mike and Beverly removed the waterproof backpacks and took out their weapons and the explosives. From her training, Beverly knew exactly where they should be placed for maximum effect. They quickly placed the charges and set the timers. That completed, they left the engine room with no further confrontation to complete the remainder of their mission.

With all the crew that was supposed to be on board, they were amazed that they were not confronted by anyone while on their way to the stateroom, where they hoped to find Sabas Gonzalez and his six drug generals. Mike considered that over-confidence was due to complacency induced by the fact that over the years, the crew were never interrupted or challenged.

They entered the large stateroom unobserved and stood aghast at the lavish display of luxury. Sabas Gonzalez was seated in a revolving throne-like chair with his six generals comfortably seated in a semicircle before him. He was speaking in a low tone, and the conversation was all in Spanish. There was a round table in the center of the room some distance away from that gathering, around which were three people, one an elderly gentleman in earnest discussion with a Cuban and a turbaned Middle East person. A map was spread out before them.

Sabas Gonzales swiveled his chair around and was the first to notice the intruders. The surprised look on his face as he stared into the business end of the Bren Ten and the Mauser C-96 could not be described by words.

The unexpected day of reckoning had arrived.

Beverly moved away from the entrance of the room to a position where she effectively covered everyone in the room and could not be surprised by anyone entering through the door.

Mike's curiosity regarding the people around the table got the better of him. He went over and stood staring at the map. The map was a detail description of industrial centers of South Florida. Two circles in red depicted Port Everglades Shipping Terminal and the Turkey Point Nuclear Power Station. Speaking to the Middle East person, he said, "Anwar Mustaffe Assan, the Iranian terrorist explosive export, topping Interpol's Most Wanted List. What are you planning to blow up this time? Let's see." Mike bent down and examined the map they were discussing. "I see you are undecided between our nuclear power station and our shipping terminal. Well, for your information, none of it is going to happen because as of now, you boys are permanently out of business. I will just have to assume that we have stumbled upon a nest of terrorist agents planning to blow up our most vital industries. So as good American citizens and having no time to take you all in for a proper trial, I hereby sentence you to death."

Mike glanced at his watch and realized that the time set on the timers was running out. He quickly backed toward the door. Beverly, being aware of the emergency, did likewise.

"Whoever you are, how do you expect to leave this vessel alive?" Sabas Gonzalez, who was finally able to overcome his surprise, asked.

"Just the same way we came," Mike replied.

"No, you don't!" Perez shouted. He found it necessary to impress Sabas Gonzalez since he had assumed the number one position after cleverly planning Donaldo Santiago's removal.

He reached in his waist for his pistol but was much too slow. The thunderous roar of Cannon's Bren Ten split the silence of the night, as a bullet penetrated Pepe's forehead and blew off the back of his head. The force of the bullet drove him and the chair across the room.

Another goon stood up and tried for his weapon, but was immediately cut down by the powerful Mauser C-96 in the hands of Beverly, who calmly stood leaning against the wall.

Knowing that the shooting would bring the crew down upon them, Mike raced across the room and seized Sabas Gonzalez. "You are coming with me. You are our passport out of here." He placed the gun to his head and used him as a shield. As they cleared the door, they faced his three bodyguards with guns drawn. "Tell them to drop their weapons and move out before us."

Sabas Gonzalez did as he was told, and the three men reluctantly obeyed.

Beverly back-walked and brought up the rear, covering their retreat, in case the remainder in the stateroom had any ideas.

Once on deck, they met the remainder of the crew assembled, ready to do battle. Mike ordered them to throw their weapons over the rails and ordered the entire group back below. A bodyguard, in a moment of ill-advised zeal, attempted to disobey. To reinforce the order, Mike shot him in the stomach twice. Led by Sabas Gonzalez, the remainder made a mad rush toward the stairs, falling over each other.

Beverly glanced at her watch and shouted, "It's got to be now. Let's go!" With that, they both dived off the deck and swam with all their strength toward shore.

A little after they were in the water, the men returned on deck and started shooting randomly. Bullets spattered all around, some dangerously close. They were less than three minutes in the water when they heard the first explosion.

The Austrian waved the flashlight as arranged, and they swam toward the raft. When they climbed aboard and looked back at the Ocean Rose, it was a gigantic fireball that lit up the sky. There were several more explosions when the fuel tanks exploded, and before they reached shore, what was left of the vessel sank to the bottom of Biscayne Bay.

The following morning, an unexplained explosion on the Ocean Rose, taking the lives of all aboard, was front-page news on the radio and also on television. Sagas Gonzalez was an unavoidable nuisance and an embarrassment to the government. It was uncertain whether they ever mounted any meaningful investigation to ascertain the cause of the explosion.

Chapter 16

It was hard for Goldie Lee to accept the violent death of her brother. According to her, Wang Lee was kind and compassionate to her and his daughter Su Lee. She sat by Wang Lee's body and wept the remainder of the night. Early the next morning, she went to the living quarters of Tai and solicited his assistance. The body had to be removed and the bloodstains cleaned from the floor before Su Lee got out of bed and came downstairs.

When Tai saw the body of his beloved master, he wept bitterly, and his grief could not be contained. Learning of the circumstances that surrounded his death, he silently swore revenge.

Wang Lee was wrapped in canvas and buried under an oak tree deep in the forested area of the estate. After the grave was covered, with tears rolling down her cheeks, Goldie said, "Tai, I need you to go on an errand."

"Where to, Goldie?" he asked.

"I need for you to go to Miami and find Inspector Mike Cannon. I do not know how you will achieve this, but you must find a way."

"Whatever it takes, I will find him."

"In three days, Ten is leaving for California. He will be away for ten days. You will leave then and bring Inspector Cannon here before he returns."

***

Mike sat around the desk at their headquarters. Facing him was Beverly holding a two-day-old copy of a newspaper. There were five instances of unexplained violent behaviors resulting in multiple killings by apparently quiet individuals with no previous criminal or violent records.

"The Jamaican Posse is back in business. This cannot continue. They are like an octopus with many tentacles. We close down one operation, they just surface somewhere else. We could take out the boss, Mr. Wall, but he is gone underground in the drug world. And I believe if we take him out, he would only be replaced. My contact can find no trace of his whereabouts. He is moving from place to place like a wandering nomad ever since we disposed of most of his men."

"What do you have in mind?" asked a curious Beverly.

"How do you kill a giant octopus? You go right in and strike at the heart. I am going directly into Fidel Castro's backyard and prove to him he is not in control," Mike replied. He flashed an ironic grin. "How do you feel about traveling to sunny Jamaica?"

"What for, are we going to take a vacation?" Beverly joked.

"No, we are going to remove the source of Jack Wall's cocaine supply. That's the only way."

"I have never been to Jamaica. Quite time I did."

"Neither have I," Mike responded. "But I know exactly where they take delivery of the cocaine coming out of Cuba. A Cuban coast guard vessel delivers two hundred and fifty kilos of the shit twice per month a few hundred yard off the beach of a hotel in Ocho Rios called the Buccaneer Cove, ninety miles from the Cuban coast. The Cubans are operating right under the nose of the Jamaican government."

"Then how do they get it here?"

"There is a small airport called Boscobel Airport, just minutes away from the hotel, managed by a staff, some of which are involved in the drug operation. It is capable of accommodating sizable aircrafts. Drug dealers fly in at nights and transact their business at the hotel, then refuel and fly out before daybreak. A cool setup if there ever was one. I think it is quite time we become guests of the Buccaneer Cove Hotel."

American Airlines flight from Miami International Airport to Montego Bay in Jamaica touched down at 9:30 a.m. on Friday. The aircraft taxied to a point of disembarkation about a hundred yards from the main buildings. The mobile steps rolled up to the aircraft's exit door, and the passengers went down the steps in single file.

It was a mild windy day, and Beverly got her first experience of the crisp, clean Caribbean Island breeze. She followed the crowd across the tarmac to the immigration desk and joined the line that marked Visitors. She waited her turn, then stood before a pleasant young man. He looked at her passport then at her and repeated that procedure two or three times. Finally after observing some resemblance, asked, "Business or pleasure?"

"Pleasure," she replied.

"Ms. Johns, how long will you be staying?"

"About ten days."

The young man gave her a welcoming smile and said, "Enjoy your vacation in Jamaica."

From there Beverly proceeded to where the passengers' travel luggage were being dumped from a chute onto the floor. She saw her suitcase, placed it on a trolley, and wheeled it to where it would be examined. She placed the suitcase on a bench, and a lady in a gray uniform with a badge marked Customs asked, "Anything to declare?"

Beverly hesitated because she had a pistol concealed among her clothes. She answered, "I am on vacation, not business."

The lady said, "Move on. Enjoy your stay."

She breathed a sigh of relief and followed a line of people to the exit door.

Outside on the pavement, a youngster wearing striped Bermuda shorts, a white-and-red shirt, and sandals came up to her and asked if she wanted a taxi. He commenced to take her luggage.

She held on tightly and asked, "Where is your taxi?"

He pointed to an old black-and-white Chevrolet parked behind other prospects. It turned out he was not the owner but was canvassing for customers. The owner was a jolly middle-aged plump gentleman, who asked," Where to, pretty lady?"

"To Ocho Rios, the Buccaneer Cove Hotel."

The taxi driver stared at her long and hard, then said, "I know the place, are you sure?"

Beverly said, "Very sure."

"Okay, lady, if you say so." He took her suitcase, placed it in the trunk compartment, and opened the rear door for her. She went in and sat down.

It is said that one cannot judge a book by its cover. Well, that could be said of that dilapidated-looking taxi. When the vehicle started, the engine purred as if it was new. There were no rattling doors or windows as one would expect. In short, its performance was a delightful surprise.

They followed a well-paved road at a steady pace about fifty miles per hour, along the north coast of the island going east. At times the sea was not more than ten yards away from the road, separated by a low concrete wall. There was no air-conditioning in the taxi, but after rolling down the windows, she didn't mind. They passed many fishing villages, sometimes leaving the coast to climb steep hills, then back to the coast. The driver told her that the particular region was near to the Cockpit Country where the legendary slave and freedom fighter, Captain Kojo, and his army of Western Maroons had their stronghold. Beverly looked toward the hills and observed a series of densely forested conical mountains and understood why the freedom fighter would have chosen to be there.

After passing the famous tourist attraction Dunn's River Falls, they finally arrived at the resort town of Ocho Rios. A mile and a half outside the town, they came upon the Buccaneer Cove Hotel sign with an arrow pointing toward the sea. They turned off and followed an unpaved road that led to the entrance of the hotel.

The hotel was constructed against the side of a cliff overlooking the sea. The top floor was level with the entrance road. There were four other floors going down to the first floor, from where one would step out onto the hotel's own private beach. There were balconies facing the sea on all floors, and these could only be seen if viewed from the sea. The construction was for ultimate privacy and amply suited to foster the drug-smuggling industry.

Beverly paid the taxi driver twenty United States dollars, went into the lobby, and stood before Mr. Charles, the desk clerk. Mr. Charles asked her on which floor she wished to have accommodation.

"Do I have a choice?" she asked.

"Today, yes, you have. Tomorrow, no, you don't. Our weekends are always crowded. I will give you a tour seeing that I have nothing else to do." Mr. Charles was a small gentleman of East Indian descent in his early forties. He took her on a grand tour, and on the second floor on which there was the swimming pool, she decided on a room.

In a corner of the balcony on the same floor, seated around a table drinking a beer, was Mike Cannon.

"This is Mr. Bill Hanson. He came in this morning. He is also from the States. He has a room on this floor." As Beverly passed Mike, Mr. Charles said, "Mr. Hanson, meet Ms. Carol Miller. She will be your neighbor."

Mike said, "Hello, Ms. Carol Miller."

"Hello, Mr. Bill Hanson," she responded and smiled.

Mr. Charles was pleased with himself in making what he assumed a worthwhile introduction.

Mike had arrived earlier on an Eastern Airlines flight at the Norman Manley Airport in Kingston at seven that morning. He took a taxi that should take him via the Junction Pass to Ocho Rios and then to the hotel. He had previously experienced many dangerous encounters, but nothing to be compared with that forty-five-minute journey in that taxicab. The Junction Pass road was engineered from the edge of a mountain and not more than twenty feet wide in some places, with a sheer drop on one side of a thousand feet or more. The driver, a young Jamaican of not more than twenty years old, was negotiating dangerous curves at more than fifty miles per hour; and at the very same speed passing on the cliff side were trucks and buses with less than three inches to spare between them.

At one stage of the journey, they approached a wide clearing in the side of the mountain where there was a bakery and a grocery store that served alcoholic beverages. The young driver stopped by the store and went into the area where the alcohol was served. After drinking rapidly two bottles of beer, they were able to resume their journey. Encouraged by the alcohol, the driver increase speed to nearly sixty miles per hour, and Mike was relieved when they stopped by a screeching of brakes before the entrance of the Buccaneer Cove Hotel. He thankfully paid the driver and, with his travel bag, approached the desk in the lobby, behind which stood a middle-aged attendant, to whom he introduced himself as Bill Hanson.

Mr. Charles proved a veritable encyclopedia of information after the donation of a generous tip of ten dollars. That morning, Mike learnt most of what he had to know, including that no vessel larger than a small motorboat can pass over the reef to come into the cove. There was a very narrow passage, but it was only known by a few fishermen, and it was very dangerous to navigate especially at night. The reef was about one thousand yards from the shore and acted as a natural breakwater barrier against high seas. Therefore, incoming vessels must anchor outside the reef.

***

In spite of the ill-fated deliveries of his merchandise in Miami, Jack Wall had no difficulty collecting enough funds to make his first payment on the Fidel Castro agreement. He would make the payment in person and in cash to the Cubans when they made their next delivery in the next three days. He would board the drug pickup plane at its base in South Florida and a few hours later conveniently land at the Boscobel Airport.

Chapter 17

Beverly slept late the next day after her arrival at the Buc-caneer Cove. In spite of the scanty staff, her accommodation was reasonably comfortable. There was a knock at her door, and before she could inquire who it was, a voice said, "Housekeeping."

She got out of bed, opened the door, and went back to lie down. In walked one of the most beautiful colored girls she had ever seen. With the most captivating smile, she said, "I am Jennifer Blake, I am in charge of housekeeping. I wish to know if you find your accommodation satisfactory."

Beverly sat up to get a better look at the charming young woman. "Goodness gracious, you are beautiful!" she exclaimed.

"That is exactly what Dave, my boyfriend, said the first time he saw me," Jennifer said and burst into tears.

Beverly hastily got up from the bed and helped the young woman to a chair. Whatever caused her to lose control so sud-denly must be overwhelmingly distressful. She was surprised after all her military conditioning that she could still be touched with compassion for another person's pain. "Whatever it is can't be all that bad. Mind telling me about it?"

It was some time before the young woman regained her composure, and after much encouragement, she decided to share her grief.

"It is my boyfriend. He was in jail in the Sates facing the death penalty. But he was not guilty, he could not have killed anyone. He didn't even have a gun. I know."

"Who was he supposed to have killed?"

"Two policemen."

"It suddenly dawned on Beverly that the young woman was speaking of her boyfriend in the past tense. "What was his name?"

"Dave, David Shon."

"Let me see, that name rings a bell. Was he the pilot of the drug plane that crashed?"

"Yes, but he did not have a gun with him. I know because I have his gun. He forgot it on the dresser in my room."

"Did his attorney know this?"

"I don't think he had an attorney, only the one the state gave him. He could not afford a good one on his own. Jack Wall turned his back on him and would not help. If he stood by him, he would not have hung himself. They left him to take the rap. Or maybe they got him killed to shut him up. I keep thinking all sorts of things."

"I am sorry. I did not know he was dead."

"Yes, he is, and left me carrying his baby. But Jack will get what's coming to him. If it's the last thing I do, I am going to see that he gets his." With those words, she again burst out in tears and ran from the room.

**

There was a jetty that stretched from the hotel beach to about fifty yards into the sea. Mike sat at the edge, captivated by the peacefulness of the waves breaking on the reef, the turquoise waters, and the white-sanded beach. He was deep in thought. The entire picture of serene peacefulness seemed unreal when compared to the existence of death and suffering that was his world. Why couldn't it be like this always? Or why wasn't there a door that I could walk through to another world and never look back, leaving the ugliness behind? And that would be the real world. And this world that we kill and die for is just an illusion.

Those were his thoughts when he heard the sound of feet on the boardwalk approaching, and he looked to see Beverly. She sat down beside him and told him of the encounter in her room with the young woman. "You know, she could be important. At least we have something in common—a dislike for Jack Wall."

Mike said, "I am thinking of encouraging the relationship and find out if she could be helpful in any way in directing us to some explosives."

Beverly said, "Give it a try."

Mike advised, "And see where it leads. It could be the answer to our major problem. I am going down to the town and see if I can get a vehicle to rent. We will need one, or else we may have to steal one when the time comes."

***

It was about 3:00 p.m., and Jennifer Blake had just completed her inspection of all the rooms in the hotel, those that had been used the night before and those that would be occupied for the busy weekend ahead. She was leaning over the counter in her little office, drinking a soda from the bottle.

Beverly pretended she had just happened by. "Oh, there you are. Are you feeling any better?"

"I must apologize for this morning. I—"

"Don't give it a thought. What are friends for? Think of me as a friend. We girls must stick together," Beverly said, interrupted her apology. "Am I interrupting your work?"

"Oh no, I am through for the day. I am on from seven in the morning to three in the afternoon," Jennifer replied.

"What will you then be doing with yourself for the rest of the day?"

"Nothing in particular. Would you like me to show you around? I have a car. We could go into town."

"Super! Then I could get myself some souvenirs. I won't be long. Let me get my bag from my room, and we can be on our way."

Jennifer drove Beverly into Ocho Rios and luckily found parking for her small Toyota just off the main street. A large cruise ship was in port, docked almost up to the street, and the shopping areas were crowded with tourists. On both sides of the street were boutiques and stores stocked with the latest Caribbean fashions. The pavements were full of stalls with local carvings, handcrafted items of straw, and seashells, as well as every conceivable creation one could think of, designed from local materials. The entire square was truly a wonderland of delightful items.

Beverly found the varieties of ladies' fashions displayed in the boutiques interesting and took the opportunity to make several purchases for herself and an equal amount for Jennifer.

The young woman was so overcome with gratitude that she could hardly contain herself.

After two hours of shopping and wandering around, they became hungry and thirsty, so they went into a Burger King fast-food restaurant for refreshment.

After eating, Beverly said, "Tell me about your David Shon, if you promise not to weep."

Jennifer promised and explained how they met at the hotel two years before, and after that, once per month when he flew in for drugs. Sometimes the weather was bad, or there were delays in pressing and packaging the marijuana, and he would stay over for a few extra days. He looked after her because her wages from the hotel was small. Dave Shon had planned to marry her before the baby was born and take her back to the United States. He had planned to retire from the smuggling business and told this to Jack Wall, who was angry for days.

"How often do you see Jack Wall?" Beverly asked.

"He comes in often, whenever he has to make payments. He should be coming in tomorrow night. He leaves on the plane after the cocaine is loaded. The cocaine comes in on the Cuban boat and docks outside the reef."

"Tell me, Jennifer. What would you like to see done to Jack for what he did to Dave?"

Jennifer was silent for a long time. As if she was afraid to hear herself speak what was really in her mind. Then finally she said, in slow deliberate words, "I would like to see him dead."

"Are you certain about that?"

"Yes, very certain," she replied with a vengeful look invading her attractive features. "I would too, if he did that to my man.

But I would do much more. I would blow up the Cuban boat with the cocaine to see him suffer before I kill him."

"Yes!" Jennifer exclaimed. "That I would like to do if I could."

"I could help you. I could, with a friend of mine. But we would have to get explosives, something like dynamite or C-2 or anything like that."

Jennifer hesitated at first, but with a steely glint in her eyes, she decided then and there that she wanted revenge on Jack Wall.

"I can get explosives. My father worked with the engineers when they were dynamiting the hills to build houses. After the construction was finished, a lot of the stuff was left with my father. He has it in an outhouse at home."

"Where is your father now?"

"He is working in Kingston building houses. But it doesn't matter. I could show you, and you can get what you want."

Beverly could not believe her ears. It was almost too good to be true.

"Let's go, what are we waiting for?"

Jennifer and Beverly drove out of town toward a small township in the hills called Harmony Hall. Jennifer's father's house was a comfortable one-family residence built against the side of a hill. They drove up onto the driveway and parked. Jennifer went into the house for the key to a shed some distance away from the house and in the back of the premises.

When they entered the shed, Beverly was surprised at the quality and quantity of different types of explosives that she found. She found a small wooden box with a lid and packed everything she thought she would need. They then drove back to the hotel.

On their way back, Beverly asked, "When is your day off?"

"This weekend is my weekend off. I get one weekend off every month."

"I am going to give you a weekend in Montego Bay. All-expense paid and money to spend. How is that? I do not want you to be here. Then no one can say you were a part of it."

"Will you do all that for me?"

"You wait and see. We are friends, remember?" Beverly answered.

At 8:00 p.m. later that night, Jennifer knocked on Beverly's room door. In the room with her was Mike. She opened the door and let her in. Jennifer was frightened as she did not expect to see anyone else.

"Don't be afraid, this is my friend. He is going to help us."

"Now, Jennifer, I want you to begin your vacation tonight. Here is ten thousand dollars for yourself and another ten for the baby. Call it a present from us," Mike said, handing her the cash in United States hundred dollar bills.

Jennifer's eyes bulged with surprise.

"Don't you worry, there is plenty more where that is coming from. Now get going. And for your own good, forget you had ever spoken to any of us."

Jennifer stuck the money into her bosom and dashed through the door, beaming. After she left, Beverly commenced putting together the charges they required to blow up the Cuban coast guard vessel and its cargo. She also contrived a quantity of devices that could be used like hand grenades for emergencies, should there be a situation that demanded their use.

It was midnight, and the parking lot in front of the Buccaneer Cove Hotel was crowded with vehicles. Vehicles were also parked along the side of the dirt road leading to its entrance. Youngsters were seated on the hood of many of the vehicles smoking pot.

Beverly had almost completed preparing for the next night's encounter, so Mike, who was assisting her, came out of her room and ascended the short flight of stairs that led to the upper floor where the lobby the bar were located. All the stools at the counter were taken, and almost all the tables were occupied. More than 50 percent of the customers were Dreadlocks, speaking loudly a mixture of Jamaican patois and a street language that his undercover experience made him understand.

He chose a table in the very back and signaled a waitress, who immediately came over. He placed an order, and in a minute or so, the waitress returned with a double Johnnie Walker Black on the rocks. He gave her five dollars and told her to keep the change. She told him there was no change. He took back the five and gave her ten. She asked if she should still keep the change, and he nodded. She walked away from the table, looked back, smiled invitingly at him, and gave him the eye.

The kitchen was on the lower floor, and there was a caravan of waitresses taking food up the stairs and placing it on tables. As soon as the food on a table was eaten, another course was ordered. Seafood, curried goat meat, and rice seemed to be the favorite choice required to satisfy the appetite of the clientele after a session of pot smoking, which appeared to be without ceasing. A table of four easily consumed four dozen bottles of the native Red Stripe Beer. Although the crowd was loud and boisterous, there was no evidence of violence among the customers, men and women, who seemed to enjoy a sort of communal comradeship. All the men seemed to carry automatic weapons. The Glock-9MM seemed their favorite.

An English couple in their early twenties, guests of the hotel, looked around for a table to sit and saw Mike sitting alone. The young man approached the table, hesitated, then said, "If these chairs are not taken, may we sit here?"

Mike answered in the affirmative and told them that a friend would be joining him later. There was still an empty chair remaining.

"You are an American, aren't you?" the young woman asked.

"That's what it states on my passport, and from Miami, before you ask."

The young woman laughed and said, "That would be my next question. But you must forgive my inquisitiveness. I am from a small village just outside of Leeds in Yorkshire, England, where everyone knows everyone's business. And sometimes I forget I am not still at home. I am Jane Ashford, and this is my husband John. We are here for two weeks, and this is our third day." She stretched her hand toward Mike, who shook it and then shook her husband's hand.

"Do you come here often?" Mike asked.

"This is our second visit," John replied. "We have a lot of black friends at home, most of them Jamaicans. They told us of this place where the pot is good quality and cheap. Not the junk we get at home. Are you also here for the pot?"

Mike thought before he answered. "You may say so, in a roundabout sort of way. But this is my first time, and I do not have any contacts."

"Don't worry about that. Tomorrow we will be going to Saint Ann, not far from here, where you can get the best stuff, sensamena, with buds this big." John held up both hands to describe the size of the marijuana buds. "If you are up early, you are welcome to join us."

Before Mike could respond, a Jamaican female with locks down to her waist came up to the table and called them away. She had a spliff in her hand almost the size of a Cuban cigar.

At one thirty, Beverly joined him. He was still nursing the scotch. She ordered a piña colada and paid for it. The waitress asked if she could keep the change, and Beverly told her she could not. She made the change from a pocket in the front of her apron, scowled at Beverly, and walked off.

Suddenly there was a hush, and all talking ceased. Two large Dreadlocks came through the hotel entrance and entered the lobby armed with AK- 47 assault rifles. They were followed by Jack Wall and three other well-dressed men with shoulder-length locks, each carrying a leather bag. Bringing up the rear were two other Dreadlocks, also with AK-47 assault rifles. They marched through the crowded lobby in military fashion toward rooms to the left, reserved for them at the end of a passage. Two of the armed men stood in the passage, their backs against the wall. There they would remain until relieved by the others.

The militancy would continue for the next twenty-four hours, until the Cuban vessel arrived, delivered its cargo, and Castro's officials on board got paid for five hundred kilos of cocaine.

Mike and Beverly observed those details and would decide on what appropriate action to take.

The following night, Mike and Beverly sat at a table in a corner of the balcony on the second floor and peered through the blanket of darkness that hung over the ocean. Sometime that night, a Cuban gunboat would approach the other side of the reef and drop anchor. On that same floor was the swimming pool, and dozens of revelers, some nude, had taken their late-night swim and left. They were alone, and between each other, there was very little to say. They waited in eager anticipation for the first glimpse of the enemy craft.

They did not have long to wait. There appeared a small light in the distance that became larger as the Cuban vessel approached slowly. And then a searchlight on its deck played upon the surface of the water until they saw the waves breaking upon the reef.

It was 11:30 p.m. on Sunday when the Cuban coast guard vessel dropped anchor. Thirty minutes after, Jack and two men approached the vessel in a small motor-powered raft and went aboard. They remained for about thirty minutes checking the cargo. The Cubans lowered a military-type motorized rubber raft, and both crafts with a total of seven men went back to the hotel.

The time for the assault on the enemy craft came, and Beverly lowered herself in the water on the side of the jetty where she could not be observed by anyone coming out of the hotel onto the beach. She walked until the water was to her neck, then she started to swim, carrying a waterproof plastic bag. It was low tide, and when she reached the reef, she could stand on the corals and wade for about twenty yards. She then swam the remaining fifty yards toward the Cuban vessel. There was a rope ladder hanging over the side. She carefully climbed up, holding the plastic bag in one hand and her combat knife between her teeth.

She peeped over the side of the deck to see if any of the remaining four men were near. She saw no one, so she climbed over. She was on the deck less than ten seconds when she saw a sailor in white uniform walking toward her. She was not yet seen, but there was nowhere to conceal herself. She thought, This guy must not make a single sound. It has to be a silent kill, and it must be now. With lightning speed, she rushed forward. She quickly balanced the knife in her hand, aimed for his neck, threw it, and it found its mark. The Cuban momentarily saw the flash of steel, but that was all. He died without making a sound.

Catlike, Beverly retrieved her knife and wiped the blade on the dead man's uniform. She stealthily crept below. The other three men were seated on a bench, eating food placed on a counter, with their backs toward her. The sound of a shot would alert the others in the hotel, and the element of surprise in accomplishing their plan of action would be lost. They were all armed. So she decided on a diversion.

Beside the stairs was an oil drum. She back-walked and hid behind the drum. There was a bottle of liquid of some sort beside the drum. She took it up and threw it to land on the deck above. The three men spun around but did not get up. One shouted the name of the dead man on the deck, and when he got no response, he got up to have a look. He climbed the stairs with Beverly silently following. As they were out of sight of those remaining below, she jumped on him from behind and locked on a choke hold. The sailor struggled violently when he realized he was losing consciousness. She kicked him behind the knee, and he went down on one leg under her weight. They rolled over onto the deck, giving her a chance to lock her legs around his waist. She squeezed with all her strength and at the same time tightened the choke hold. The Cuban's life slowly drained out of his body. She held him there until it did.

Beverly stood up and waited. She knew that it would only be a matter of time before one or both of the others would get curious and come to investigate. She did not have long to wait. They raced up the steps toward the deck, one behind the other. When the one in front saw her, he went for a gun in a holster on his hip. This time she aimed for the heart and, with tremendous force, threw the knife. The blade of the weapon found its way between the ribs and sank almost to the handle in his chest. He lost the use of the muscles of his body, as if paralyzed. He fell backward, knocking his companion back down the stairs. The companion hit his head on the steel floor as he fell and was temporarily winded.

Beverly jumped from the top of the stairs and landed feet first on the abdomen of the sailor. She quickly reached for a fire extinguisher that hung at arm's reach and smashed him on the forehead. After that, he did not move.

She returned on deck where she had dropped the waterproof plastic bag with the explosives. She lit the wick of six sticks of dynamite tied together and threw it in the hold where the cocaine was stored. She then lit the wick of another bundle and threw it in the engine room. After that, she knew there was not much time.

She dived off the deck and swam underwater with all her strength toward the jetty. She surfaced a few yards from the piles that supported the structure and heard and felt the shock of the first explosion. She had barely recovered from the effect of the first when there was the second, which lifted the vessel almost out of the water. She sought the shadows of the jetty and walked toward the shore unseen.

The explosion brought almost everyone down to the beach. Mike, who was waiting to hear the explosions, removed the Bren Ten from the shoulder holster concealed under his leather jacket. In the confusion, no one saw him going toward the passage that led to the room where Jack had the money for the Cuban payoff. He tried the door and found it locked. He knew that one or more persons were behind that door guarding the cash.

With a powerful kick, the door crashed open. He jumped sideways just in time. The Dreadlock opened up with the AK-

47. So scared, he did not stop until he had emptied the entire clip. Then he threw the rifle aside and went for his handgun.

Mike stepped in the opening and blasted away before he could get off a shot. The Dreadlock fell dead over the four leather bags. Just in time, a wet and dripping Beverly appeared holding a gun to the head of a burly Dreadlock.

"Is everything okay?" she asked.

"Everything is going just fine," Mike replied.

"Come on, big fellow. Grab two of those bags."

The frightened Dreadlock took up the bags, and Mike took up the other two. They walked out of the room with Beverly holding the gun against the back of the Dreadlock. As they got to the end of the passage, they met Jack running toward them. There was a gun in his hand. He realized what was happening and was hastening to save his cash. He hesitated for a brief moment to get a clear shot at Beverly, who was partly shielded by the Dreadlock. He realized he would be given only one chance to make his shot good.

Beverly did not hesitate. She pointed the Beretta toward Jack and fired. He took the bullet in his shoulder, and the gun fell from his hand. In desperation, he threw himself to the ground and retrieved the weapon. Beverly fired again, and that time the bullet struck him in the chest. She looked down at him, and his eyes met hers. He said something that sounded like profanity, but the words were too faint to be clearly understood. He struggled against the approaching death as he sensed the life draining out of his body. He finally made a defiant effort and fired a shot harmlessly into the ceiling.

Beverly smirked and shot him again, that time in the forehead. Jack stretched out and died. The remainder of the crowd, seeing their hero lie dead, lost their nerve and scattered.

Before they regained their courage and regrouped, Mike hurried to the car in the parking lot that he rented the day before and stored the money in the trunk compartment. He said, "Now, Dread, you sit in the passenger seat and direct me along the shortest route to the airport."

"The shortest route is from here to the main road, and turn east for about one mile," the Dreadlock said.

Mike sat behind the steering wheel and pressed the accelerator to the floor. He could hear the noise of a commotion getting closer and realized that the followers of Jack had overcome their shock of seeing their leader dead and had regrouped. The small vehicle sped out of the parking area, and its front wheel struck the curb when Mike turned on to the dirt road. Halfway up the road there was a load bang as the tire exploded. The vehicle turned across the road and came to a stop.

"Mike, they are coming after us!" Beverly exclaimed as she saw the headlights of a car approaching at top speed and heard gunfire coming from the approaching vehicle.

"Everyone out! Get the bags from the trunk and follow me!" Mike shouted.

They rushed from the disabled vehicle and ran through the bushes at the side of the road toward the direction of the approaching car. The driver stopped about thirty yards from the car that blocked the road. Mike guessed that was what they would do, thinking they would be still in the vehicle. Four armed Dreadlocks and two Cubans came out of a Chevy Impala and menacingly approached the disabled car. The Cubans were armed with AK-47 assault rifles. As they advanced, they fired a barrage into the vehicle until the headlights went out, and both doors facing them fell off. When they were convinced that no one inside could have survived, they ceased firing and rushed to confirm the kill.

The Chevy Impala had stopped opposite to where Mike, Beverly and the young Dread were hiding.

"Can you drive a car?" Mike asked the Dread.

"Yes, boss," he replied.

"The road up ahead is blocked. Can you get us to the main road through the bushes? I will make it worth your while. Your boss is dead. This is to your advantage. We are all you've got. Do something for yourself."

"Sure, boss. It will be rough, but I can get you to the main road, driving through the backyards of those houses."

"Beverly, where are those homemade grenades you made?" Mike asked as he tossed the bags with the money into the Impala.

"They are right here," Beverly replied. "I told you they may come in useful." She gave two to Mike.

As the young Dread sat behind the steering wheel, they noticed the confusion ahead as the men discovered no dead bodies. They bunched together, discussing what to do next, and appeared as if they were considering going back to their car.

Mike and Beverly both tossed the grenades at once. The explosions took the men by surprise. Those who were not dead or wounded ran for cover in the nearby bushes.

The young Dread started the Impala, and they headed through the backyards of the houses toward the main road. One of the Cubans was unhurt, and being a military man, he guessed what had taken place. He aimed his weapon at the fleeing Impala and commenced shooting. A bullet shattered the rear windshield and grazed Beverly John's shoulder. She felt the sharp pain but said nothing.

The Impala ploughed through the fences, knocked down outhouses and chicken coops, and finally emerged on the main road, with only one headlight intact. A portion of a picket fence went through the grill and pierced the radiator. Steam and water came back onto the windshield, affecting the Dreadlock's vision. The Dread held his head outside the window and kept speeding toward the airport.

The pilot was sitting on a stool awaiting Jack and the consignment of cocaine when they drove onto the runway. The plane was refueled and ready. He heard the distant explosions and wondered what had taken place. "Where is Jack?" he asked the Dread.

"Change of plans," Mike said and pointed the Bren Ten in his face. "Now you two place the bags in the plane. We are taking off right now."

Both men did as they were told; they were given no options. Mike Cannon, for the first time, saw the blood-soaked shirt of Beverly and realized she was hit. He rushed toward her, concerned.

"That's nothing to worry about. It is only a scratch and has already stopped bleeding," she said.

Mike opened her shirt and examined the wound. It was a flesh wound and not very serious.

The pilot went into the plane and sat in the pilot's seat, and Beverly climbed in as copilot. As the plane was about to take off, Mike, true to his promise, opened one of the bags and threw four bundles of notes to the Dreadlock standing on the runway. The plane took off, circled the airport once, and headed low over the sea, toward the United States.

Chapter 18

It had been one week since the Caribbean encounter, and Mike took a well-earned vacation. There was a rear door to his apartment that opened onto a deck that protruded over the Miami River. That Sunday morning, there was no commercial traffic, only the occasional pleasure boats on their way to the ocean. He sat there on a wooden recliner, a large cup of coffee beside him, and read from a copy of that day's newspaper. He felt compensated to read several letters of gratitude from various charitable organizations thanking the anonymous donors of very large cash contributions to their causes. One beneficiary, a children cancer research organization that was in the final stage of closing because of lack of funds, was extra grateful. Their letter touched a part of him he thought had died with his own losses.

He wondered if Beverly had seen the letters. He knew she would be satisfied, knowing that her personal contribution to their humanitarian causes was well worth the effort. Alone and staring into the dark waters of the river that flowed beneath him, he was overcome by a depressive spirit, which was made worse by his pensive dispossession. Often he struggled against the ensuing wave of loneliness he wished to avoid, but never could until it had run its course.

Deep in thought, he felt a certain amount of uneasiness, considering he was never challenged by his department for any of his actions. He reasoned that at sometime or another, he would be required to give some account. Would those in power accept that it was in the interest of law and order? On the other hand, if his agenda was allowed to continue unchallenged, it was evident he was playing an important part in someone's game, and that someone had to be very important.

That night Mike turned on his small television set and idly flicked the remote to find a channel of interest before retiring to bed. He paused on the late news that reported the disappearance of retired Brigadier General Stanley Fraser. On the screen was a recent image of the retired general. He pondered where he had seen him recently.

Then it came to him. The general was the elderly man sitting around the table with three others studying a map of South Florida in the stateroom of the ill-fated Ocean Rose!

He took up the telephone and called Beverly. "Did I wake you up?"

"You did not. What's up?" she asked.

"Do you know Brigadier General Stanley Fraser?"

"Not personally. But I have heard of him. He was before my time. He was forced into retirement because of some scandal while he was serving in South Korea. What has he got to do with you?"

"I just saw the news reporting him missing. He was the elderly gent studying the map in the stateroom of the Ocean Rose that got blown up."

"I be damned!" exclaimed Beverly. "This thing is getting more complicated each day. We must meet tomorrow. I have been doing some thinking. And I believe you must be too. I think we are being set up."

***

It was four the next morning, and the telephone rang twice. Mike lifted the receiver and listened.

"This is Jay."

"Okay," Mike answered.

"Do you know an Oriental called Tai?"

"And if I do?"

"He has a message for you. Should I set up a meeting?"

"Yes, but be extra careful."

Jay hung up.

***

At 9:00 a.m., Beverly raised the garage door and drove into their Cannon Force headquarters. She drove in and lowered the door behind her. Mike was waiting.

"I hope you haven't had coffee yet. I brought an extra hot one."

"You are reading my mind. That is just what I need to start this day," Mike said.

"Does that mean that you are hooked?"

"Not really. I can take it or leave it."

They sipped their coffees in silence and peered at each other over their cups, as if trying to read each other's mind.

Finally Mike drained his cup and flipped it into the wastebasket.

"What do you believe is happening, Mike?" Beverly asked. She had her opinion, but preferred to hear his first.

202

"I believe the powers that be, whoever they are, want us to continue what we are doing until we have completed what they want us to do. I think they know about you. If our meeting was not by accident, I would say it was arranged. It's just too neat. I believe everything is joined together. Don't ask me how or why. I just know."

"When it is all over, if we are still alive, what do you believe will happen?" asked Beverly; a serious expression came over her countenance.

"I believe we may be held accountable. We could be the fall guys. They will have got what they wanted. Then they may throw us to the wolves. That is, if we live that long."

"No, Mike. Not if I can help it. They taught me too damned well. That was their big mistake."

Mike listened to the words of Beverly with keen interest. There was no doubt in his mind that she was not bluffing. Looking back on her actions over the past thirty days convinced him she could do whatever she had a mind to do—and succeed doing it. Her overall capabilities were on a level unparalleled.

Beverly was annoyed. She said, "Whatever force or forces behind this are above the ordinary authoritative level. To survive, we must find a way to convince them that to expose us negatively would be to expose themselves. They use us, we use them. It works both ways."

"How the hell are we to do that? May be it goes all the way up to the White House?"

"Don't care how high it goes. We are dealing with people. They have personalities, weaknesses, skeletons in their cup-boards, and glass windows. We will survive. If we stop now, we will not. We have to continue playing their game. Whatever they are using us to cover up is their weakness. We must find whatever it is, expose it, or neutralize it. In a nutshell, Mike, that is our assignment."

Mike and Beverly agreed from then onward to be together on all their future assignments. As they had proved to themselves, working together, they were almost invincible. Their mission that day was to accept the invitation of Goldie Lee. They thought that damsel was in distress and may have a lot to say.

On their way they stopped at a service station to gas up the Cadillac, and Beverly went into the restroom to freshen up. In spite of her lethal and destructive capabilities, she would not allow her femininity to be compromised. She considered her charm and beauty also an effective weapon. To this, Mike agreed without reservation.

The sign on their approach to the service station read 180 Miles to Gainsville. Their destination was fifty miles out of the town. To be there on time, it would be necessary to increase speed to an even eighty to ninety miles per hour. On the way earlier, he had the suspicious feeling of being followed. But he dismissed the feeling and contributed it to overcaution. If he was right, whoever was doing the tailing had to be a real pro.

Mike removed the pump nozzle from the tank and felt an overwhelming presence of danger. He knew whatever the eminent confrontation, it was near. Through the reflection in the rear-door window, he saw the two suited figures emerge from a parked black Buick and approach him from behind, carrying drawn guns with silencers attached. He did not turn around. He was planning his play. They moved with the grace and assurance of professionals—unafraid, focused, and straight toward the target. They were well dressed like New York hit men.

But they made the fatal error of getting too close. One of the gunmen heard the sound of Beverly's shoes on the concrete pavement as she approached and turned to deal with her. She had observed the situation as she came out of the restroom. She decided to engage and smiled in anticipation of the dangerous encounter.

"Stay out of this, babe. This has nothing to do with you, except if you wish to make it your business," the gunman said. Overconfident, he did not notice the sudden flick of a foot, and the next moment her shoe was in her hand, and the sharp pointed heel was buried deep in his temple, blood pumping from his face.

Simultaneously, there was a flurry of motion, and the gunman's weapon was in her other hand, taken from him before he was aware he was not still in possession of it.

"You made it my business," she said as she fired two bullets into his chest, killing him on the spot.

Momentarily distracted by the unexpected action taking place behind him, the gunman holding the weapon on Mike failed to see the nozzle of the gas pump on its way to smash into his face. Simultaneously, Cannon's sledgehammer left fist crashed down on the top of his head. He lost consciousness and slowly folded up onto the pavement.

Beverly calmly walked up and pumped two bullets into the unconscious body. "We do not take prisoners," she said as she released the clip, threw the empty weapon on his body, and walked away.

Another customer at another pump saw it all and explained to the manager and service station attendants what took place. "The couple took away their guns and shot them dead. I have never seen anything like that before," the witness said.

Mike and Beverly climbed into the Cadillac and continued on their journey, as if nothing spectacular had occurred.

Midafternoon found them driving through the impressive entrance of the Ten Lee Estate. They slowly drove up the drive and parked close to the entrance to the main house. Coming up the drive, the large white building looked even more impressive than before.

Before they came out of the car, Tai emerged from the front door and greeted them. He looked scared. He said his boss had cut short his stay in California and was due back anytime.

Mike and Beverly followed him to the room where Wang Lee was murdered, and he asked them to be seated. Moments later, Goldie Lee entered the room and bowed gracefully in customary Oriental fashion before she sat. Mike introduced Beverly as his associate, and Goldie Lee, without further formality or hesitation, commenced to narrate the incident that led up to the death of her brother. Frequently she would pause to regain her composure as she was still emotionally distressed by the tragedy.

"Mr. Cannon, Ms. Johns, I must be short, but forgive me. We do not have much time. My brother has cut short his business trip and will be back at anytime. Should he know that I am asking your assistance or warning you of the threat on your life, I will be in mortal danger. For this very reason my brother was killed. This place is not what it seems. It directly controls the lives of many thousands of your people. The main people involved in this place are some of those responsible for the welfare of this nation.

"Mr. Cannon, have you ever noticed the ants in your garden? The entrance to their colony belowground is no larger than could be covered by a dime. Yet a nation consisting of many millions are at work constantly. Think of this place as the ant colony, an illusion. You are a very wise and resourceful man."

With that, she bade them farewell and left the room.

Mike and Beverly saw themselves out. They drove slowly down the drive from the house and onto the highway on their way back to South Miami. Neither spoke. They were analyzing the gravity of every statement Goldie Lee made. In the brief dialogue, she said so much in so very few words. But from what was said, and what remained unsaid, they were conscious of a gigantic conspiracy of national proportion.

"What do we do next, Mike? We will be confronting very powerful heavyweights in high places," Beverly said, breaking the silence.

"Beverly, the man who has the answer to your question is Captain Abe Duncan."

Chapter 19

Carved on a large slab of white stone conspicuously displayed on the lawn was the name ABDUN RETREAT, and below were the numbers 88430. Beverly stopped by the large iron sliding gates and observed the meticulously manicured lawn surrounding the large two-story gray building. The outside walls were covered by creepers, giving the building an aged and sinister appearance. The drive from the gate up to the front of the house was recently done in interlocking gray pavers.

Beverly thought someone had gone to a lot of trouble to create an ominously unwelcome appearance. The Old Cutler area could not have maintained a more descriptive name; every one made special efforts to epitomize the term ancient. Some may say the effort created an appearance of affluence.

Beverly came out of her BMW and walked to the neighbor's fence, where an old lady had just cleared her mailbox and was closing her gate. She pressed her face against the metal rail and said, "Excuse me, may I have a word?"

The old lady hesitated, looked at her car, then at her, and said, "Certainly." She walked toward Beverly.

"My house is just a few blocks from here, and I wonder if you could help me. I have creepers growing on my wall just as your neighbor's. Except mine is overgrown and needs trimming. Do you know what day the gardener comes so I can ask him to take a look at mine?"

"Certainly. Not that he has anything to do. He is there every Thursday. He walks around doing nothing and turns up the radio in his van, disturbing the neighborhood."

Beverly laughed. "He will have a lot to do at my house. Thanks very much for the information. Have a nice day." She went into her car and drove off, leaving the old lady to make her final observation.

Thursday at 10:00 a.m., Mike drove up to number 88430 and parked the van marked National Security Alarms by the gate. He walked up to the gate with his notepad in his hand and knocked on the iron rail to attract the attention of the gardener, who was trying to look busy pulling out tiny weeds from among the well-trimmed hedge. The gardener walked toward him and wiped his hands on his overalls as he came.

"What a beautiful lawn. Are you the lawn maintenance expert?"

"I am," the gardener answered with pride. "What can I do for you?"

"I am from the Security Alarm Company, and I am here to check if the recent rains had done harm to the system. Mr. Duncan contacted the office. I will examine only the outside today. Inside will have to remain until he is at home. "

"Can't see any harm in that. Just the outside, you say?"

"That's it, just the outside," Mike replied.

The gardener opened the gate, and Mike went in and examined the house. There was no alarm system. He went to the rear door, and the lock was an old type that could be opened with no effort. There were no dogs, so he walked around to appear real, thanked the gardener, and left. Before he left the area, he drove and examined the road behind the house and noted that a large empty lot was directly behind. This seemed as an untended park, judging from the vast amount of banyan trees with overgrown branches almost touching the ground.

Satisfied, he returned to the Cannon Force headquarters where Beverly was waiting.

At 10:00 p.m., Mike and Beverly drove into the untended park in Old Cutler and concealed the Cadillac beneath the branches of one of the banyan trees. They removed their gears from the trunk compartment and proceeded toward the wall that separated the park from the house he cased earlier that day. They scaled the wall and landed onto the rear of the premises. As discovered earlier, the lock on the rear door was easily picked.

They entered the house and walked up a passage that led to an open kitchen and breakfast area. Beyond that was a large family room with a very low ceiling. The furniture was old and chunky, and the pictures on the walls were original nineteenth century oil paintings. It was evident that particular room was hardly used, judging from the heavy formation of dust that settled on the dining table and chairs.

They walked from there into the combination family and sitting area. A very impressive staircase led upstairs to the sleeping areas. The furniture in this area was heavy and old but comfortable. There were family pictures on the wall and a heavy and expensive area rug on the tiled floor. On one wall was a large photograph of Abe Duncan in uniform with several army buddies.

Beverly removed her special night camera from her kit bag and took pictures of the gathering. They entered the private study, which had a large desk and locked drawers. Mike pried open the drawers, and Beverly took pictures of files and the pages of what appeared to be a book of codes.

A car drove up toward the house. The beams of the headlights penetrated the drapery and lit up the room. They concealed themselves behind the drapes and waited with weapons drawn. The front door opened and closed, and the light in the passage went on. Two individuals stood in the doorway to the study. They peered from behind the curtains and observed Captain Duncan and a young army officer in full uniform in a passionate embrace. In a moment of impatience, the captain commenced to hastily unbutton the officer's tunic while they kissed. The young officer dropped his pants onto the floor and stepped out of them.

Beverly removed herself from behind the curtain and began clicking away with her camera. Mike walked toward the middle of the study and commenced clapping. It took some time for both men to overcome their fright and try to regain some composure. The captain, in a desperate moment of disappointment and rage, went for his pistol in its holster, but Mike pointed the Bren Ten at him and said, "I think I will take that, Captain." He approached Captain Duncan and took the pistol. He ordered both men into the study and told them to sit down together and turned on the lights. Beverly took more pictures.

Mike said, "Well, Captain, I see you are a man of many surprises. Make yourselves comfortable, we have a long night ahead."

Beverly retrieved the officer's pants from the floor in the passage, threw it at him, and said, "Put these on. I hate to see you like that."

The officer stood up and got dressed.

Mike sat on the desk and looked down disdainfully at the couple seated together on the love seat. Captain Duncan turned his face to the wall and refused to look at them. Mike said, "Lieutenant, I am sorry you had to be caught up in this. Nothing personal, but you are just in the wrong place at the wrong time."

The young officer started to sob and covered his face with his hands.

Moved with compassion for his lover, Captain Duncan said, "I know I may die tonight, but can you find it in your heart to spare my friend's life? He has a wife and two young children."

"That is a hard one, Captain. Leaving witnesses is a bit unprofessional. And you must have noticed that since your people murdered my family, I have become quite a professional in this line of work. In short, we do not take prisoners. But on the other hand, being the businessman that I have become, if you have something to bargain with, we are all ears. But it has to be good because both your lives have no further value to us. It is much easier to finish it here and now. I told you the last time we met that I would kill you when I have the proof I needed. Well, that is now."

Mike got up from where he was seated on the desk and pointed his weapon threateningly at the two men, as if ready to take their lives.

The young officer whimpered in anticipation of the inevitable.

Beverly quickly crossed the room, held his gun hand, and said, "Hold on a bit, Mike, maybe they can shed some light on that Ten Lee situation."

"What can they tell us that we have not already found out? That they deal in drugs?" Mike asked.

Captain Duncan saw the opportunity to possibly save his life and that of his lover and seized it immediately.

"She is right, Cannon. What I can tell you will shock the world. Let us walk, give me the negative in the camera, and I will tell you things you never guessed could happen in this country. I may lose my position and place myself in danger, but it will be worth it."

Mike and Beverly both took chairs and sat across from Captain Duncan and his friend and waited on what he had to say. The anxiety in pleading for their lives diminished as he realized that Mike may possibly be interested in his story.

"Wait a minute, since you have to talk, let's have it on tape." Mike rummaged through his pack bag, found a small tape recorder, turned it on, and placed it on the desk. "Now let's have it," he said.

"It happened while I was on active duty in Nam. I was only twenty-one years old and had just been promoted to corporal. We went out on a search-and-destroy mission to find out where Charlie was getting their supplies from, enabling them to operate so far from their main base. On the third day out, we walked into an ambush, and the lieutenant caught one in the head. The sergeant, a good man from Kentucky, caught a grenade fragment in the hip and had to be supported. So the responsibility fell on me to get our group back to base. I believed Charlie knew the route we had to take and planned another ambush. So I took the long way against the foothills so we could scout around them and avoid a confrontation.

"It was then we came upon a village we did not know existed. In the center of the village were several bales of rice waiting to be collected by the enemy. I ordered them burned. An old woman rushed out of a hut with a sword and stabbed one of the men destroying the rice, and he died on the spot. The men, tired and hungry, lost it and opened fire. When it was over, everyone in the village was dead. So we thought. We burnt the village to the ground.

"After our troops pulled out of Nam, I could not get passage for my Vietnamese wife, so I hung around, doing what I could to survive. Finally I drifted into Hong Kong, where I found a job as a supervisor in an American security company. At that time, the army was on their witch hunt and punishing war criminals that carried out atrocities against Vietnamese nationals just to appease the victorious North Vietnamese government, in exchange for soldiers missing in action and still in their slave camps.

"One day on a train, I met a young Vietnamese who claimed he witnessed me giving the orders to destroy the village and that he was the sole survivor. I had on the uniform of the security company, and two days after, I was arrested and handed over to the army.

"While awaiting trial, Ten Lee came to see me. That was the first time I met him. He said if I would join his organization, he could make my charges go away. I was looking at life. I had no choice. I agreed, and before the trial, the witness against me disappeared. That witness is Tai.

"His organization was international arms and drug smuggling. I stayed with him for three years, and one morning I decided I had enough. I disappeared and made my way to Los Angeles, and then crossed country to Miami. I wanted to put as much distance between us as possible.

"Four years ago, after I became captain, one day he and Tai turned up at headquarters, and the blackmail started all over.

"It so happened that during the periods of the Korean and Vietnam wars, a total of more than fifty thousand missing soldiers from the United States and other allied countries are still being held as slaves in work camps, factories, and mines in China, North Korea, and North Vietnam. It was a plan of the enemy to capture the young enlisted men who were not yet seasoned to jungle warfare and hold them for slave labor. That would free up their regulars for active duty. To assist morale, most of the soldiers reported by the army killed in action were really captured.

"After the end of hostilities, the war department struck a deal with various factions holding the soldiers, that if they were allowed to establish the opium trade in various parts of the States unobstructed, they would, over a period of ten years, systematically arrange the release of all the prisoners held. So far they have been living up to their word, except for one problem. Ten Lee, who is in charge of this side of the operation, has slowed down the release of the prisoners to extend the ten-year agreement. I do not know why he had to do that, but he must have had a valid reason. I am supposed to remove the drug competition in South Florida. If I do not cooperate, my past goes to the army. You can figure out the rest for yourself. You were getting too close to the arrangement, and it had to be kept secret from the public. You were doing your job too well. I suspect there is some sort of a private deal with someone high up in the army, and that person gave orders that the threat you propose must be terminated for the welfare of the agreement."

"So I am caught in the middle," Mike said. "On one hand, I am aiding Ten Lee and his group to distribute drugs to our people, and on the other, I was unconsciously supporting the army's top secret arrangement for the release of our boys. What a place to be. That is why we got no interference from the feds or the department. Ten Lee is being protected all the way."

"Do you see what that means, Mike? Our hands are tied. We can do nothing," Beverly said disappointingly.

"Not if the captain and his girlfriend here work along with us. We must find a way to force Ten Lee to keep his side of the bargain so the blackmail can work the way it was designed to benefit the American people. Ten Lee gets South Florida for his opium trade, and we get back our prisoners of war. My god, what a world we do live in!"

"This is how I see it," Beverly said. "Captain Duncan and his girlfriend walk tonight, and we find a way to get Ten Lee off his back. Captain, you continue doing what you are supposed to do, and from now on, we work together for the USA."

Mike, satisfied with the way things eventually turned out, said to Captain Duncan, "Captain, when you do all you are supposed to do for us, we give you the negatives. That is our insurance that you play ball with us. Or you and Frankie here make the headlines."

"Okay, Mike, I can live with that. I have nothing to complain about. This thing started halfway around the world and more than two decades ago. If I get the chance to make things right, I will do all I can. Ten Lee has the military behind him. You have to be careful you do not turn out to be the bad guys."

That was Captain Duncan's story. For the first time in years, he felt relieved of the heavy burden he carried. His skeleton was out of the closet, and he could abandon the thought of suicide he so frequently contemplated.

Lieutenant Frank Sandi listened attentively to all that was being said and experienced a certain amount of insecurity in the arrangement. Holding Captain Duncan by the shoulders and shaking him, he said, "Abe, that is all well and good for you, but without the negatives, I will be exposing my career and my family. I am offering you no support in this matter. And in a matter of fact, our personal relationship will be seriously affected."

No one expected the impact the lieutenant's threat would have on the captain. Upon hearing the lieutenant's remarks, he immediately fell on his knees and beseeched Mike to give up the negatives.

The pathetic actions of Captain Duncan so disgusted Mike that he and Beverly immediately left the house. When they entered the car, Beverly said to Cannon, "Mike, take it from a woman, Abe Duncan is now a dangerous enemy. He will try to get you killed for jeopardizing his love affair. Frank Sandi will see to that. Frank Sandi's lifestyle will make him very influential friends in the army. It is not healthy to be on their wrong side."

Chapter 20

The next day, Mike and Beverly sat across the desk in the office of their Cannon Force headquarters and reiterated the account given by Captain Duncan the night before. Beverly had firsthand experience of the efficiency of the United States Military machinery. She explained that being right or wrong did not diminish the awesome power that could be brought to bear upon any opposing element. They had to find a way to convince the army they were working on their behalf and get them to agree to it. It would be useful to find out who was the military personnel in charge of the Ten Lee operation and confirm the situation described by Captain Duncan. Beverly considered the possibility of discreetly using her army connection to get confirmation before going out on a limb. She had an uncomfortable feeling that there was more to the Ten Lee operation than the captain explained.

A week had passed, and they had not formulated any workable plan of action. They met daily, made plans, and discarded them as being impractical.

Early one morning, Beverly heard a knock on the front door of her house. She looked through her window and saw an army personnel vehicle parked at her gate. When she opened the door, she was greeted by an army sergeant and a corporal. The sergeant said, "Captain Johns? Are you Captain Beverly Johns?"

Beverly answered, "Yes, I am Captain Beverly Johns."

"You are wanted at army headquarters. My order is to escort you without delay. We will be waiting outside by the vehicle." Both soldiers stood by the vehicle and waited while she got dressed. She called Mike and informed him. She was escorted to army headquarters and, without explanation, within the hour was aboard an army helicopter bound for an unknown destination in Virginia.

Brigadier General Carol Newton examined the service record of AD3044, Captain Beverly Johns, for the fourth time and found no reason to change his mind. Apart from the fact that AD3044 was the best qualified and most aggressive officer for the assignment, there was the all-important matter of absolute secrecy. She had no family ties and no reported vices. He knew AD3044 was on the base and would be shown into his office any moment. His personal interests were at stake, and he pondered over the most direct way to present the assignment so it would not appear too much of a direct order. Her dedication to the undertaking and usual personal zeal would be important for its success.

Beverly entered the building and saw Second Lieutenant Tyrone Little seated at his desk. They immediately recognized each other. Second Lieutenant Tyrone Little was on the training course that Beverly took, but did not make it beyond the first week.

"Is that you, Johns? My god, you look great."

"You look great yourself," Beverly lied. She thought desk boredom had taken its toll on him. It showed in most places.

"So you are that special someone the general is expecting?"

"You flatter me, Tyrone Little. Anyway, it's good to know I am special."

Lieutenant Tyrone Little smiled, opened the door to the general's office, and announced her.

Beverly stood behind the chair opposite Brigadier General Carol Newton and waited for him to cease pretending being busy. Finally he looked up and said, "Have a seat, AD3044."

Beverly sat and waited.

"I trust you are well and in good shape. This meeting is for an important assignment for which you will be briefed." He was surprised at what he said. That was not how he wanted it to come out. But since it did, he may as well continue.

"I am well and in excellent shape, General."

"Well, you will need to be," the general continued. "I see here that you have three more months to go. The army will be trespassing on your last days and require that you carry out one last important assignment." There, that sounded more like it. Not ordering and not asking, the general thought.

"There is a privately operated international organization here in the United States. Its uninterrupted operation and success is of national interest to our government. It is reported that certain terrorist elements are planning a strike against it. The operation is located in a secluded forested area of five thousand acres. We do not have the information when a strike will occur—it could be next month, next year, anytime. The order is that the army must protect this establishment, day and night. This assignment is at top-secret level, and all aspects of it must be kept out of the media. There must be no civilian involvement. The leader of the suspected terrorist movement is reported to be military trained and is responsible for many atrocities in South Florida. Needless to say, an end to him and his activities is of vital importance.

"This is where you come in. The military personnel assigned to secure this establishment will be men long removed from civilian life with no ties to the public. Have you seen the movie The Dirty Dozen with Lee Marvin?"

"Yes, I have, General," Beverly replied.

"Well, you will be our Lee Marvin. These men will be military prisoners, desperate and dangerous. We have selected sixty men. Of these we need the best thirty. Fill them with as much of what you know as possible. You have a free hand to use your own initiative. You may have to resort to drastic measures to set examples. The army will understand and stand behind you. We have assigned a staff sergeant to assist you on this assignment. This is how important it is. Do you have any questions?"

"No questions, General," Beverly answered.

"Well then, the lieutenant will fill you in. You are dismissed, AD3044."

Beverly saluted the general and left his office. She embraced the opportunity her new assignment would provide, to find out more about the Ten Lee affair, and how much the army was really involved.

The next morning, Beverly entered a large briefing room. Staff Sergeant Adrian Boone, after briefing the men regarding what the training was about and the terms of engagement, was standing at one corner of the room looking scornfully at the collection of army misfits. They were seated one to each small desk. Beverly was in full combat gear; she did not underestimate her task. It could be difficult.

She stood by her desk at the head of the assembly and waited to get their attention. Some of the men did; some pretended she was not there. Staff Sergeant Boone smiled. He heard of her reputation and knew she needed no assistance.

She banged her hand on the top of the desk. "I am Captain Beverly Johns. You will address me as Captain from now on," she said loudly.

A monster of a man seated at the back of the group laughed, pushed back his chair noisily, and placed both feet on top of the desk. He broke the pencil that was on the desk for taking notes, threw one half across the room, and placed the remainder in his mouth.

The staff sergeant moved toward him, but Beverly signaled him to stay. "Stand up, soldier!" Beverly ordered the soldier.

He heard the order, but he remained seated, chewing on the bit of pencil. Without warning, there was an explosion, and the bullet from her weapon splintered the remainder of the pencil in the soldier's mouth. Frightened, he fell backward in the chair, his hand covering his face. He hastily got to his feet and stared at the gun in Beverly John's hand.

"I see. What you are saying to yourself is 'That it is not fair.' I am armed, and you are not. Well, I will change that." Beverly placed her weapon on her desk and moved away in the open, about ten feet. "Now you are saying that I still have my combat knife, and you have nothing. Well, we can change that too." With lightning speed, she drew the knife and threw it to bury its point in the desk before the soldier. "Now, soldier, you will take that knife and defend yourself." She said it slowly. Her speech had deadly effect. "But I must warn you, if you do take it up, I will take it from you, and this day will be your last because I will kill you with it. But if you wisely think of saving your life by not taking it up, go over to the staff sergeant now, surrender yourself, and be taken back to prison."

All eyes were on the soldier, and his ego only gave him one way out. Beverly suspected what that was.

With exceptional speed for a big man, the soldier seized the knife and threw it with deadly accuracy. Everyone saw the knife as it sailed through the air, but no one saw when it was caught in midair and thrown back at the sailor with such force that when it found its mark, only the handle could be seen. The blade was deeply buried in the soldier's chest.

The soldier looked down at the blood pouring from his wound in disbelief, then fell backward and died. The efficiency of the execution was so astounding that no one moved. Fear and amazement was mirrored on the faces of the stunned soldiers. They were appalled by the lack of emotion displayed by Beverly, as if nothing out of the ordinary had happened.

The message was understood loud and clear.

Beverly said, "Now, that will be all for today. If anyone wishes to withdraw from the training, please inform the staff sergeant before assembly tomorrow morning. I do not wish having to make another demonstration. Tomorrow, train-ing begins in earnest." She casually walked toward the dead soldier, retrieved her knife from his body, cleaned the blade on his clothes, and left the room without a backward glance.

For many weeks, Mike waited on Captain Duncan to return any of his many phone calls. He concluded that the assistance he promised was difficult to provide. He thought of the negative conclusions he had previously entertained regarding the cap-tain's motives, which had been proven wrong. So he decided to give the captain the benefit of the doubt, be patient, and wait.

One morning, after deciding that something was radically wrong and he should wait no longer, he called Captain Duncan at home. The phone rang many times before there was a voice at the other end. "This is Frank Sandi, how can I help you?"

At first Mike was uncertain how to reply. Then he said, "This is Mike Cannon. Get me Captain Duncan."

"Abe is indisposed. Whatever you have to say, you may say it to me."

"Are you certain about that?" Mike asked. By that time, he was becoming very angry. "Will you be serving his time for him because if he has gone back on his promises, that is what he will be doing. The army will be happy to oblige."

"The only person who will be going to prison, Inspector Mike Cannon, will be you, and maybe your female companion. You see, I have taken care of Abe's situation. He cannot be held at ransom any longer. The American government has agreed to close the file pertaining to any mistakes on his part during his military career, in exchange for something, of course. Can you guess what that something is, Inspector? Let me give you a good advice, and I would hope you take it. You are challenging something bigger than any of us. Continue in the direction you are going, and you will be consumed in a fire of your own making."

Before Mike could respond, Lieutenant Frank Sandi hung up.

From the statement of Frank Sandi, Mike realized things had taken an unexpected turn, and Beverly should be alerted. The information he had just received could place her position in danger. But he had no knowledge where she was or how she could be contacted.

It had been four weeks since Mike received the phone call from Beverly informing him that she was being recalled to duty by the army. The call was brief without details. He was reduced to thinking all sorts of negative things. Finally he decided that Beverly was accustomed to taking care of herself.

Late one night, after he had resigned himself to the idea of going back to dealing with matters alone, the telephone rang. He lifted the receiver and waited.

"Mike, this is Beverly," the voice at the other end said.

"Who is Beverly?" Mike joked.

"Stop the fooling around, Mike, this is serious. I am calling from a call box. I am not allowed to call from camp until after my assignment. It is top secret, so I am made to understand. Anyway, this information is confidential. Do not trust Captain Duncan or his girlfriend, Frank Sandi. The army was tipped off. They were informed you were a terrorist. Mike, that is bad, very bad. It may be possible that my superiors do not yet know of my involvement. Who else could it be? They are arranging a welcoming committee of crack army personnel as security. They want you dead. I was assigned to train them. I have a plan. Do nothing until I see you. I will be back in fourteen days. Have to go now."

The next day, Beverly met Lieutenant Little going toward his quarters with a box of fried chicken in his hand. She had timed the interception perfectly. "My god, Lieutenant Little, what is that in your hand, takeout dinner? I thought by now you would be comfortably married with children?" Beverly had already done her research and discovered that the lieutenant was a reluctant army bachelor who had failed at two serious attempts to get married.

"Not yet, Captain Johns, but I am working at it. I notice you have had your share of disappointments. You are still unmarried."

"Come on now, let's cut the formalities. No need for ranks off duty," said Beverly. Looking at the box of fried chicken in his hand, she said, "Care to share that at your quarters? That is, if no one is there waiting."

To Lieutenant Tyrone Little, that self-invitation was as manna falling from heaven. For the past year, he had been unsuccessful in every effort to seduce another female to cross the threshold of his quarters. And that day, out of the blue, a female with the rank of captain and physical references defying verbal descriptions was inviting herself. He asked himself, What the hell have I done to deserve this? Before Beverly could have a change of mind, Tyrone Little said, "Certainly, and I was saving just the perfect bottle of wine for this occasion."

Lieutenant Little's living accommodation was the standard army-issue bachelor apartment designed for discouraging lengthy female visitors. Beaming with delight, the lieutenant went back and forth into the kitchen, and each time he returned with something different. Finally, a bottle of wine, two small dishes, two forks, and two wineglasses were placed beside the box of chicken on the dining table. He commenced making excuses regarding the obvious inconveniences, which were promptly ignored by Beverly.

To make him feel more at ease, Beverly opened the bottle of wine, poured two glasses, and helped herself to a portion of chicken. He relaxed instantly, burst out in laughter, and commenced eating. As far as Beverly was concerned, the first phase of that evening's plan was successful.

"Tyrone, how is the army treating you? Better than how they are treating me, I hope." Beverly said, opening the conversation on the path she intended it to take.

"The army? You know the army, what it is like."

"No, I don't. The army treats most people differently. It depends on your immediate superior. How is the general treating you? Is he looking out for your future? Will he be recommending you for promotion? Or maybe because you are so damned good at what you do, he does not want to lose you?"

"That is striking the nail on the head. The brass looks after brass. But no one looks after you if you are out of that circle."

"Tyrone, you have to look after yourself. If you don't, no one will. Take me, for example. I have something on the side going. It keeps me comfortable. When I am out of here, I will do it full time."

"What is that?" asked Lieutenant Little.

Beverly poured herself another glass of wine and poured one for her host. "What am I doing on the side? I am a part-time journalist. At this time, I am doing a piece on the army and its faithful underpaid aides who keep the generals successfully protecting the country."

"Where do you get your material?"

"There is a special account from which the people I interview or who give me information are paid. You would be surprised the people who cash my checks. Some people prefer to remain anonymous if the information they give is confidential. They make the most money. Sometimes, they are paid thousands of dollars. Depending on the information they provide."

"Are you serious?"

"I am very serious," Beverly replied.

"Suppose I wish to make some money with you? That is, only supposing, of course. Would you be interesting in information concerning General Newton? Of course, all information can be useful."

"If I do not need it immediately, perhaps in a couple of months when I am ready to do an article on this operation, I will need it. So what I do, in an instance such as this, I get the information and store it for future use. I still pay you your check or cash, whichever suits you."

"So what are we waiting for? Let's do it," said an eager Lieutenant Little.

"Well, get me pen and paper. I will write down the information that is generally useful. Some may be of a confidential nature. The more confidential the information, the more expensive it is. And the more money it will mean to you. You may qualify for thousands."

Lieutenant Little, had recently experienced a costly engagement that did not materialize in its matrimonial expectations. A chance to recover his losses without any dangerous exposure could not be refused. Whatever information Beverly found useful, he was willing to provide, as long as he would be sufficiently compensated.

The next evening, Beverly met Lieutenant Little at his quarters. His excitement could not be contained. He handed Beverly a file. Beverly timely examined the documents and gave Lieutenant Little a nod of approval.

"Was it difficult to get these?"

"No, it was not difficult at all. What do you believe these will be worth?" he asked, trying to conceal his eagerness.

"Let's see, how about paying you twenty thousand dollars?"

"What?" the Lieutenant asked, scarcely believing what he heard.

"In cash," replied Beverly. She opened a leather pouch she carried, paid the lieutenant the money, and placed the pile of papers in the pouch.

She was about to leave when Lieutenant Little asked, "By the way, how is the training going?"

"Better than expected," Beverly replied. "There is one soldier who I think was some sort of military agent before he went to prison. You should know. You were responsible for recruiting them. His name is Tele De Soto. He is head and shoulders above the rest. The others look toward him as their leader. He is very intelligent. I think he should be watched closely."

Chapter 21

It was late before Lieutenant Tyrone Little fell asleep that night. Every word Beverly Johns said came back to him with added forcefulness. With an added unexpected twenty thousand dollars to prove her point, his appetite for much more was wetted, and his brain went into action.

Earlier that day, he was informed that the men being trained by Beverly Johns would be serving in Florida. At that time, the information had no significance. Still it could be a coincidence. He aimed to find out the nature of their service. A surge of ambition that he was unaware he possessed invaded his mind. His career in the army that was, until then, a monotonous day-to-day existence had never seemed so prosperous.

***

Finally, after almost six weeks, Mike and Beverly were together again in their Cannon Force headquarters. The military convicts she had trained were dispatched along with equipment to control security on Ten Lee's five-thousand-acre estate. Beverly reported that the men were efficient and were capable of carrying out the duties to which they were assigned. As a reward for satisfactory services, all charges against them would be dropped.

Mike sat down and examined the documents given to him by Beverly. He read the many pages over and over, and the astounding evidence against the generals left him stunned. When he overcame his astonishment, he said, "We have in our hands what we need to make the army sit back and listen."

"But how will we use it to our advantage?" Beverly asked. "This is powerful stuff, and to underestimate the awesome power of retaliation capable by the military brass especially when their peers are challenged is a fatal error."

"That I know, Beverly. But nothing or no one is as powerful as public opinion influenced by the press. We will seek the attention of the American people before we make our move, and to get that attention, I know the very individual who can do that for us."

Jerry Slater sat at dinner with Mike and Beverly and listened attentively to their story—from the murder of Cannon's family to that present time. He was sympathetic and shared their concerns. They had his full cooperation and promised dedication to the cause, which was the eventual release of American prisoners of war being held in slave camps in the Orient.

Jerry carefully folded the documents given to him and placed them in his attaché case. In reference to the documents, Mike said, "These are our insurance if anything goes wrong and in the unlikely event that we lose our lives doing what we have to do. Use them as you see fit. If we did not believe in you, we would not be sitting here."

Jerry closed his eyes, as if absorbing mentally the responsibility placed upon him, and said, "No greater honor could be bestowed on an individual than the trust you two citizens have placed in me. If the occasion arises, I will do you proud." He arose from the table, shook both their hands, and left.

Jerry Slater was a man of outstanding integrity who refused to compromise his principles. His insatiable appetite for the exposure of any form of deceit or injustice on a national level had placed him in the upper echelon of journalism. They felt satisfied they had done the right thing.

***

Ten Lee drove a half of a mile into the interior of his estate and saw the elaborate security preparation being arranged by the army in setting up their military camp. What appeared as an invasion frightened him, and he wondered whether the army's effort was for his protection or a show of strength for the protection of their interests. He noticed the two armored light mechanized units and the arrogant disposition of the military personnel. There was no doubt in his mind whatsoever that the intention of the army was an overt takeover.

The more he thought of it, the more he blamed himself for being influenced by Captain Duncan, who reported the imminent danger of an attack on his drug industry, causing him to request protection from the army.

Day two after the military support had arrived, the perimeter around Ten Lee's estate was satisfactorily secured. Ten Lee awoke that morning to find an M113 armored personnel carrier parked in the rear of his home, with three operators aboard. The radio operator was in communication with another armored personnel carrier somewhere else on the estate.

Later that day, soldiers in military Jeeps could be seen patrolling the estate at regular intervals. That was to be the pattern of surveillance twenty-four hours per day, seven days per week, for an indefinite period. Ten Lee was informed that the officer in charge was the newly appointed Second Lieutenant Elle De Soto, and his orders were directly from Brigadier General Carol Newton's office. Ten Lee was inconvenienced, but he could not complain.

***

Two weeks had passed, and Mike Cannon received a call in the middle of the night from Jay. Tai had made contact with him in person and wished to discuss a matter of grave importance. Mike realized that the matter of importance would concern in one way or the other Ten Lee's organization. So he advised Jay to arrange a meeting place where Tai could be met. Mike immediately contacted Beverly, who agreed to be present.

Mike, Beverly, and Tai sat in a crowded park off Brickell Avenue in downtown Miami. Where they were was only a stone's throw from the water of Biscayne Bay. Tai was seriously distressed. Mike waited for him to speak. Through tradition, he bowed to Beverly, then to Mike.

"Mr. Cannon, they have taken the master and my mistress prisoner."

Cannon's eyes met those of Beverly John's. "Tai, would you mind saying that again?" Mike requested.

"The soldiers came into the house and took Mr. Ten and Miss Goldie prisoner."

"Can you say why they were taken prisoner?"

"They are locked up in the house under guard until the new boss from Virginia comes tomorrow."

"New boss? Do you know what his name is?"

"No, Mr. Cannon. Miss Goldie placed a note in a loaf of sliced bread at breakfast. Here is the note." He handed Mike a crumpled bit of paper from his pocket.

Mike read it and handed it to Beverly. The note read, "Go to Mr. Cannon, and tell him what is happening."

"Did the soldiers hurt any of them?"

"No, they told Mr. Ten if he gave them any trouble, they would shoot Miss Goldie."

"How did you get to Miami?"

"I came on the bus. I must get back before they know that I am not there."

"But they must have missed you by now. It takes nearly four hours to get here."

"No, Mr. Cannon. They say no one must wait on the boss or Miss Goldie. They threw me out of the house last night."

"Do you know where they are holding your boss and Miss Goldie?"

"In the day, they are in the parlor. In the night, they possibly could still be held there," Tai replied. His concerns could be heard in his voice.

"Okay, Tai, you go back and tell Miss Goldie if you possibly can that we will take care of things."

That evening, Mike and Beverly met at the Cannon Force headquarters to plan their strategy. It was agreed that as painful as his decision would be, their first obligation to the cause was to free Ten Lee and his sister. If anyone would know the true facts, they would.

"Mike, why would the general choose to rock the boat at this time? It doesn't make sense to me. Ten Lee is the main man in the entire affair. Without his cooperation, nothing happens. Except someone else wants to be the main man, and Ten Lee refuses to hand over control."

"The only way to find out is to ask Ten Lee. Beverly, what kind of equipment would they have guarding the house?"

"I would expect at least an armored personnel carrier with at least a dozen men outside securing the area. There will be two or three guarding the prisoners inside," Beverly answered.

"We have to get inside the house. I know my way around inside. We must rescue the prisoners and be out again without any harm coming to them. That won't be easy. We will be facing trained soldiers, but that is our objective. One good thing in our favor, Ten Lee can take care of himself. He is something like you," Mike said.

"Then that won't be too hard since he is inside. But we must create a diversion. We need explosives. That will draw away the armored carrier and give us a chance to enter the house. Or else we may have to seek another entry. One they will not expect."

Mike kept the Cadillac at a steady sixty. The idea was to start the assault on the house after midnight. The trunk compartment was loaded with whatever Beverly thought would be needed. She was the expert on military engagements, and she was the one who trained and instructed the solders how best to counter assaults such as the one they were planning.

They were exceptionally silent, both having their private concerns. One concern they shared was their hesitation to kill American soldiers, although a few must be sacrificed to save the many.

About ten miles from their destination, they came upon a disabled transport bus laden with passengers parked at the side of the road. Mike stopped to see if anyone was hurt. He learnt that their problem was mechanical and drove on. About five miles farther, they came upon a lone individual walking. They drove past, only to discover it was Tai, who was a passenger on the bus and was walking the remainder of the way to the house. That was their good fortune.

Seated in the back of the car, Tai contributed to solving their worst problem. There was a secret entrance near one of the outbuildings, close to the main house. They outlined their plan to Tai, who considered it to be sound and workable, except he advised them to leave the house through the same secret entrance. By so doing, the only confrontation would be with the soldiers in the house. That way, a diversion may not even be necessary.

At twelve thirty, they drove past the main entrance to Ten Lee's residence and turned onto a narrow unpaved road almost obscured by trees with very low overhanging branches. Shrubs on both sides came together to give an appearance that the road was not there. In fact, if one did not know it existed, it could be mistaken for a narrow footpath. That was intentionally done when the opium drug operation did not enjoy the protection of the government, and secrecy in entering and leaving the operation was necessary. Twenty yards up the path, and the vehicle was totally hidden.

They came out of the car and took from the trunk whatever they thought may be necessary for the engagement. They walked about a thousand yards when they abruptly came upon a stout metal door set into a ten-foot-high wall that secured the compound. The door was cleverly paved over with concrete on both sides. You had to know it was there, or you could mistake it for a portion of the wall.

Tai told Mike and Beverly to wait by the door. He disappeared beneath the bushes and soon reappeared with a large metal key shaped like a T. He inserted the sharp end into a hole in the door and gave it a twist. The door swung open. They entered the compound and walked closely to the wall in the shadows to avoid the security lights. They ducked when a patrolling jeep with two soldiers inspecting the compound drove by.

Tai turned into a covered paved passage, stopped opposite a door, took a key from his pocket, and entered his quarters. His accommodation was very comfortably furnished, consisting of a bedroom, a combination sitting and dining area, and a kitchenette. Tai opened a drawer in a cabinet in the dining area and armed himself with a World War II German luger and a large hunting knife. He assumed a completely different facial expression then and looked the part of a dangerous Viet Cong guerilla fighter.

"I am taking you to where we will kill the soldiers who hold Mr. Ten and Miss Goldie," Tai said in a vengeful, determined tone.

Mike and Beverly checked their weapons and followed him. By that time, they were inside the main building. Tai signaled for them to stop. In the kitchen area seated on a chair with his back turned toward them was a soldier asleep. Beside him on a table was a half-finished meal.

Tai, with knife in hand, stealthily approached the soldier, held his head from behind, surgically decapitated him, and scornfully threw the head to the floor. The blood gushed from the headless body and sprayed the room in all directions, drenching Tai almost completely, who did not seem to mind. It was evident he had done that before.

In the parlor, Ten Lee and his sister Goldie were sitting on a leather sofa, bound. There was no one in the parlor with them. Goldie Lee was the first to see their reflection in a mirror on the wall. She gave her brother a sharp nudge. Ten Lee saw them and smiled with relief.

Ten Lee signaled with his eyes to say that the men holding them as hostages were in the adjoining room. Tai rushed forward and released him while Beverly untied Goldie Lee. Ten Lee held up three fingers informing them that there were three soldiers. He took the hunting knife from Tai and walked toward the room. Mike hastened to join him.

The three soldiers were seated but not sleeping. They saw the two men approaching through the door. All three went for their weapons at once. Mike threw his knife with deadly accuracy, just as Ten Lee became airborne. Simultaneously, he killed both soldiers. One died with the knife through his neck, and the other by a sharp chop with the hand across the base of the nose. The three men died without a sound.

Mike turned and looked at Ten Lee and was grateful they were, for the time being, on the same side.

Ten Lee and Goldie Lee hastened upstairs to their separate rooms and reappeared with two traveling bags. Tai stopped by his room and hastily changed his blood-soaked clothes. Without questions, all five left the building by the secret door and into Mike's waiting car.

Before sunrise, Ten Lee, Goldie Lee, and Tai were safely accommodated at the Miami Hilton Hotel. During the journey, Ten Lee told Mike and Beverly what happened, up to the time they were taken captive.

Leaving, Mike said to Ten Lee, "Do not make any calls before we speak later."

Ten Lee agreed.

***

It was morning on the Ten Lee estate, and no one was aware of the tragic occurrences during the night. Second Lieutenant Tele De Soto, who was given full control of the security force by Brigadier General Carol Newton's office, knocked on the door of the main building to inquire of the welfare of the two detainees. When he could get no response from the soldiers inside who were given the responsibility to guard the prisoners, he ordered the door forced open.

Inside he found four dead soldiers and no prisoners. Infuriated, he ordered the building searched, and then the entire compound. The search continued for the better part of the day before Tele De Soto concluded that the prisoners had made good their escape. He was at a loss to understand how, after removing all weapons from the house, a man and a woman could overpower four of his best men, kill them, and escape unobserved from the premises.

The day after Lieutenant Tyrone Little obtained certain confidential documents relating to the brigadier general and his superior, a copy of which he sold to Beverly Johns, he paid a visit to Tele De Soto, who was still undergoing special training. They formulated a conspiracy of a mutinous nature, which was to take control of Ten Lee's organization and hold him captive until he agreed to organizational changes. The other soldiers under his command, knowing that the order was from the general's office, supported him. They were unaware that whatever the major financial advantages to be derived from that venture would be mainly to the benefit of Lieutenant Tyrone Little and Tele De Soto.

***

After the security force and military equipment had departed to Florida, Lieutenant Tyrone Little demanded a private meeting with the brigadier general. The general informed him that he had a previous personal engagement, and whatever it was should be postponed for the next day.

"No, it won't," Lieutenant Little said to the amazed general. "It is to your advantage that you listen to me now, or you may be looking at your court-martial."

No commissioned officer had ever addressed the general in that manner before, so he realized that the officer before him was either insane or had something of a serious nature on him. The general was speechless, and Lieutenant Little observed the evidence of his fear.

The lieutenant, taking advantage of the occasion, removed certain documents from a large envelope and placed them in front of the general. The general's hand trembled as he recognized their contents and asked in a broken voice, "How did you get these?"

"It does not matter how. The important thing is that I have them. And also, a trustworthy associates of mine has copies for safekeeping," the lieutenant replied.

"And what do you intend to do with them?"

"That depends on you and your accomplice. You will take me in as an equal partner. And I will control the Florida operation with the China man. I do not trust you two. You will continue to be the army's representative, of course, and Washington will not be the wiser. My share of the balance in the Cayman bank is retroactive. I will give you the coordinates of my offshore account. Better still, I think I will make the transfers myself. You may advise Major General Martin Shayne, your accomplice, of the new restructuring. And for your information, one of my associates with copies of these documents is with the New York Times. He awaits my instructions."

"And what if the China man does not agree?"

"Don't worry about that, partner, he will. In fact, I will go down and persuade him myself. My main objective is business as usual," Lieutenant Little responded. Observing the impact his presentation had on the general, he knew he was in the driver's seat. So he made arrangement to travel to Florida and confront Ten Lee with a proposal he made certain he had to accept.

***v

Captain Abe Duncan was on his way to Ten Lee's house, which he was required to do once every month. He was unaware of the many unexpected changes that had taken place. On that particular visit, he had with him his new personal advisor and intimate associate, the young Lieutenant Frank Sandi.

Frank Sandi had been instrumental in removing the object of blackmail that Ten Lee had used for years to keep the captain under his control. They were also partially responsible for causing the military protection so adequately provided by the army against what they termed an eminent threat made by Mike. With those things in his mind, and Ten Lee being indebted to him, he looked forward to the new experience of facing him as an equal.

On entering the driveway to the main house, the captain was greeted by the expected military presence. He and his companion came out of their car and walked toward the entrance door. There they were intercepted by a uniformed soldier. The soldier, observing the insignia on the lieutenant's uniform, saluted respectfully and asked the purpose of their visit.

Captain Duncan informed him that he was expected by Ten Lee, and he was a frequent visitor on business. The soldier went to the front door and knocked. A disgruntled Tele De Soto answered the door, and upon seeing the lieutenant, he allowed them in.

Captain Duncan introduced himself and explained the purpose of his visit. He followed Tele De Soto into the parlor where he saw Lieutenant Tyrone Little, but no Ten Lee. Captain Duncan asked for an explanation regarding his absence. It was obvious to the others that Captain Duncan was unaware of the recent occurrences. It was not long before Captain Duncan began to suspect that something was unusually wrong.

Lieutenant Tyrone Little had arrived by army helicopter that morning. He was about to be briefed regarding the unexplained disappearance of Ten Lee and his sister and the death of four soldiers when Captain Duncan and Lieutenant Frank Sandi made their untimely visit. A bewildered Tele De Soto for the first time explained to the present company what he had discovered that morning and confessed that he had no acceptable explanation.

The disappearance of Ten Lee and his sister Goldie had a more devastating effect on Lieutenant Little than it had on the others. He knew he had burnt his bridges behind him, and there was no going back to his former position as the general's aide. After coming to terms with the existing situation, he said, "Well, gentlemen, without Ten Lee, we are all in a lot of trouble. Those of us who will not be shot for mutiny will spend the remainder of our lives in prison for conspiracy to incite mutiny and all the various charges the army can devise to throw upon us. We are faced with an unfortunate dilemma. Unless we can produce Ten Lee alive and in one piece, we are doomed. If the general becomes aware of the situation, we will have very little to bargain with, and all our plans are down the drain. I explained at the start how important it was that every detail planned should be in place. Now it turns out that the subject of importance is missing."

It was the first time Captain Duncan would be learning of the conspiracy, and he spent no time arriving at his own conclusions. Needless to say, the conspirators had made serious errors in constructing their plans, which, in his opinion, was doomed to failure from the start.

Remaining quiet so far, he amazed everyone with his bold statement when he said, "I know who is responsible for the disappearance of Ten Lee and his sister and the killing of the soldiers. Only one person I know of who could accomplish this so-called impossibility, and now that he has allied himself with a she-monster as himself, we will all be dead very soon if they have a mind to kill us."

"And who the hell is this superman and this female?" inquired Lieutenant Tyrone Little.

"His name is Detective Inspector Mike Cannon, and I have recently learned that his companion is an expert Special Services trained army captain Beverly Johns. Those two together are unstop—"

Before Captain Duncan could complete his statement, both Tele De Soto and Lieutenant Tyrone Little jumped to their feet, as if death sentences were just pronounced upon them.

"Gracious god! Little, what the hell have you got us into?"

Lieutenant Little was speechless. He realized he had been tricked by Beverly and was possibly lured into a trap.

"I must get out of here. I must think of a way out of this situation. I have made a serious mistake," a confused Lieutenant Little said, gathering his belongings.

"No, you don't. Nobody leaves here," Tele De Soto said, pulling out his pistol. "I would be a fool to allow you to return to the general so you can manufacture some statement to clear yourself and leave us down here to face the music. No, sir, here you stay and get us out of this mess you have got us into. If we go down, you go with us. And that goes for the remainder of you."

Still covering them with his weapon, he opened the front door and called in the guard. "Get me four armed men in here. On the double, soldier!"

In an instant, four armed soldiers entered the parlor.

"Relieve them of their weapons and lock them away somewhere. If you lose any of them, I will shoot you myself," ordered Tele De Soto.

The soldiers obeyed and took them away to another room.

One soldier went into the room and examined the only window through which the detainees could escape. He saw that the window had an iron grill securely fixed into the wall from the outside and was confident that no escape would be possible. The room had served as a library, with hundreds of books stocked on shelves attached high on the walls. There were two reading tables with two upholstered armchairs each. The tables were bare except for carved wooden ashtrays. The only lighting in the room would be from standing reading lamps beside each table. The soldier was satisfied, and he closed and locked the door behind him.

Captain Duncan and Frank Sandi sat at one table, and after a while, Lieutenant Little sat down heavily in a chair at the other, an expression of hopelessness on his face. The captain asked Lieutenant Little, "How the hell did you get yourself in such a mess? You do understand you will not get out of this in one piece."

Lieutenant Little looked across the room at the serious expression on the captain's face and felt the tightening up of his stomach from the fear that permeated his body.

"If De Soto does not kill you, Mike Cannon will. And if by some miracle you escape Mike Cannon, how do you expect to avoid the army?"

Lieutenant Little could think of no feasible answer, so he did not reply.

Lieutenant Frank Sandi, fear stricken, said to the captain, "Abe, what do you think will become of me? There are my wife and children, my mother and my grandfather who assisted me in becoming an officer. When they learn of this horrible thing, it will break their hearts. And to think, none of this had to happen. I have only myself to blame. I insisted on coming here with you."

In response to Lieutenant Sandi's statement, Captain Duncan, burdened by concern over the dilemma confronting his friend, said, "Frank, it does not matter where death finds us, but as soldiers, let us die honorably. At least we will be facing it together."

Those were not encouraging words for the other two men. The finality of the captain's statement got to them, and they began weeping uncontrollably.

Captain Duncan embraced Frank Sandi and tried to offer as much comforts as he possibly could under the circumstances. Finally he settled down to face whatever fate had in store for him.

Tele De Soto sat in a room by himself with the door closed. Somewhere from the dark recesses of his mind, gloom emerged to overshadow his confidence, and he envisaged the culmination of his life. At his court-martial when he was pronounced guilty and sentenced to serve the remainder of his life in confinement, he had declared war upon his world, which was the American Military Establishment. Until that day, he had believed that no force on earth could overcome the reality of truth. But truth in his case had failed to assert itself, and the military had abandoned one of its fairest sons.

In his mind, he went back to the time and place his world came to an abrupt end.

***

It was August 1976, and the place was Cairo. The heat that day had rolled across the desert sands and refused to continue any farther. So it settled over the ancient city like an invisible monster, sucking the moisture from every living creature. He was a young flight second lieutenant, and he was proud of his uniform, so he wore it everywhere he was permitted to. He was an American military personnel, and no one could be more proud. He was the best he could be.

He had about six beers trying to combat the heat and humidity and decided those were enough for the evening. He stepped out of the side door of the bar and into the alley on his way to hail a taxi that would take him back to base. From the shadows, he heard a female cry for help. He turned to see an American soldier in uniform ripping the clothes from a young Egyptian woman. Instinctively, he turned to assist when the soldier attacked him with a knife. In the ensuing confrontation, the soldier got killed. When it was over, he was found standing over the body stunned; he had never killed anyone before. The young female had disappeared, and no one remained to collaborate his story. That was his last day of freedom. So he was condemned to spend the remainder of his life in confinement by the institution he had worshipped above God.

Yes, he was bitter. Over the years, he became hardened by association with his peers—real killers, traitors, and rebels. There in his new environment, he was forced to kill to remain alive. Every day was a confrontation with death. He had forgotten who he was and had resigned himself to an existence of obscurity.

And then unexpectedly, the army gave him a second chance. He was resurrected, and for a brief moment in time, he felt being alive. But the years of confinement and negative association had robbed him of his moral values, and he had no defense against people such as Lieutenant Tyrone Little and his temptation. He was shown how he could get even for the years he was innocently confined and, in the process, become wealthy. But he was mistaken and threw away his last chance.

Now he had to resort to an existence based on deceit he thought he had left behind. But even that was better than nothing, and he was reluctant to allow it to slip out of his hands.

Assessing the current situation, the negatives had to be turned around to work in his favor.

***

In the back of Tyrone Little's mind, some vestige of truth that still remained told him it would not happen. But he was out of options, and the seemingly improbable was all that remained. Like a rat caught in a trap and awaiting its capturer, he planned his final desperate move.

Chapter 22

It was midday before Mike and Beverly returned to the Miami Hilton Hotel where Ten Lee was staying. On the way there, Mike gave thought to the fact he was on his way to aid the very person who was instrumental in giving the order to murder him and his family.

The memory of that day returned with all its painful vividness. His whole being cried out for revenge. The effort to adjust to the emotional turbulence left him physically weak and unfocused. He reached out to Beverly for help.

In response, she said, "Mike, we are not the same. I told you once I think as a soldier and act as one. I can experience no difficulty in arriving at decisions because they were already made for me. But you are different. You are a free spirit, a man at war with your values. This could be one of your most profound tests as a human being. From where you are, you either rise above the emotions of your animal ego, or forever consider yourself a reproach. You alone must make that decision, and it must be now. What would Kim wish you to be?"

When she asked that question, he thought of Kim and her innocence and compassion, and a warm feeling flowed over him, melting the ice his personality had become. He also saw the larger picture and the place he was occupying in it. The cause was bigger than personal satisfaction. For the greater good, Ten Lee must live, guilty or not.

"Thanks, Beverly. Let's go and cure the world," Mike said, not being certain whether it was he who said it or another someone inside he thought had died.

When they got to the Hilton, Ten Lee, Goldie, and Tai had just finished lunch. Mike had abandoned his emotions in favor of his responsibility, and there remained no noticeable evidence of his recent indecision. So he accepted their invitation to join their table.

"I suppose you have given the situation a lot of thought. What have you decided to do?" Mike asked Ten Lee.

"I know I wish to get from under this military invasion and continue business fulfilling my agreement to the army without interference. Only, I don't know how to get it done."

"Well, I do. And I will. But I must make one thing quite plain so you will understand where I stand. I do not like you. I am disgusted of what you are and what you are doing to my country and my people. Under different circumstances, I would have killed you. But at the moment, you are the lesser evil. I want my enslaved countrymen back home."

Ten Lee met Mike's eyes and cringed before his defiance. He said nothing in response to Mike's statement.

"Can you reach the general from here?" Mike asked.

"Yes, I can," Ten Lee replied. "I have a private number."

"Then let's go up to your suite. We will contact him from there."

In Ten Lee's suite, Mike said, "Make the call and give Beverly the phone. Beverly, you introduce me to the general, say what you believe is necessary to defuse the situation, and then hand the phone to me."

Ten Lee dialed a number, and the general promptly answered. "General Newton, this is Ten Lee. I have some one here you will want to speak with."

Before the general could respond, Ten Lee handed the receiver to Beverly.

"General Newton, this is AD 3044, Beverly Johns."

"Good gracious, AD3044, how did you get mixed up in this?"

Call me Beverly, General. Remember, I am no longer in the military. I am a civilian now. I know you are having problems, and my associate and I believe we can get you out of it in one piece."

"You are too late. Major General Martin Shayne shot himself this morning. Thanks to that traitor Lieutenant Tyrone Little. As for myself, I do not know what I am thinking."

"Please don't, General. Have a talk with my associate." Beverly quickly handed the receiver to Mike. "Mike, he is contemplating suicide. Speak to him," a concerned Beverly said.

"General Newton, my name is Mike Cannon, Detective Inspector Mike Cannon of the Miami Police Force. I believe you have heard of me. Say nothing, General, just listen. Disregard the negative information that I am a terrorist. Firstly, we all make mistakes, and you have made yours. That is a part of being human. America needs you now to get our prisoners of war back. That is my interest in this affair. The price I have paid for my involvement is the death of my entire family. I am now trying to forgive. Beverly and I will take care of Lieutenant Little and his renegade army. We will replace Ten Lee as principal of his organization. In turn, you will discontinue your personal interests in the drug trade and give whatever you have in your Cayman account to a worthwhile charitable organization and let it stop at that. The army does not have to be the wiser. General, this is your way out. Do this for yourself and our prisoners of war in slave camps who have lost hope of ever returning home. Remember, you are a soldier."

When Mike finished speaking, the general said, "Give me AD3044, I mean Beverly Johns." The sobbing could be heard in his voice.

Cannon handed the receiver to Beverly.

"Your friend, is he serious? Can he do what he says he can do?"

"Yes, he can, General. And he will do whatever he promises. That is who he is. We work together."

"Tell him thanks for giving me back my life. Inform him that he will have the full backing of the army in whatever you two have to do to clean up this unfortunate mess. Keep my private number, call me anytime, and let me know when it is over."

"Okay, General. Rest assured we will take care of it," Beverly said to the general. She repeated what the general had said so that all could hear.

Mike said, "Tai, go back today and enter the compound. Contact me by telephone, and let me know whatever is taking place as soon as you get there. If you do not get me, telephone your boss. Be careful, and don't get yourself killed."

"Don't worry about Tai, he can take care of himself. He was accustomed to doing that as a sniper in the jungle when he was in the North Vietnamese Army," Ten Lee said.

With that understanding, Mike and Beverly left the hotel to commence preparation for putting an end to the mutiny of Lieutenant Tyrone Little and his renegade army.

On the way back to their headquarters, Beverly could not help but notice the confused look on Cannon's face. "What is it, Mike?" she asked.

He replied, "Beverly, I have spent the majority of my adult life detecting guilt and arresting criminals. But whenever I am face-to-face with Ten Lee, I fail to detect the feeling of guilt in him. Yet the evidence says otherwise. I am trained to follow the evidence. What do you think?"

"Let us play it by ear for the time being. The truth will present itself. You have made your decision. From now on, your feelings are irrelevant."

"You are right, how I feel is no longer important," Mike said, deciding to put the thought to rest.

***

At 10:00 p.m., Tele De Soto approached the room where Lieutenant Tyrone Little and the others were confined under guard. He was aware how influential words could be. And since they were all he had at his disposal, he intended to make them work for him. In prison, in desperate life-and-death situations, they had worked for him before.

On entering the room, he said, "Gentlemen, have my apology. Overcome by frustration caused by the unacceptable recent occurrences, we failed to observe the wonderful opportunity that still exists in our favor. Let us sit down as professional soldiers and examine this situation as it is. But before we do that, we will enjoy the comforts of the China man's parlor, have some refreshments, and plan our success. I am certain you are as famished as I am."

A soldier brought in food he had requested for the occasion and placed it on a table in the center of the parlor. That was the final setting of the stage. But as hungry as the hostages may have been, none of them had the appetite to eat.

De Soto, although disappointed, ate sumptuously as if he had no urgent concerns. He hoped to impress his audience of his assurance of success. There was no doubt whatsoever that under pressure, Tele De Soto's capability as a leader excelled.

"Gentlemen, let us examine our many assets as they truly are." As he began to speak, it was evident that they were mentally dependent upon his resourcefulness for their salvation. They were listening attentively.

"We have the valuable opium-processing plant of Mr. Ten Lee in our possession. And as you can see, it is being protected by some of the finest of the United States Army. The government had made a secret agreement to compromise their anti-drug policy in exchange for the return of American prisoners of war. As far as they are concerned, that agreement still exists. To safeguard against political criticism, this operation is top secret. That is our protection. As powerful as the army is, they cannot make public our actions here.

"What then is missing? Mr. Ten Lee. He is the ace in the pack that is missing. Whatever action Mike Cannon, and the invincible Captain Beverly Johns mount against us, it has to be limited to avoid publicity by the media. So what do we do? We already know that there will be a creative attempt to retake this place. So we set our trap and wait. We have the equipment, we have men. Mike and Beverly Johns are only humans. They are dispensable. But we do need Ten Lee with his Oriental connections to make this operation a success. Then there will be business as usual with us as his partners. The army or no one has to be the wiser."

"My god!" exclaimed Lieutenant Little. "Brilliant idea, explained that way. Why didn't I think of that?"

There was a period of silence, during which the statement of Tele De Soto was being considered, and to some, it was a ray of hope.

And then Captain Duncan spoke, deflating their bubble. "That is an excellent suggestion. But one thing is very wrong, and that is what you said about Mike Cannon. You do not know Mike Cannon as I do. You will not be able to kill Mike Cannon easily. Many have tried, and many have died trying. And now that he has linked up with Beverly Johns, there is not much of a chance doing that. Believe me, he has already worked out what your plans are, and at this very moment, he is counter-planning. He is a strategist. That is what he was trained to be. "

"Then what would you suggest?" asked Tele De Soto sarcastically.

"There is only one chance to remain alive," Captain Duncan replied. "And I would suggest you take it. Surrender to him. The only reason why this operation is not already reduced to a pile of rubble is because he has compromised his policy to aid the return of the prisoners of war. De Soto, he may spare your life if you agree to disappear. That goes for you too, Little. Abandon your delusions of riches in exchange for your lives. The soldiers will remain as the army planned, things will return to normal, and no one outside will be the wiser that all this happened. I am quite certain the army will not be at a loss over your disappearances. As for me, whatever happens to me depends on his disposition when he finds me. I will wait right here and see."

"Never in a thousand years!" De Soto shouted in objection. "With all we have going for us, surrendering to him will never happen. We can come out of this situation as winners. What do you think, Little?"

Lieutenant Little did not reply at once. He was deep in thought. What Captain Duncan suggested made sense to him the more he thought of it. If he was given the opportunity to walk away with his life, he would take it. He could still try to make a fortune somewhere else, another day. To avoid the publicity, the army may allow him to do just that.

Meeting De Soto's gaze squarely, he said, "Duncan makes sense. He seems to know Cannon better than anyone else here. If I am allowed to surrender, I will."

At his decision, De Soto went into an uncontrollable rage. "You yellow coward, you are the one who talked me into this. Good men are already dead because of you, and perhaps more will. Now you are trying to weasel yourself out of it to save your own cowardly hide. Not a chance."

So saying, unexpectedly, De Soto drew his weapon and shot Lieutenant Little at point-blank range between the eyes. He died instantly where he sat.

With the weapon still in his hand, he turned toward Captain Duncan and aimed it at him. Captain Duncan braced himself for the inevitable. Then De Soto hesitated and said, "What the hell, you are not even a part of this." He then walked away.

Lieutenant Frank Sandi, who thought it wise not to be a part of the discussion, gave a sigh of relief at the sparing of Captain Duncan's life. His only reason he accompanied Captain Duncan was to ensure that no opportunity in getting the negatives from Mike would be overlooked.

***

At 1:00 a.m., Mike received the call he expected from Tai. He had left the compound through the secret exit and walked four miles to the nearest highway truck stop to make the call. He could not risk making one from the compound as no one knew he was there.

Tai was excited. He said, "Mr. Cannon, all hell has broken loose. De Soto shot and killed the army man Little, who came in the helicopter. He is holding Captain Duncan and his army friend prisoners. After the shooting, four of the soldiers stole the helicopter and deserted. I heard some of the soldiers talking. They do not want to fight against Miss Beverly. They believe they do not stand a chance. De Soto had a meeting after the soldiers stole the helicopter and told those remaining that he is setting a trap for you, and if they fight with him, he would make them all very rich very soon. He also told them that the boss must not be hurt. Only six promised to help him. The others believe you and Miss Beverly may be on the compound already and could kill them at any time. They plan secretly to steal the boss's truck and leave. Mr. Cannon, what do you want me to do?"

"Wait for us inside the compound. Your boss will take us in through the secret door. I do not wish to fight against the soldiers who want to leave. After they are gone, we will take out the others and Mr. Tele De Soto. We will be there presently. Good job, Tai."

Before daybreak, Mike, Beverly, Ten Lee, and Goldie Lee entered the compound through the secret entrance. Tai was waiting for them. Goldie Lee asked to remain in Tai's quarters, as it would be safer there. Tai told them that the soldiers had taken the big truck and headed north. At the gate, the guard, one of those who had promised to remain loyal to Tele De Soto, tried to stop them by shooting at the truck. They ran him over,

256

and he was critically wounded and not expected to survive. Tai did not know where De Soto and the other five soldiers were at that time, nor did he know where they were keeping Captain Duncan and his lieutenant friend.

Mike did not wish Captain Duncan to be harmed; his continued presence as part of the overall plan was vital. Mike said, "They are planning to surprise us. We have to flush them out. But how do we do that without danger to the captain? You can bet they are holding him and Frank as hostages."

Beverly, in full combat uniform and fully armed for an assault, said, "Tai, do you understand grenades?" She handed Tai a grenade.

"Of course I do, Miss Beverly. I was a soldier."

"That's good. Find a personnel carrier and blow it up. I will find the other. We don't want them to have that firepower. Mike, let's hope they come looking for us when they hear the explosion. That's the only way to flush them out."

As Tai prepared to carry out his assignment, Ten Lee said, "Wait, Tai, I am coming with you."

Beverly handed him her backup Beretta.

"No need for that," Ten Lee said, smiling. "These are enough." He showed both hands.

By the pool, Tai and Ten Lee found the first personnel carrier. The vehicle was sabotaged and disabled. Someone had removed two of its wheels. Tai pulled the pin and threw the grenade where the gun was mounted. The explosion shattered the silence of the early morning.

Beverly, searching for the other vehicle, heard the roar of engines as a vehicle sped toward the direction of the explosion. It slowed down to make a deep turn around the corner of a building. Three soldiers were inside. They saw a figure running directly toward the speeding vehicle, but were confused by the madness. It was happening so fast, they had no time to think or shoot.

About ten feet from the vehicle striking her head-on, Beverly leapt several feet into the air, somersaulted, and dropped both grenades as the vehicle passed beneath her. It happened so fast, the occupants could do nothing except wait for the explosion. When it occurred, the speeding vehicle was lifted high off the ground, rolled over many times, and burst into a huge ball of fire.

Ten Lee and Tai, who witnessed it from where they took cover, stood aghast at the daring and unbelievable feat.

Tele De Soto heard the two explosions. It did not take him long to reason that Mike and Beverly were already on the compound and that more of his men were either dead or wounded. He was counting on heavy fire from the gun mounted on the carriers. He thought he could lure Mike and Beverly into the open, searching from building to building for them. The order was to shoot anything that moved.

He found himself at a disadvantage, with only two men with him and two hostages. Those were not the odds he counted on. Neither did the remaining two soldiers who had pledged to be faithful to him. They did not have the displeasure of experiencing Mike in action, but if he was even closely as good as Beverly, they reasoned the odds against them were too great.

The two soldiers looked at each other and nodded. They had silently made the same decision. Whatever they had to do, it had to be then. They drew their weapons, stuck them into De Soto's back, and ordered him to drop his. They gave him no alternative.

He placed his gun on the ground. They knew he had a knife and a backup weapon. "The others!" one of the soldiers ordered. De Soto relieved himself of the other weapons.

Mike, Beverly, Ten Lee, and Tai were in an outbuilding contemplating where De Soto and his men would be holding the hostages when they heard a voice calling, "Captain Johns! Captain Johns! We are coming out. De Soto is our prisoner. The hostages are unharmed."

"Wait!" said Captain Duncan. "Circumstance has just given you a way out. If you do not kill Cannon now, you will be going back to prison. And you, De Soto, will be facing the death sentence for murdering Lieutenant Little. Give us back our guns, which we will conceal. Pretend that we are still your prisoners. They will not expect us to be armed. We will surprise Cannon and the woman. Once they are dead, the others will bargain. They know you have nothing against them." Captain Duncan was playing a desperate game, but any chance taken to appease Frank Sandi and restore intimate relationship with him was worth it. The lieutenant wanted the negatives, and continued intimacy was conditional upon receiving them.

The soldiers gave his suggestion some thought, but remembered the capability of Beverly Johns. "Not a chance," one of the soldiers said. "It will be our way. If it does not work, we are dead. I cannot afford the gamble."

Hearing the soldier's response, Captain Duncan realized his hope of seeing Mike dead was shattered.

"Send out the hostages first," Mike ordered the soldier.

Captain Duncan and Lieutenant Sandi came through the door and walked out into the open with their hands raised.

"Walk toward us," Mike said.

They walked toward the door and entered the room where the order came from. Tai pushed them against the wall, searched them, and then covered them with his weapon. He stared aggressively at Captain Duncan.

"Now, send De Soto out, with his hands in the air."

De Soto came out with his hands raised.

"Get down on the ground and stay there. Now, you two drop your weapons, come out slowly, and get down beside De Soto. If I find as much as a pocketknife on any of you, you are dead."

The two soldiers did as they were ordered.

Mike then said, "De Soto, these two will be going back to prison to serve out their sentences. But you will be charged with murdering Lieutenant Little. This is the end of the trail for you."

De Soto thought of facing trial and being sentenced to death and decided it was not an option. If he was going to die, he would prefer it to be then and there and take the one of most importance to the army with him.

He waited for a chance and noticed that Tai held his weapon quite loosely. He made a desperate dash toward Tai and took him down. He easily relieved Tai of his weapon and aimed it at Ten Lee. He reasoned that killing Ten Lee would be the greatest loss.

But he miscalculated the physical capabilities of his target. In a split second, Ten Lee dropped to the floor and swept De Soto's legs from under him. He fell backward as the gun went off. Ten Lee flipped to his feet and dived, aiming his outstretched fingers at De Soto's throat. De Soto tried to twist his upper body away from the lethal thrust, but already his larynx was crushed, closing off the air going to his lungs. He rolled around on the ground, fighting against his imminent death.

Ten Lee walked toward the agonized body, jumped high into the air, and landed with both feet in his sternum. De Soto's body twitched, and it died.

No one had noticed that as Captain Duncan turned to get out of the way, the bullet that was intended for Ten Lee had struck him and penetrated his liver. When Mike learnt of the accident, already the Captain's blood, almost black in color, was flowing profusely from the wound unto the ground. Mike suggested that he be immediately taken to the hospital. But Captain Duncan, being experienced to seeing various types of wounds while in combat, told Mike to leave him where he was as he was ready to face the end, and he would be dead within twenty minutes.

Mike stooped down and took Captain Duncan's hand; it was cold and damp, and in his eyes, he saw the empty stare of death. Mike said, "I am sorry it had to end like this, Captain, with so many unanswered questions." Mike hoped that if the captain had any burden on his mind, he would not wish to take it with him. The question regarding the one responsible for the death of his family was foremost on his mind and still unanswered.

The captain tried to answer, but his voice was too weak to be understood. So Mike placed his ears close to his lips and was able to hear his parting words. He squeezed Cannon's hand feebly and whispered, "Mike, all that glitters is not gold."

Then he died.

Frank Sandi held him in his arms and wept bitterly until the end. In spite of his questionable involvement, Captain Duncan in death displayed the courage that was evidence of his real self.

Tai, who had secretly cherished the idea of someday killing the captain himself for the massacre of his people in the Viet Nam village, showed no sympathy. Although he seemed satisfied with the untimely death of the captain, he could not conceal the noticeable disappointment on his face as he walked away.

Mike stood over the distraught Lieutenant Sandi and handed him the negatives that were once the object of his concerns. "Take these. It is all over now," he said to the lieutenant.

The lieutenant looked up at him and said, "You are correct, Inspector Cannon, it is all over for us. But for you, it's just begun. Evil is like an octopus, it has many tentacles."

Mike looked at Beverly, as if he expected her to interpret the meaning of the lieutenant's statements, but there was no response from her. So they both walked away, leaving the lieutenant to his moment of grief.

"What did the captain whisper in your ear, Mike, or is it a secret between you two?" Beverly asked.

"Kind of, just something Shakespeare once said." Mike considered the captain's words a parting gift he wished to hold on to for a while before sharing. That was all he had to show for almost a lifetime of friendship.

Mike noticed a troubled expression on Ten Lee's countenance. He noticed the manner in which he looked at Tai, as if he was uncertain about something. Ten Lee failed to understand how a trained and experienced jungle fighter could have allowed De Soto to so easily relieve him of his weapon. He knew that Tai had a backup pistol and also a knife. He had trained Ten Lee in the art of knife fighting. In hand-to-hand combat, he was one of the best and could have taken De Soto in seconds.

As Ten Lee walked away, he was joined by Mike and Beverly. Something was missing, and both sensed it was something of importance.

"What will be your next move, now that events have resolved themselves?" Mike asked.

"It was my intention to spend another ten days in Los Angeles to complete very important business, but I am not so certain that I should now," Ten Lee said.

Mike and Beverly looked at each other. They had similar thoughts. "Where is Goldie?" Beverly asked. "I believe Tai is gone to get her," Ten Lee replied and walked dejectedly toward the entrance to the main building.

Mike asked Beverly, "Do you know what I am thinking?"

Beverly answered, "Yes, I do. I think we have been taken."

"Did any of the documents specifically state that Ten Lee was the only partner of the general?" asked Mike.

"No, not really," Beverly replied. "We just took it for granted. Did you notice that Tai had arranged that we rescue Ten Lee and Goldie and take them off the compound before Lieutenant Little came down? We were not supposed to speak with him. I believe Captain Duncan was getting too close to the truth, and that's one of the reasons why Goldie and Tai wanted him dead. I do not believe we have all of the details, but I do believe the originator of this conspiracy is Goldie Lee. I do not know for certain what Tai is, but both of them are in it together. Another thing, when we went to the Hilton Hotel, there were two rooms with one king-size bed each. Since Tai occupied one room, who occupied the other?" Beverly asked. "Following my woman's intuition, I do not believe Ten and Goldie are brother and sister. I believe they are husband and wife. I also think the quarrel between Wang Lee and Ten Lee originated from something much deeper than the reason Goldie gave us. I believe Wang Lee was Goldie's secret lover, and somehow, Ten Lee found out. You know what I think? They plan to murder Ten Lee."

"Then we better find him before that happens," Mike advised.

They immediately began to search for him and heard a shot. Hurrying toward the sound, they saw Ten Lee on the ground bleeding. Tai came out of the main building, followed by Goldie Lee. A German luger in his hand was aimed at Ten Lee. Goldie also had a weapon. They were so intent in finishing what they had planned, they failed to notice Mike and Beverly observing.

Goldie Lee, while walking toward Ten Lee, said, "The day I buried Wang, I promised him I would avenge his death. This is for him."

Mike and Beverly, concerned for Ten Lee's life, fired several shots. Mike, intending only to discourage them, fired to miss. But Beverly had no such intention after seeing Tai shoot Ten Lee. She was shooting to kill. A bullet from Beverly's gun hit Tai, and he fell to the ground fatally wounded. Infuriated, Goldie Lee uttered a loud cry of anguish, aimed her weapon at Mike, and commenced walking toward him.

At that moment, Mike understood the meaning of Captain Duncan's last words. Approaching him was the materialization of his agony and mental grief. His heart pumped the fluid of retribution to his brain. He embraced the moment of revenge as he again heard the cries of his loved ones on that dreadful day.

He pointed the Bren Ten at her chest and, his finger on the trigger, commenced to obey his command. The moment had arrived.

Then he hesitated.

Beverly, observing, saw the deadly intent in Goldie Lee's eyes and shouted, "Mike, shoot! Shoot her!"

But Mike stood staring at Goldie Lee as if he was frozen.

Beverly could not understand.

Goldie Lee's eyes narrowed, and a distorted grimace re-placed her usually deceptive soft countenance. She stopped and tensed for the kill.

At that moment, Beverly fired. The bullet struck Goldie in the chest, and she reeled from the impact, but was still standing. She swung around and, with superhuman effort, again aimed her weapon at Mike.

Beverly stared in amazement at the unbelievable power she was receiving from the evil intent motivating her actions. Without further hesitation, she fired a second time. The next bullet penetrated Goldie Lee's heart. The force spun her around, and she fell dead.

Beverly angrily approached Mike, slapped him across the face twice, and shouted, "What the hell is the matter with you? Why did you want her to kill you? Do you have a death wish or something? Answer me! Answer me, damn it!"

Mike did not answer at once. And when he did, he said, "I don't know. At that particular moment, I just felt I had enough."

They stood there staring at each other, saying nothing. He tried to conceal the tears in his eyes from Beverly, who turned away to spare him any embarrassment.

Mike approached Ten Lee, bent down, and helped him to his feet.

Ten Lee covered a wound in his shoulder with his hand, and blood flowed through his fingers onto his clothes. Ten Lee said, "Thank you both for saving my life. Mr. Cannon, justice has been served. It will not bring back your family, but you have been avenged. Where I am concerned, I suspected all along my wife and her brother wanted to take over. But I just did not believe they would have taken it this far."

In response to that statement, Mike said, "Once the scheming started, they had to follow it through. To think of it, they almost succeeded. She certainly had me fooled. But when I looked into her eyes, I knew then and there she was the one who ordered the hit on my family. She wanted me dead to finish the job. At that time, I could not want to kill her more. But then something happened. Standing between us were Kim, Dianna, and Tommy staring up at me, pleading for her life. In their eyes, I saw the pity they felt for me and my suffering, and I froze. Thinking about it now, it is difficult to believe it happened, but at that moment, it was real. And something else has happened to me. I feel clean, very clean. Just as if I had a cleansing bath in a sparkling pool. Thank god it's over."

Beverly, concerned about Ten Lee, said to him, "You better see to that wound before you bleed to death."

"It is just a flesh wound, the bullet went straight through. I can take care of it myself. Remember, I am a medical doctor."

Mike stared at the two bodies on the ground and then at Ten Lee and asked, "For the record, what part did Goldie and Tai play in all this? Why did they also want you dead?"

Ten Lee hesitated to reply. Answering Cannon's question would disclose information he had pledged to secrecy. But present circumstances gave him no option. Mike and Beverly earned the right to know.

He said, "Goldie and her brother, Tai, were the children of a general of the North Viet Cong Army. Before their people were massacred and their village was burned by Captain Duncan, Goldie was sent to an uncle in China to avoid the war. Tai, her older brother, was left in the village to assist his mother on the farm. Their father owned an opium operation along with other top military officials. After the American military pulled out of Saigon, they established a prisoner of war slave camp, which provided labor for the extension of their operation.

"I met Goldie while practicing medicine in Hong Kong. She introduced me to her father and Tai. That is how I got caught up in the opium business and the exchange of the prisoners of war arrangement with the War Department. The opium industry is highly competitive over there. America is the most profitable outlet. Tai and Goldie were hard-core enemies of the United States. They were reluctant to speed up the release of the prisoners and would have done anything to slow it down. They believed the generals over here were earning too much from the operation, and as I found out, they had their own private arrangement sharing what was paid to them. My brother was also involved. He and my wife were lovers. I know I am still committed to fulfill my obligation to the army, but I can't wait for when all this is over, and I can return to living a normal life. I will still be a young man."

***

That night, Mike Cannon, for the first time, was able to place a value on events that had so dramatically affected his life. He reasoned that every value had a price, and all, in one form or another, had to pay. Some paid more than others, as was the inestimable price he paid toward the gift of freedom for the welfare of others who were unknown to him.

He thought fondly of Captain Duncan, whom he wished had lived, but in conflicts of that nature, there had to be collateral damages. For the first time since he had lost his family, he was at peace with himself. The anger was gone and replaced by an irresistible commitment to be useful.

Satisfied with the culmination of events, he visualized seeing in the near future an army transport aircraft landing at a United States Army air base. Standing by and waiting eagerly were men, women, and children of different ages and of many races. Their eyes were focused on the men emerging from the plane. They were the final batch of prisoners released from slave camps. Many were aged and feeble and had to be supported. There was a gleam on all their faces because they were finally home.

Mike slept peacefully that night, comforted by the thought that he had done his part.

At the Cannon Force headquarters the next day, Beverly Johns, in the presence of Mike Cannon, spoke with Brigadier General Carol Newton. The general was relieved to learn that the crisis was over. She emphasized that what was most important to all concerned was that the prisoners of war would eventually be coming home. Beverly assured the general that they would personally see to that.

General Newton asked that a full report of the events be sent to him immediately so that the army could advise the FBI to clear things with the local authorities.

Mike was much relieved with that promise. The general said before he hung up, "AD3044, with people as yourself and Mike Cannon keeping watch, America has nothing to fear."

Mike leaned back in his chair and looked at Beverly. He sensed a warm feeling toward her he had not experienced before, and there was an unusually wide grin on his face. "Are you ready?" he asked her.

"Am I ready for what?"

"Our next assignment," he replied.

"I thought you would never ask. What are we waiting for? Let's get on with it."